THE
BLACK
BLOSSOM

THE HEALER SERIES

C.J. ANAYA

CONTENTS

Glossary of Characters and Japanese Terms

Kami – a god, deity, divinity, or spirit. Kami are believed to be "hidden" from this world and inhabit a complementary existence that mirrors our own.

Mikomi – The Healer and the Japanese word for Hope. Also known as Hope in the first book in The Healer Series.

Musubi-no-kami – The Japanese god of love and marriage. He is also known as Tie Hart in the first book of The Healer Series.

Masaru Katsu – a warrior god descended from Bishamonten, the god of war and warriors. He is also known as Victor in the first book of The Healer Series.

Hachiman – Shinto god of war and divine protector of Japan.

Fukurokuju – Japanese god of health and longevity. Also the emperor of Kagami and Mikomi's father.

Chinatsu Mori –Empress of Kagami and Mikomi's Mother.

Amatsu-Mikaboshi – Demon god and Lord of the underworld.

Daiki – Innkeeper and Mikomi's surrogate father.

Hatsumi – Daiki's wife and Mikomi's surrogate mother.

Akane – General of the samurai insurgents and leader of the rebellion.

Saigo – Mikomi's brother.

Kenji – Mikomi's tutor.

Aiko – Mikomi's maid.

Kushi - Decorative combs used in traditional Japanese hairstyles.

Kojai – Decorative hairsticks also used in traditional Japanese hairstyles.

Furisode – A more formal, decorative kimono.

Geta – Japanese shoes or platform sandals often worn with kimonos.

Zango – Specific Japanese fighting style.

Hachi Kata – a fixed pattern of fighting used to teach basic elements of swordsmanship.

Katana – A traditionally made Japanese sword used in feudal Japan. Also known as a samurai sword.

Nakago – Unpolished part of a blade concealed by the hilt; the actual hilt of a sword.

Tsuba – A round or squarish hand guard at the end of the grip of bladed Japanese weapons.

Obi – A sash worn for traditional Japanese martial arts.

Saya – The scabbard for a sword or knife.

Prologue:

The God of Love and Marriage, 700 A.D.

Musubi-no-Kami, the god of love and marriage, was preparing to make a deal with the devil...literally.

Stone steps crunched beneath his sandaled feet, and the temperature dropped with his slow yet determined descent. The path he took now was one he never would have considered a millennium ago. He never would have considered it a *month* ago, but Edana was gone, dead by her own hand, and someone needed to pay. That someone was Masaru Katsu, warrior god and keeper of the Grass Cutter Sword.

Musubi had done his best to curb Katsu's inappropriate relationships with human women. He'd tried thousands of times over the past centuries to help the warrior god understand the kind of devastation he left in his wake every time a heart was broken and another girl abandoned. It left his job of helping these women find their soul mates virtually impossible. They became unwilling to ever open up and trust again.

It was selfish of Katsu. He was one of the few kami in all of creation destined to have a soul mate, destined to have the kind of love and companionship that Musubi could merely dream of and never hope to achieve. Yet the warrior god showed very little emotion whenever his future bride was mentioned. He clearly took his good fortune for granted. He didn't even care, and now he'd gone too far. Edana was gone and it was Katsu's fault.

He ground his teeth together as he continued to descend the

cold, black stone steps to the underworld. His previous existence had centered solely on bringing happiness and joy to others. He'd done it for thousands of years and always assumed it would be the only thing he would ever desire. Now, the only thing he desired was revenge.

Musubi took his very last step into the underworld and waited. The nekomata, one of the demon god's trained assassins, had been very specific in their previous conversation. Musubi was to wait there until he was sent for. Wandering off and getting lost in the underworld was not only unwise but hazardous to one's health, even for an immortal being.

He didn't have to wait long. Despite the dense darkness surrounding him, he was able to hear the padded approach of one of the demon god's servants. He hoped it was a servant and nothing else. The padding came to an abrupt halt a few feet in front of him. A small flame pierced the oppressive blackness, and a torch was lit, illuminating the desolate cavern.

He eyed the nekomata critically. The depraved soul had once been a kami himself, but he'd defected centuries ago, never to be heard from again.

"Musubi, it's been a long time," it hissed.

"I have a meeting with your master," was Musubi's short reply.

The nekomata's cat-like eye narrowed and then seemed to glow a deep green color.

"Of course, I shall take you to him now." He turned and motioned for Musubi to follow. "I must admit, the news of your arrival here has created quite a stir, but I for one am not surprised. It's always the best of us that falls the hardest."

Musubi suppressed an angry response and followed his guide deeper into the dark recesses of the underworld. Before long, he was led into a large opening. Lighted torches hung on black metallic posts in the air. The black stone surrounding them seemed to absorb any light the fire from the torches created. They were in some kind of dungeon, to be sure, but one that no longer resided in the world of the living. A black throne lay thirty feet ahead of them, and seated on its edge was the demon god and lord of the underworld, Amatsu-no-kami.

He thought he was prepared for the sight of the demon god, but at that moment he doubted anyone could be completely unaffected by the pure malevolence that radiated from the god of the underworld.

It was difficult to take in the fallen deity's appearance because he had the same face and form as always, and yet here he sat, horrifically different from the day Musubi witnessed him cast out of Heaven. The whiteness of his skin was just as blinding as ever, but he was and had always been, a devastatingly handsome individual with jet black hair and eyes, a strong chin and firm cheekbones. He still wore his sparkling white robe almost as if he were mocking the Parents who originally bestowed such pureness upon him.

His appearance suggested power, aggression, and absolute dominance. He was someone you might mistakenly consider as a trustworthy leader, a valuable asset, an individual you hoped to have on your side. A demon in angel's clothing. The juxtaposition was jarring.

"It's been such a very long time since I've basked in the presence of the god of love and marriage," Amatsu said. There was a mocking lilt to his tone.

"Seems like an eternity," was Musubi's clipped response. He noticed Amatsu's eyebrow rise in amusement.

"Tell me, dear Musubi, what brings you from the land of the living? Why this completely unexpected honor?"

"I think you know why I'm here." He tried his best to look unaffected as Amatsu scrutinized him with his scalding gaze.

"Revenge," Amatsu said, almost laughing. "Seems a bit beneath you, punishing Katsu for the death of your one true love."

Musubi held his tongue at Amatsu's flippant remark.

"You won't help me then?" Musubi held his ground but began to taste the bitterness of defeat. If the demon god wouldn't help him, he didn't know what path he could take next.

"I said it was beneath *you*. I, however, have never turned my back on the idea of giving others exactly what they deserve."

Musubi tried not to let his relief show.

"I am extremely curious as to what exactly you have in mind for our dear Katsu, and how you think I could possibly help you. I am, after all, trapped here." Amatsu's voice took on a scary edge. Signs of his displeasure with his lot in life seeped through the calm mask of indifference he held.

"Katsu has to pay for what he did to Edana. He took away the woman I love, and now I'm going to take away the woman he loves." It sounded worse saying it out loud than it had merely thinking and plotting it in his head, but thoughts of Edana steeled his resolve, and he didn't lower his eyes when Amatsu studied him again.

"Katsu loves no one. Of this I am certain. So again, I ask you, what is it that you require from me?" Amatsu's tone was becoming less pleasant.

"Katsu loves no one at the moment, but it is prophesied that he will."

The demon god's eyes seemed to flash with a strange green light. "The Healer," he whispered to no one in particular.

Musubi nodded. "I'm sure you wondered why I would take such a huge risk in coming here. I know my revenge will not only benefit me, but will also eliminate a problem you have no doubt wished to remedy since the day the prophecy of The Healer was given utterance."

"You want to kill The Healer? The Savior of the living? The half-mortal child destined to heal the veil between the living and the dead?" Amatsu began to laugh quietly to himself, and then the laughter grew louder until it echoed against the blackness of the stone walls. "You have wasted my time and yours, Musubi. The child cannot be slain. Her immortal paternity has ensured that nothing save a sword forged from this land can kill her. Do you have any idea how difficult it is to send an assassin through the veil?"

"I didn't say I wanted to kill her."

"Then what—"

"I want to take her for myself. How can she heal the veil if she is never bound to Katsu?"

Amatsu raised his head, and for the first time showed some real interest in what Musubi had to say.

"An interesting proposition, but tell me how you plan to woo The Healer away from the one she is destined to love and belong to. She will be created specifically for Katsu. Denying one's soul mate in favor of someone else? You and I know that this is as impossible as killing the child and being done with it."

"I agree with you, which is why I need your help. I need something that will sever her connection to Katsu and make her fall in love with me."

Amatsu looked triumphant, though nothing had been decided or resolved. "Something that can sever the link between soul mates? Now that *is* an idea, and quite a nasty one if you don't mind my saying so. Not like you at all, really."

"And yet, here I am."

"Indeed." Amatsu gave Musubi an appreciative look. "I may have something capable of accomplishing exactly what you propose, but I warn you, it will come with a price."

Musubi let out an impatient grunt. "Name your price, and I'll pay it."

"Well, obviously money is out of the question. What would I need that for in this place?" The demon god let out a perverse laugh. It was as if its facetiousness was all the more macabre due to its infrequent occurrence. "And having you here serving me prevents us both from getting what we want. So here is what I propose. Once the deed is done, the girl has fallen for you and her connection to Katsu has been irrevocably severed, you will deliver her to me and walk away without a backward glance."

"Fine," was all Musubi had to say.

"Yes, you say that now, but I'm afraid I will need to ensure that if I grant you this favor, you don't suddenly become consumed with a guilt-ridden conscience and go back on our deal."

"What more can I do to prove I will uphold my end of this transaction?"

Amatsu merely smiled, a smile that sent rippling chills up

C.J. Anaya

and down Musubi's spine. He held his hand open, palm up, and then flipped it with a flourish. When his hand came to rest palm up again, there stood, levitating above it, the blackest flower Musubi had ever seen. It pulsated with darkness.

"What is that?"

"This is a black cherry blossom, the solution to both our unfortunate situations."

Musubi shook his head. "I don't understand. How does this—"

"The black cherry blossom is an interesting piece of magic, very old magic, mind you, something I'm sure not even our First Parents are aware exists."

"How could they not know about this?"

"Why, because I created it. This cherry blossom has the power to sever the connection between two soul mates by literally changing the destiny of the one who holds it. Come forward, please."

Musubi walked to Amatsu slowly, never taking his eyes off the black, floating flower.

"Hold out your hand."

He did as he was told. Amatsu moved his hand away from the blossom, but it still remained suspended in mid-air. Then it began to move toward Musubi's outstretched hand. The blackened stem grew longer as it descended, and then wrapped itself around his wrist. He looked on in fascination as the stem continued to creep its way up his arm, under his clothing and toward his chest.

And then it struck.

The stem embedded itself within his heart, and the pain was like nothing the god had ever before felt. He let out a strangled cry and nearly staggered to the floor, but just as quickly as the pain took hold of him it let go. He closed his eyes and opened them slowly, seeing his surroundings in a new light. He felt... different; things were different. It was as if his heart and mind had been violently disconnected. He looked at his outstretched arm and watched the cherry blossom continue to hover above his hand.

"What have you done to me?" His question came out hollow.

"Oh, that? I merely blackened your heart a little, enough to taint it. Subduing your conscience is necessary, really. You do-gooders always manage to ruin the most wonderfully laid out plans, and we can't have that now, can we?" Amatsu gave him an evil grin. "This cherry blossom serves another purpose, however. Now that it is a part of you, it will also connect you to whomever you wish. In other words, once you give it to the young girl of prophecy and she accepts it, her connection to Katsu will be cut, and she will be bound to you forever, doing anything and everything you wish, including aligning herself with me." Amatsu clapped his hands in utter delight.

"You just happened to have something like this on hand?"

"You're not the only one to have had an epiphany, realizing the only way to destroy the girl of prophecy was to alter her destiny. I've had quite a bit of time to troubleshoot such an annoying issue. I just never realized I'd have my very own minion working out the kinks for me. It is so delightful, the kind of actions revenge and hate can produce, and to have the god of love and marriage possessing an item capable of ripping soul mates from one another?" Amatsu rubbed his hands together gleefully and let out a slow, deliberate chuckle. "Well, let's just say the irony isn't lost on me."

Part of Musubi's mind, the part holding a small remnant of the kami he used to be, wondered if maybe he'd taken things too far. The errant thought flickered like a small candle in the wind and was extinguished by another thought much more insistent and pervasive.

Revenge.

S neaking out of the imperial palace, without my guards the wiser, had been much more difficult this night than any other, and the complications and delays couldn't have come at a more inconvenient time.

I could feel Hatsumi's birthing pains ripping into my abdomen as if they were my own. It was the empath in me, and an unfortunate side effect of healing that occurred after the first time I connected to someone's ki or life force. My ki would stay very much tied to theirs until their pains were taken care of.

Unfortunately, trying to help a bedridden woman prevent her child from being born prematurely was an arduous and ongoing battle, both physically and emotionally for Hatsumi and myself due to the fact that I had connected with her ki three months ago when her baby had tried to come at five months. I'd been able to feel her labor pains coming on every few weeks since then and was seriously considering never having children of my own. If my father had his wish, I would never be capable of having them anyway.

I had to stop on the grassy path to Hatsumi's momentarily and grab hold of an uprooted tree stump for support as another contraction ripped through my abdomen. I nearly screamed out with the pain of it but bit my lip instead and tried to remember that I was most likely not alone in the forested area, even if the night was quiet and still. Samurai rebels littered these wooded areas, and although I had no problems with their mission or their desire to usurp my father's throne and take over the empire themselves, I couldn't afford to be held up at the moment. Hatsumi's baby was coming. I sensed there would be no stopping it this time.

I bit my lip hard as another tearing pain hit me and tasted blood. I nearly panicked thinking that my poor, dear friend was having to do this without me.

After two quick breaths I pressed forward, running as fast as my sandaled feet would carry me. I needed to cover more ground between these debilitating contractions, or I would never reach her in time.

The night air had chilled considerably despite the warmth of the day, but I hardly felt its coldness due to the amount of strain Hatsumi was experiencing. Sweat had already left my underthings damp, clinging to my aching back.

I nearly stopped short when I heard a crash of branches behind me. It may have been a rebel, or it just as easily could have been a forest animal. There were a number of nocturnal creatures scampering out and about. I couldn't pay attention to what was happening behind me with so much at stake before me.

I increased my speed and prayed to the gods I wouldn't trip over the many tree roots that tended to protrude along the path. The moon was a slight crescent amidst the stars in the sky and gave off very little light.

White, hot pain shot to my back and radiated forward. I dropped to my knees and let out a muffled scream, grinding my jaw together and digging my nails into the dark earth before me. That contraction had not been normal. I may never have experienced child birth personally, but I had served as midwife enough in the village to know the difference between birthing pains and pain originating from a situation far more serious. I wouldn't be certain until I was with the mother, but I had a terrifying thought that the baby's watery home had separated itself from the lining of Hatsumi's uterus and the placenta was torn.

I was up and running like the very demons of the underworld were mere inches from my heels, roots and tree limbs be hanged! The palace and the small village of Yanbaro were separated by a small wooded forest, and although the forest by anyone's standards wasn't large compared to most, with so much at stake, it might as well have traversed all of Japan.

I had to reach Hatsumi in time.

I was so relieved to see the small flicker of firelight as I made my way around a bend in the path that tears seeped from my tired eyes. I continued running forward and managed to make it into the village before the next wave of pain hit, dropping me to the ground. I let out an awful scream this time, and breathed in the frosty night air as I tried to pull myself to my feet.

"Did you injure yourself?" a soft male voice said from behind me. I felt myself being pulled to my feet and turned awkwardly around.

Eyes the color of frothy blue waves glinted in the firelight, flickering just above us from a hanging luminary on a bamboo street post.

I'd never before seen eyes the color of a frozen winter sky, but had often heard that men and women far to the west were born with such eyes. His face was much lighter than the olive skin of my countrymen, and his hair was the color of the rising sun. I felt myself drawn to him almost immediately and stood momentarily stunned at my own emotional and physical response to this complete and total stranger.

His concerned eyes narrowed as he took me in. "Did you hurt your ankle when you fell?"

His words broke me out of my moment of stupor, and I felt monumentally guilty for losing sight of my purpose even for one second. Not to mention the level of uncertainty I felt at the physical contact. No man was allowed to touch me. Most men wouldn't have considered touching a strange woman either way, but now he had spoken directly to me, and our social customs dictated that I show respect and answer the man's question.

I couldn't waste time with social etiquette at this point. Not when Hatsumi's life depended solely on the timing of my arrival. I moved to break away from the tight hold he had on my arms and doubled over as another wave of excruciating pain pummeled into my lower back.

"Clearly you've been injured far worse than I originally thought. Come, I will take you back to my camp and find someone to assist you."

"No," I fairly screamed as I wrenched myself from his grasp, turned on my heels and ran as fast as I could toward the small tavern where Hatsumi and her husband lived.

"Wait." I heard the young man call out. The loud pounding of his feet indicated he was close behind me. It was strange that he would pursue a woman whom he deemed ill. In my culture, a woman wasn't important enough to speak to directly, let alone be the focus of a stranger's concern. I might have wondered at it a bit longer, but more debilitating waves of pain coursed through me, and the exotic-looking young man was momentarily forgotten.

These pains Hatsumi bore did not bode well for her or the baby. Every second I lost would determine whether or not I would be able to save either one of them. I reached the front door of the tavern and wrenched it open, not bothering to knock when another pain ripped into my back, making me feel as if my body were tearing in two. My cries echoed that of Hatsumi's from the room connected to the back of the tavern.

"You've arrived, young healer. I knew you would," Daiki said, Hatsumi's husband, just as I was grabbed and lifted into the air by a pair of strong hands. I let out a muffled squeal of surprise as the young man whom I had previously run into held me close to his chest and refused to release me, even after I forcefully pushed against him.

"Musubi, you must let the girl down," Daiki urged.

My captor didn't respond nor loosen his hold on me. I looked up at him and noted a small lift to the side of his mouth. His eyes studied me in such a frank manner that my attention was instantly captivated. I couldn't wrench my glance away from the commanding fire of his gaze, but I should have. I wasn't allowed to look a man directly in the eye without his express approval, but he had immediate and total control over me and held me as no man had ever been allowed to hold me before.

This foreign contact with a member of the male species, combined with my desperate need to escape his unrelenting perusal of my body, and my complete panic at the thought of losing Hatsumi had an incredibly surprising effect on my behavior. Without considering the consequences of my actions, I rounded my fist, pulled it back as far as it would allow, and threw it at his chin with such force that the contact cracked the top of my knuckle and actually threw his head to the side. I was so shocked by my behavior that I barely registered the pain in my broken fist or the fact that my ki had immediately begun healing it.

He turned his head and glanced at me in surprise, and then threw it backward, letting out the most lighthearted laugh I had ever heard.

"I told you to put her down." Daiki chuckled.

"I'm so sorry," I sputtered. "I...please forgive me, it's just that...ahhhhh."

I crumpled forward and felt his arms tighten around me protectively.

"You must put me down," I yelled. I groaned a little at the relentless pain and was pulled closer to his chest. I felt angry all over again by his persistence and my reaction to him. "Please." I beat against his chest and struggled to escape his hold on me both physically and emotionally. "I must attend to Hatsumi."

Instead of letting me go, the young man looked up at the innkeeper. "Daiki, do you know this female?"

I was surprised these two knew each other by name and felt close enough to use them.

"You must let her go. Hatsumi will deliver, and this is the midwife."

I looked at Daiki and nodded my thanks, appreciating his discretion. There were very few people who knew my identity, and

Daiki had kept my secret for several years.

"This child is the midwife?" The man let out a disbelieving snort. "She hardly seems capable."

I considered hitting him again, but my hand hadn't healed completely. Fortunately, he set me down more gently than I would have expected, and my anger with him dissolved almost instantly. Hatsumi and her baby were all I could and should be focusing on.

I took two steps forward and dropped to the floor as the searing heat in my back hit me again. Both Hatsumi and I let out pain-filled cries.

"You see," the young man said. "She clearly needs a person of medicine herself." He moved to pick me up again, but I crawled forward and held my hand up to stop him.

"I feel her pain. It is as simple as that," I shouted it as loud as I dared.

He ignored me and reached for me again, but Daiki stepped between us and held up his hand. "Musubi, you will have to trust me and let the midwife do her job."

"She can barely walk, Daiki. What can she possibly do to help?"

"Bring her to my wife, and you will see." He stepped out of the way and motioned Musubi forward. I gave Daiki a nervous look. I did not want to be held by this distracting individual again, and I didn't think it wise to perform a healing in front of him either. Daiki had no idea how precarious his wife's situation had become. I would be doing much more than simply aiding the birth of her baby.

My old friend gave me an encouraging look as Musubi reached for me again and lifted me into his arms. It was strange to feel secure and safe in the arms of someone I barely knew, but I didn't have time to dwell on it.

Upon entering Hatsumi's bedroom the strong odor of blood filled my nostrils and Hatsumi's soft moans and labored breathing pierced my heart. My mind cleared as I scrambled quickly out of Musubi's arms and sat down on the bed next to the struggling mother.

I couldn't hold her head between my hands with the young man present, so I grabbed Hatsumi's hands in my own and looked into her eyes as I willed myself to connect with her ki. It would have been better to hold her head and close my eyes to concentrate, but I couldn't let this man...this Musubi, know who I was.

It took a few moments, but I finally latched on to her ki with my own and felt pain and nausea hit me with such force I nearly toppled over. Just as I had feared, part of the baby's small home had ripped away from the lining of the womb. It was significant enough to prevent the baby from receiving as much oxygen as it needed to survive, and the heartbeat was irregular. I could sense the baby's distress and even its fear, something I had never felt before. Even the unborn child was aware that all was not well. I instructed her ki to reattach the bag of waters to the lining of the womb and to heal the blood vessels that had been broken. I received no response.

I couldn't understand why her ki was ignoring my instructions. I hadn't for one single moment felt that Hatsumi or her baby were meant to perish during this delivery. Her ki should have been able to respond and repair the damage. I searched for more answers and found that the bag of waters was beginning to dry out and the baby's head was already firmly placed in the birth canal. Even if the bag had been repaired and reattached there was simply no way to stop this labor. Not even healing powers could stop nature from taking its course.

We had to get the baby out, but Hatsumi was nowhere near ready to deliver. I couldn't wait for her body to ready itself fully. This baby had to be delivered now. I did not want to do what I felt was the only recourse we had, but I instructed her ki to prepare her body for delivery, knowing that the pain we would both feel as her body accomplished in only a few seconds what usually took several hours would be the worst kind of pain either one of us had ever felt. There was simply no time to lessen it.

C.J. Anaya

I maintained eye contact with the poor mother and gave her my most confident smile.

"Hatsumi, we will deliver this baby right now. Are you ready?"

She nodded as sweat and tears rolled down the sides of her pale cheeks. I gave her ki the instructions it needed and held fast to her hands as both our bodies were hit with wave after wave of the most debilitating labor pains a woman could ever experience. I did my best to keep my own pain to myself and focused on the baby as it slowly traveled closer to its birth. Its heart rate dropped so low at one point I had to slow down everything and take time to increase the beats of the tiny child's heart before it died.

Sensing it was time, I let go of her hands and checked the baby's progress.

"It is time for you to push, Hatsumi."

She was pushing before I even finished my sentence. The child was small and frail and came rapidly as a result. I wrapped the tiny baby in a cloth and quickly connected to it, making sure the heartbeats were steady and strong and the lungs were taking in the oxygen needed before handing it over to the mother.

"He's fine, Hatsumi. Your baby boy is just fine."

She let out a tired laugh as she snuggled closer to her son and then wept softly.

I felt a huge weight lift from my shoulders as I watched her hold her firstborn child, a child that she and Daiki had tried and failed to have for many years now. Finally, the fight was over. A soft tear ran down my face as I took in the beautiful picture before me.

"We have a son, then?"

I turned to see the happy face of Daiki as he rushed to the side of his wife's bed. I had completely forgotten he was there. I'd even forgotten the young man standing in the corner until his hand came to rest on my shoulder.

The light contact was more than inappropriate, and I tried my best to keep my eyes averted from his handsome face. I thought about shrugging his hand away, but couldn't find the willpower to do so; not when this connection made me feel as if I had just found my way home. It was a disturbing thought to have, considering who I was and what my future held for me.

"That was quite possibly the worst thing I have ever before seen, and I've witnessed countless gory wounds in battle. The way you handled that was…impressive."

His coloring appeared quite pale but had been slightly light to begin with. I wondered at his background and means of work. He certainly didn't look like a regular soldier, but his long cloak covered his clothing underneath.

I hesitated, still uncertain as to whether or not he wished for me to speak. I glanced at him below lowered lashes, and found my answer as his gaze locked with mine. "Ah, yes, childbirth. It is not for the faint of heart." I gave him a small smile and then hurriedly averted my gaze when he returned my smile with one of his own. I felt his hand tighten ever so slightly on my shoulder and then he withdrew.

I couldn't account for the feeling of loss that descended upon me in that moment, but it was clear that remaining in this man's presence was simply not good for me. I folded my arms across my chest. It was then that I realized my cloak and arms were covered in blood. There was always blood in childbirth, but I was soaked in it. I raised my arms up and studied the front of my cloak.

Blood everywhere.

"Hatsumi," I said, glancing at the young woman's small form. Blood continued to coat the bedding beneath her, dripping to the floor. I could see a glassy look begin to grow in her eyes.

I rushed over to the bed and motioned for Daiki to take the baby. Then I grabbed Hatsumi's hands in my own.

"No! Hatsumi, you focus on me. You look at me, right now!"

I grabbed her ki with my own and saw that she was hemorrhaging. Her blood would not thicken due to the amount she had lost. I could stop the bleeding, but I wasn't sure I would be able to repair the blood loss before her organs went into shock and she died. I instructed her ki to repair the damage, and then went to work trying to help her poor, weak body replace the blood she had lost.

I felt Musubi's presence close to me as I worked, and knew his eyes were studying every move I made, every facet of the situation. I did my best to look like I was examining her so he wouldn't assume I was simply sitting there watching her bleed to death.

I worked with her body for ten minutes when the first of her organs, her left kidney, began to shut down.

"No!"

"What is happening, child?" Daiki asked.

"She's lost too much blood, and her body is struggling to hold on."

There was real fear in Daiki's eyes. "What can I do?"

"You and this young man need to leave so that I can work." Daiki was the only man I had ever felt comfortable speaking so frankly with. It probably seemed unusual for Musubi to watch me throw orders at Daiki, and though most men made me nervous, I knew I could count on Daiki to take seriously the danger his wife now faced.

He nodded his understanding, turned swiftly with the baby in hand and directed Musubi out the door. I had to admire him for his absolute faith in me. Most men would have balked at such an order, demanding to stay and oversee the process.

"Daiki, this is madness. Your wife needs a more experienced person of medicine if her bleeding is internal. What can a midwife do?"

"We must go now." Daiki insisted.

I thought I heard Musubi protesting about leaving Hatsumi's life in the hands of a child, but I was too focused on keeping her organs functioning to feel offended by the slight.

It was difficult work and a sort of mental juggling act to keep her organs operating and help her body replenish the blood she had lost all at the same time. Her body could only produce the blood at a specific rate without compromising its other functions or damaging her organs, but without the blood there to help the organs function they would begin to fail, and I would have to stop what I was doing to revive them again.

I wasn't sure how much time had passed as I continued to help Hatsumi fight for her life and her right to raise her first child, but soon there was enough blood in her system that her organs could function without my help. I withdrew my shaking, bloodied hands from her head and looked at her peacefully sleeping face. She felt no pain, and for that I was grateful. If I had had more time to ease the pain first, the whole experience would have been less traumatic for both of us, but when you have a choice between easing pain and saving lives your path as a healer is clear.

I took a moment to collect myself and then began cleaning up the blood on the floor by using my own sodden cloak and other linens in the bedroom. I woke Hatsumi only long enough to help her remove her soiled clothing and bed linens and to clean her up as best I could.

We spoke very little. Hatsumi looked as if she might die right before my eyes, and I had to keep checking her ki to reassure myself everything within her body was functioning as it should.

She was like a mother to me; more of a mother than my own ever could be, and I wouldn't lose her. I laid her back down upon her bed and drew new blankets over her body. She grabbed my hand in her weak ones and squeezed them gently.

"You saved my life and the life of my baby. Thank you so much, dear friend." I could tell it was a struggle for her to remain awake after everything she had been through.

"Of course, Hatsumi. I would not have let anything happen to you or your precious child. You must sleep now." After smoothing back her hair, I stood up and tiredly headed for the door.

"My son...can I see him?"

I turned to Hatsumi and nodded. "I will send Daiki in with your son as soon as you have rested for a short time." I swallowed back a lump in my throat when she gave me a questioning look. "It was very close this time, Hatsumi. Too close. Just rest for a few minutes and then you can hold your son." She nodded her understanding and closed her eyes. I knew she was sleeping even before I left her room.

The moment I stepped into the serving area of the tavern, Daiki met me with his sweet newborn son cradled in his arms and an anxious look upon his face. He was only ten years my senior, but the hard life of an innkeeper had aged him dramatically. Fine lines covered the corners of his slanted eyes and large mouth, but his positive attitude in the face of insurmountable poverty kept a smile on his round face.

The last two years had been especially difficult for him, though I hadn't been able to find the source of what troubled him. Every time I asked, he would tell me money was tight and times were hard, but I always suspected there was more to the story, and that perhaps he was protecting me from something.

Though he looked older than his twenty-seven years, he was well-muscled and strong. He would have looked more natural with a sword in his hand than he did serving food or managing his business.

"She will be fine," I said quickly. "Her bleeding was not as severe as I had thought it to be. Within an hour you should take your son in to nurse. She should be up to the task by then." I didn't think it wise to advise him of how close he came to losing Hatsumi and his son tonight with the young soldier sitting at a table to our right.

Daiki seemed to understand the need to lighten the mood in front of Musubi, though why he had let him stay during his son's chaotic birth was a mystery to me.

"Come. Sit at table with Musubi and myself."

I barely suppressed a raised eyebrow at this. I had sat at table with Hatsumi and Daiki many times throughout the course of our friendship, but being invited to sit at table with a stranger here was unprecedented and quite dangerous. I couldn't afford to have anyone recognize me for fear of my parents discovering my late night excursions to homes in need of healings.

Technically, my powers for healing were meant for something

completely different. As the daughter of Emperor Fukurokuju and Empress Chinatsu there was much expected of me, but my destiny was much more complex and demanding than any other imperial princesses might be.

According to a prophecy written thousands of years ago, a princess would be born to a god and a mortal, possessing healing capabilities that would be used to help the guardian of the Grass Cutter Sword heal and strengthen the veil between our world and the world of the dead. I had been raised to believe that this princess of prophecy, this healer, was me.

Suffice it to say, healing peasants and wives of innkeepers were not the kinds of activities the imperial family would have supported, and that was putting it mildly. My father would have beaten me until I was black and blue, and my mother would have made her normal indifferent treatment of me even icier than usual.

My role was simple and clear—marry the warrior god, Masaru Katsu, and spend the rest of eternity helping him heal the veil.

The end.

I held some deep reservations where my duty and destiny were concerned.

"Please, sit with us," he said as he drew me to the table and offered me a bench. He placed me across from Musubi and then sat down next to me.

I was able to study the soldier's features more thoroughly thanks to the lamplight in the tavern. I admit, I thought him much more handsome than I had before. Of course, I was no longer distracted with the possibility of losing the most important woman in my life.

I realized I was staring, and he had caught me doing so. His lips turned up in amusement. I hurriedly lowered my eyes to the table, feeling myself grow warm at the same time.

I marveled at the small smile he shared with me. It was strange to see any expression other than anger on his features considering the bitter feelings I felt rolling off of his ki for reasons known only to himself.

"My dear friend, Musubi was curious as to the pain you felt earlier. I explained to him you are an empath, but he worried you might actually be suffering from some illness."

I noted Daiki failed to address me by my given name. I was grateful for that.

"It is obvious she is just fine now," Musubi said, directing his comment to Daiki. "I've never heard of a midwife also being an empath. It seems like an undesirable trait to possess considering her line of work."

"Oh, no. It is just the opposite," I blurted out. "The pain allows me to sense when and where I'm needed." I bit down on my tongue and lowered my eyes to the table again. It wasn't common knowledge that the famed healer of prophecy was also an empath, and it certainly wasn't mentioned in the prophecy, but letting anyone know I could do things most people couldn't wasn't the smartest of ideas either. The less I talked, the better my chances were of maintaining my secrets.

As it stood, only Daiki and his wife, my brother Saigo, my maid Aiko, and our tutor Kenji had any idea that I ventured out of the palace walls in the middle of the night, disguised as a woman of medicine to heal the sick and suffering in the empire.

Another strike against me was my gender. A woman speaking out of turn in my society was an uncommon occurrence, and although Musubi was talking *about* me, his comments had not been directed *toward* me. I'd had no right to voice my thoughts. Then again, I'd had no right to hit him in the face. My behavior around this man was unorthodox at best.

I felt his steady gaze bearing down upon the top of my head and wished Daiki had not invited me to sit with him and his friend. I needed to get back to the palace before dawn, and the rising sun was due merely two hours from now.

"You mean to tell me you could feel Hatsumi's labor pains from your own personal dwelling, and that's how you knew to come?" Musubi asked.

"Yes," I replied reluctantly, keeping my eyes glued to the table.

"Daiki didn't send for you?"

I shook my head in response. I was nervous being asked all of these questions. Daiki must have sensed my anxiety because he placed a calming hand upon my shoulder.

"He means you no harm. I promise you can trust young Musubi. He's been fighting with the samurai insurgents for a few months now and is very much a man of honor and integrity."

An aura of chagrin surged from Musubi's person. I couldn't tell if the praise embarrassed him or if he simply didn't agree with Daiki's assessment of his character. I was happy to hear of his involvement with the rebels, however. Anyone fighting against my father was someone I considered a friend.

"I wonder...are there limits to your empathic abilities?" Musubi asked.

I pondered this for a moment and dared a look in his direction. "To the best of my knowledge, as long as I have had the opportunity to meet the person in question, I can generally feel when they are distressed, in pain or in need of any medicinal administrations no matter the distance between us, but I have only ever been acquainted with the people of this village."

I failed to mention those who lived in the palace. I also failed to mention that my empathic abilities only worked with people I had already connected to as far as sensing pain went, and once their problem was resolved I didn't feel the connection any longer. Unfortunately, I tended to absorb others' emotions regardless of whether I had connected to their ki or not.

Musubi's anger, for example, was fairly distracting me with its intensity. I wondered if all soldiers survived war by carrying around a healthy dose of suppressed rage. Perhaps it fueled their ability to fight.

"Intriguing," was all he said. He sat back in his seat, but continued to study me directly.

"You seem to have an idea brewing, Musubi," Daiki said. "What are you thinking?"

"I'm thinking that I'm crazy, and that a war zone is no place for a female such as this small, defenseless little girl."

I felt myself prickle at his comment. "You feel I am unequal to the task of administering to the sick and injured due to my size? I can assure you, a war zone would cause little trouble for me."

I bit down on my tongue again as Musubi's frosty eyes flashed to mine. Where had my caution flown to? I needed to stop drawing his attention to my person. I could have sworn I sensed a smile lurking at the corners of his mouth. Amusement lightly skipped its way through him before the anger, his constant companion it would seem, managed to smother it.

"I think you are undeniably equal to the task...of healing, that is. However, you are untrained to defend yourself should the occasion arise, and I'm almost certain it would. There are other things to consider as well."

"You want her to live with the samurai insurgents and heal your wounded men?" Daiki let out an incredulous laugh. "It is unthinkable. She *does* have family, you know, and she is not yet eighteen. She would have to be married to a soldier or her reputation would be lost altogether."

I nearly laughed at Daiki's protests. He and I both knew my reputation mattered very little considering the matter of my betrothal to the warrior god Katsu. Nothing I did, no matter how inappropriate, would ever prevent that impending union from happening.

If I were to be honest with myself, I would have reveled in the chance to spend time healing soldiers or even fighting alongside them. I would have given up my position in the palace and my destiny at that very moment if it hadn't been for two things.

One, my father would search relentlessly for me the minute he discovered my absence, and two, I could never leave the palace for good without my maid, my brother, and our tutor, Kenji. They were some of the few people in this world who knew me and loved me for me and not my title or the birthright that came with it.

"I agree, it was a silly notion," Musubi said, stroking the fine, firm planes of his smooth jaw. "She will most certainly be missed by her family considering her station."

I looked at him in surprise. He quirked an eyebrow at me and his lips formed a half smile.

"Your kimono, child. Your state of dress clearly comes from the more affluent classes in this empire. I'm only surprised you were allowed to travel so late at night unaccompanied considering your age and station."

I squirmed under his shrewd glance. He was far more perceptive than I had given him credit for. I had forgotten my blood soaked cloak in the other room. It would do me very little good to pretend I wasn't a woman of some consequence now that he could see the fine silk of my kimono. There simply hadn't been enough time to change into the clothing I usually wore when coming to the village to heal people.

"I admit, my family is unaware of my abilities as a midwife," I managed stiffly.

He let out a soft chuckle and grabbed my chin in his hand. I gasped at the light contact. Very few men had ever taken such a liberty. My eyes met his, and he considered me thoughtfully.

"Adventurous, isn't she, Daiki? You wouldn't think it to look at her."

I dared an angry glare at him before pulling my chin from his grasp and leveling my eyes to the table.

"Stop it, Musubi. You'll scare the child, and after I just told her she has nothing to fear."

Musubi laughed out loud this time. "I get the feeling nothing scares this one." He sighed regretfully. "It's a shame she would be missed by her family. I'm sure I could find some soldier willing to marry her for the sake of our armies' well-being."

I said nothing, but was fairly certain that my anger at the moment could have rivaled his. It certainly burned just as brightly. Did everyone assume I couldn't choose a husband for myself? Did everyone assume I was only worth marrying so long as I was capable of healing?

Musubi chuckled again and placed a finger under my chin, gently raising it until our eyes met.

"I am only teasing you, little healer. I enjoy watching you fight to hold your temper in check."

I couldn't help but give him a reluctant smile in answer. It was hard to ignore his abrasive charm and joking manner.

"It was nice to have met you, young lady," he continued. "I hope our paths cross again someday."

Though his eyes remained a cold, frothy blue, the warmth I felt from his touch traveled slow and steady through the whole of me. He stood up and bowed to both Daiki and myself. I barely managed a short nod of my head, so resistant to the idea that I might miss even a moment of looking at him before he stepped out of the inn and out of my life forever.

Just as he reached the door, he turned around and took me in one more time. He looked a bit confused, and I could sense he felt it as well, almost as if he was unsure as to why he hadn't left yet.

"I never did learn your name, child," he finally managed.

"It is probably best that you never do," Daiki said.

Musubi looked at the innkeeper and nodded, then rested his eyes on me one last time before he opened the door and stepped through it.

"**Y**ou had no trouble getting away tonight?" Daiki asked.

His question pulled me from my fixation on the door through which Musubi had recently exited. I felt drawn toward that door and the idea of stepping through it to catch up to the young soldier and...and what? Discuss the frigid night air or make polite conversation about the impending fall of the empire? I nearly laughed outright at the absurdity of it all.

A woman approaching a soldier in the middle of the night and initiating a conversation—just as ludicrous to impart to him that the thought of never seeing him again disturbed me more than the idea of never breathing again.

"In truth, I was having a...meeting with my father when Hatsumi's pains came on." I kept my eyes on the table and took a sip of my tea.

"A meeting with your father?" Daiki placed a comforting hand on my shoulder. "How bad was it this time?"

"Bad." I grimaced into my cup. Daiki knew the phrase "meeting with my father" was just another way of saying my father, Emperor Fukurokuju, had once again used my healing powers for personal gain. It wasn't something I wanted to discuss further, but I knew Daiki would have questions. He always did.

I had met Daiki and his wife when I was twelve, after sneaking out of the palace in an attempt to run away from a life I felt I could no longer bear. As a child, my one thought was to escape my own personal prison as quickly as was humanly possible. It had been impulsive and ill thought out. By the time I had reached the village, I realized I had no food, water nor shelter and no money to my name. I was an imperial princess but owned nothing save it were the clothes on my back.

I had continued walking down the narrow stretch of road, wondering what my next course of action would be when I heard a scream from within the tavern to my left. Without thinking, I had run into the tavern, weaved my way silently around the many patrons, and headed to the very back where Daiki and Hatsumi's living quarters were. I could sense Hatsumi's distress and felt so pressured by it that I walked into their living quarters without asking.

Upon entering I had found Daiki doubled over on the floor with blood dripping from a wound in his thigh. I had immediately walked over, placed my hands on either side of his head and closed my eyes, connecting with his ki. I healed the wound instantly and then released him while stepping back.

I hadn't dared say anything, especially after realizing what I had done. No one outside the palace knew what the imperial princess, The Healer, looked like. I was never allowed out without a veil covering my face or several guards shadowing my every move. No one even knew my real name.

Daiki had examined his leg for several seconds before saying anything. Not even Hatsumi had been able to manage a word, and she was, as I would soon come to find out, a very vocal individual considering she was a woman.

"How is this possible, child? How...unless you are The Healer. Princess?"

I had merely nodded and kept my eyes to the floor. I knew my plans for escape had been ruined after revealing myself.

Hatsumi had rested her hand softly on my shoulder and then squeezed it gently. My own mother had never been the kind to offer much affection. As a twelve-year-old girl, on the precipice of understanding the finality of my future, I felt cold, alone, and directionless. The small gesture Hatsumi gave me was enough to open a flood of tears I must have kept stored deep within my soul for most of my life.

I fell apart in front of a couple who knew nothing about me except that I was the daughter of an emperor whom everyone detested, and that I was the famed girl of prophecy, The Healer. Hatsumi had snuggled me close in her arms and the conversation that followed was one I would never forget. I had poured my whole heart to them and divulged my plan to run away forever.

Fortunately, Daiki had a better plan. He knew of my desire to heal people and wondered if I might consider being the village healer in disguise. Whenever someone needed my help he would find a way to get a message to me at the palace. This usually involved writing a small note and concealing it under a specific rock in the open gardens at the rear of the huge edifice. It was one of the few places I was able to visit frequently outside the palace gates without an army of guards shadowing me.

I checked for messages on the first day of every week, and whenever I found one waiting for me, I felt as if my life held meaning…a real reason for living. I suspected that was exactly what Daiki had been trying to provide.

Daiki's thoughts must have been reviewing the same memories. "I sometimes wonder if I should have helped you escape five years ago. Your life would have been better, less fraught with pain and suffering."

I set my tea down and met his remorseful gaze.

"You know as well as I do that I wouldn't have been successful in my attempt at escape. My father would have found me eventually. You saved me in more ways than you or I will ever know, I'm sure."

He gave me a tight smile, but his eyes held a hint of regret.

"Who was it this time?" he asked.

I didn't want to discuss it. I didn't want to consider what I had been forced to do tonight just to gather information for my father.

"Let's not dwell on a subject so undeserving of our attention when we should be celebrating the birth of your son, Daiki. After all this time, you finally have a son."

He smiled down at the small babe nestled snug in his arms. He and Hatsumi had tried for several years to have a child, but she always miscarried before I was able to arrive and offer help. There was never enough time to fix whatever was happening within her body nor with the baby in her womb.

It was a mystery to all of us. There was nothing within her that should have prevented her from carrying a child to term, but it continued to happen with each new pregnancy. I had become more determined than ever to help her deliver a baby to term, and this time we had been successful.

"You didn't tell me the truth, did you?" he asked.

"What do you mean?"

"She lost almost all of her blood. I've fought enough in battle to know when someone is bleeding out and close to death." He lifted a shaky hand to his face and wiped a stray tear from his cheek. "You saved her tonight."

I felt guilt chafing away at my joy. "Yes, that is true. The baby's home had torn from her womb. She only had a few seconds by the time I joined with her. I should have noticed the bleeding sooner, Daiki. I am sorry."

He shook his head in surprise. "My wife and my son are alive. You should never apologize for saving lives."

I fought back the guilt and plastered a smile on my face. I then considered something he had said. "Daiki, when did you ever fight in battle?"

I saw him grimace at what he must have considered a slight slip of the tongue.

"I suppose I should have told you, but it never felt right to say. Before Hatsumi and I married I fought with the rebels against your father. This was when the rebels first organized themselves with Akane."

"Yes, I have heard of her. I must admit the idea of a female general leading a large army of Samurai into battle makes me feel as if anything is possible."

Daiki chuckled softly. "Akane makes everyone feel as if anything is possible. I ended my fighting with the rebels after marrying Hatsumi. It wasn't what I wanted, but I knew if I continued I would most likely be killed. The wound on my leg that you healed the day of our meeting...I had acquired it in battle. As soon as you used your powers, I knew I could never fight again, but I also knew I had found another way to fight against the emperor." He pointed a finger in my direction.

"Me?" I wondered.

"You. I believe you are the answer to this war between the rebels and your father. I truly believe you can bring peace to this empire. It is partly why I encouraged you to stay."

"What was the other reason?"

"You felt like my daughter, and I could tell Hatsumi felt the same way. We couldn't have let you go even if we had wanted to."

I smiled into my tea as I brought it to my lips, but before I could take another sip a thought came to me. "Daiki, have you been helping the rebels again?"

He was silent for so long I wondered if he would answer me.

"I'll admit I have provided shelter and food for some of the men over the past few years. I've even sent for you to heal some of the more badly injured ones."

I'd thought some of the men I had healed didn't look like rice farmers. Their injuries had been severe, disturbingly so. I must have been blind not to see it. Many of the wounds had to be healed slower than I would have liked in order to avoid divulging my true identity, but several wounds were life threatening and had to be dealt with quickly.

"It was good of those soldiers to refrain from voicing any suspicions they may have had concerning my identity," I said.

"They fight against your father, my child, but in many respects they fight for you. Most of the rebels believe that you are the key to harmony in this empire. The fact that you were willing to heal some of the men merely strengthened that belief and their morale."

"Why do they feel they must fight against the emperor on my behalf? My father will give the throne to my brother Saigo, and I must go live with some obscure kami who is no doubt just as cruel and unfeeling."

"Exactly. You are destined to leave, but the people need you to stay. You are capable of healing much more than the veil or the pains that life inflicts on its inhabitants. You could heal a whole nation if given the chance. The rebels are fighting to give you that chance."

"I'm just a princess trapped in a palace. The situation seems a bit hopeless."

"With Musubi joining the rebels, I think there is most certainly hope."

My ears perked up at the mention of Musubi. "Who is he, Daiki, and how do you know him?"

"He is a close friend of General Akane. I've heard stories of his prowess in battle, but wasn't aware that Akane had convinced him to come join our cause."

"Perhaps his idea of having me heal his men isn't so ridiculous."

Daiki snorted. "A young, single woman on the battlefield would not survive."

"No, but what if I learned to fight, and what if I only came when I was needed? It isn't necessary to live with the rebels in order to help their cause. Perhaps we could spin a tale that I was married and widowed within a short time."

"A very short time, considering your age," he muttered.

"I could do this. I could help!" I looked at him with fierce determination and saw that he might actually be considering my proposition, but then he shook his head.

"It isn't safe. I would worry about you, and Hatsumi would have my head if she thought I had allowed it. Even widowed, you would still be single. I'm not suggesting these soldiers are without honor, but without a man claiming you as his wife, I don't see how you would be able to keep your identity a secret, and you would have to keep it a secret amongst the rebels. The ones I brought to you were men I trust with my own life, but there could be other rebels planted as spies by your father."

I considered his arguments, and although I thought each one to be valid, I still longed to be a part of the solution.

"Maybe we could find someone you trust, someone willing to pretend a marriage with me. Claim me as his wife, and no one would be the wiser or look to unearth my background since the matter of marriage would be settled."

Daiki chuckled. "I know of no man I could trust to take on that kind of role with you. He would have to be invincible on the battlefield in order to keep you safe, and if he were killed in battle, we'd be right back where we started."

I sighed, feeling frustrated.

He tucked the cloth more firmly around his son. "Besides, I would worry about you. I may not be your father through blood, but my love for you as a father would rival that of any other. This war is best fought by those capable of doing so, and your job in this battle is to live long enough to pick up the pieces of this broken empire once your poor excuse for a father is finally out of the picture."

I shook my head, knowing the rebels' fight was futile. "My father is a god, a major kami created by our First Parents. He cannot die, he cannot be beaten. What do these samurai insurgents believe they will accomplish by fighting an immortal as strong as he?"

Daiki leveled me with a frank look. "Death is just one of many ways to overcome an opponent, and in my opinion a more merciful one. Once captured, there will be very little your father can do to stop the insurgents from handing the empire over to you."

My eyes widened at that bold statement. I didn't necessarily want the life my parents had plotted for me, the life they felt was fated through a prophecy given long ago by ancient kami, but ruling an empire as broken as this one also left me feeling overwhelmed and trapped. I was only seventeen, and though I wanted to heal everyone and everything, I couldn't imagine being in a position where I might actually be expected to do just that.

My noble desires mixed with my feelings of total inadequacy made for an uneasy mind and a troubled heart.

Daiki's son chose at that moment to let us know how hungry he was. His high-pitched cries reassured me that all would be well with him and Hatsumi.

"You had better take your son in to nurse with his mother. I should be going as well. It will soon be light outside."

"Yes, you had better return quickly. I fear I may have kept you too long this time."

I gave Daiki and his sweet babe a quick hug and headed for the door. As I stepped outside into the cold night, I thought I heard footsteps scampering to the left. I turned to look but could make out very little. Dawn would be here within the hour, but it was still quite dark outside. After standing there for a few seconds, I determined that I had most likely heard the rustling of some neighboring animal or possibly a small bird and quickly hurried to put distance between myself and the small village before any early morning risers ventured forth out of their dwellings.

Just as I was about to leave the road and enter the forest, I heard a small cry to my left and sensed another individuals fear mixed with worry. I looked and beheld a small figure lying upon the floor beneath a tree. I walked a few steps toward the cloaked mass, but I pulled back abruptly when a sword flashed from underneath the huddled cloak.

"Don't come any closer."

The voice was decidedly female but raspy. Her breathing was labored and heavy.

I lifted my hands up to show I held no weapon.

"I'm not going to hurt you. I just thought you might need some help."

"Do you know the owner of that tavern, one, Daiki, by name?"

"I do. I just came from there."

"I have heard tell of a medicine woman he uses to help people who are suffering. I need to get to his tavern, but find I am too injured to move."

"It would seem fortune has smiled upon you. I am the medicine woman you are in need of." I walked over and bent down next to the woman. She shielded her face at my approach, something I found odd. She tried to lift her sword again, possibly hoping to defend herself against an attack, but the weight of it pulled her weakened arm to the ground. She released it and sucked in air. I gently took her hand and connected with her before she could stop me.

I gritted my teeth at the pain and explored her injuries. Broken ribs, broken pelvis, broken hip, fracture on her lower spinal column. I had already gathered that this woman must have been a warrior, but I couldn't understand what would have caused such extensive damage.

"How were you injured?"

She took in shallow breaths. "Horse...spooked...by something in the forest...rolled on top of me."

I couldn't believe she had managed to drag herself to the edge of the forest with the type of injuries she had sustained. I was sure she must have damaged her back further due to the exertion. As a result she would never walk again, and now I was faced with a serious dilemma. When Daiki had me heal people who were injured, I could teach their bodies to heal slowly so it didn't look as if I had anything to do with it other than administering to their needs with herbs. I couldn't instruct this woman's ki to heal slowly and then leave her here for the next few days with no food, no water, and no shelter, and since the fracture and subsequent damage to her spine left her no option of mobility, she would stay trapped on the ground just inside the forest until she slowly healed or perished from dehydration.

Moving her to the tavern was out of the question. With the way her ribs had broken, her lungs would easily be punctured and she could bleed internally, expiring before we arrived. Besides, I knew for certain I would never have the strength to carry her dead weight. If I wanted to save her I would have to heal her immediately and risk my identity in the process. I could only hope I hadn't inadvertently run into one of my father's spies.

"What is your name?" I asked.

"That's my business and has nothing to do with your taking me to the tavern." She inhaled sharply and let out a small wet sounding breath.

I smiled at her guarded and suspicious behavior and decided I liked her. "I'm afraid moving you is out of the question. Your back is broken and prevents you from moving your legs. No... don't even try. This will only worsen your situation." At my words the young woman paused any movement she might have made and stilled. "Your ribs are broken and will puncture your lungs if you are moved."

"I don't understand...how you could know...the...extent of my injuries?"

In answer I let go of her hand and placed both of mine on either side of her head. She sucked in another shallow, wet breath in surprise, but I had already connected again. I instructed her ki to fix the ribs since one had punctured her lung in the few moments we had talked to one another. That accounted for her breathing.

We both screamed out in pain, and I realized that I had not anesthetized the area before instructing the mending of her bones. I had been so concerned with the amount of blood filling her left lung that my only thought was to remove the jagged end of the lower rib, assemble the break and redistribute the pooling blood.

I quickly instructed that her pain be blocked, but her screaming had already subsided. She had passed out from the shock of it. I continued on, feeling guilty that I had allowed her even a moment of such excruciating pain.

Once this life-threatening injury had been dealt with I focused on the small break in her lower spine. This particular break was very delicate in nature due to its position, and it wasn't as if the intelligences within the cells knew exactly what to do. I always had to be so meticulous when giving directions and mental images to anyone's ki, but especially when it came to injuries along the spine or within the heart and brain.

I could feel tiny droplets of perspiration beading along my hairline as I instructed the fusing of the fracture as carefully as possible.

This woman was a warrior, and though I had no idea if she fought for or against my father, at that moment loyalties and sides made little difference. When you stripped away titles and groupings, in the end, we were all human, and she deserved a chance to live. Without the ability to use her legs, she would never survive on her own, and I would never allow that to happen.

Not when I could help her.

It took about fifteen minutes to heal the fracture to the spinal column. Had the break been any worse, I most likely would have been missed by my father. Once I accomplished that tedious task it was only a matter of seconds for the break in her hip and pelvis to be remedied. I'd had plenty of practice mending such injuries with my father's soldiers. Of course, he would have me heal them only to break them again; one of his favorite torture methods.

I sickened at the thought and became more determined than ever to crawl out from under my father's tyranny and find some semblance of a life for myself.

Once I finished healing the most debilitating injuries, I read her ki again to make certain I hadn't missed anything that might significantly impair mobility. Other than some bruising, her body had healed perfectly. I let out a happy sigh and pulled my hands from her head. I felt the dusky light from the early morning dawn shift just a bit, and I almost lost my balance. Closing my eyes, I waited for my ki to correct the weakness in my body.

I had pushed myself to the limit within the last few hours. Upon opening my eyes again it seemed as if the sun had risen an inch in the last few seconds. I panicked, knowing I was pushing my time limit. My disappearance would be noticed within an hour. I knew I couldn't leave the poor woman on the outskirts of the forest for any traveler passing by to see and possibly attack her. I stood up and positioned myself behind her slumped over frame, then bent low, wrapping my arms around her mended chest and dragging her backward deeper within the forest.

After making sure her cloak covered her completely, and then covering her with a blanket of fallen leaves for good measure, I stood up, gave her ki a blessing of protection and continued my hurried journey toward the palace.

If I hadn't been the emperor's daughter, I could have watched over her to make sure no one disturbed her while her body recuperated. As a normal peasant girl, things could be different... easier...less complicated.

It took only a few minutes to reach the marked trail and begin my familiar journey down the path toward the palace. It was important that I reach my room before Aiko came to wake me. Even though she knew about my excursions, and sometimes accompanied me, it was her responsibility every morning to wake me and ready me for the day's events. If she could not find me, she would most assuredly be blamed for it. I quickened my pace at the thought of Aiko receiving punishment due to my tardiness.

Aiko had been my companion since I was a baby and she sixteen, a nursemaid and mother of sorts, and then trained as my handmaiden as I grew older. She was a bright light against the constant darkness within the palace walls. I never wanted to lose her, but our permanent separation was inevitable once I was united with Katsu.

She would not be allowed to come with us, and though it pained me to consider never seeing her again, I certainly didn't want her to ever face the same fate as myself. She would be able to have children when she married. Once I became a full kami, that option would no longer exist.

At least she would be free to leave the palace and make a new life for herself. With my father ruling the empire with his iron fist, there was scarcely an opportunity to experience joy or happiness. His presence always seemed to snuff out such things.

The empire of Kagami was a part of Japan within the island of Okinawa, but cloaked in a way that prevented the rest of the inhabitants of Japan from finding it. In other words this vast empire existed in a different sphere in order to keep the land of our kind hidden from the rest of the world.

All the inhabitants of Japan knew of this empire, and revered and respected its sacred purpose as a home for their gods, but very few were able to find it. The humans who lived in this empire had been brought here thousands of years ago to cultivate the land and keep it safe from outside influences.

For centuries, Kagami had been a home of peace and prosperity, ruled by Hachiman the god of war, agriculture and farming, and the divine protector of Japan and its people, until it was time for the preparation of my birth. The empire was placed in the keeping of my father, Fukurokuju, the god of health and longevity, whom it was prophesied would unite with a human empress, Chinatsu Mori, from another region of Japan, and together they would prepare the empire and its people for the birth of their savior, The Healer.

When my mother was brought to live at the Ivory Palace, she was immediately accepted by the people and loved for her role in giving birth to their savior. My tutor, Kenji, told me the events surrounding my birth were filled with happy days of prosperity for the empire and the inhabitants that dwelled therein, but soon after my birth, my father began to grow suspicious and paranoid of other kami, worried that his position as emperor would be challenged now that his duty had been performed and a daughter born.

According to Kenji, the relationship between my parents disintegrated, if there ever was one to begin with. Arranged marriages were not known for giving consideration to the preferences or personalities of the parties involved. My father became obsessed with power and greed, and the empire slowly dwindled to what it was now—a province full of repression and injustice, ruled by a tyrannical emperor.

The Samurai Wars started two years after my birth and had

continued ever since. Though I hoped and prayed that one day the rebels would have the power to overthrow my father's claim to the throne, I understood the gravity of the situation.

Breaching the palace walls was a near impossibility. Only a kami's blood would be recognized by the walls of the palace. In the real world, palaces that lived and breathed were completely nonexistent, but in the empire of Kagami, The Ivory Palace contained its very own ki, or life force, and recognized that its purpose was to protect the kami that dwelled within.

If a samurai rebel did manage to find a way to breach the walls of the palace, he would be forever lost within its vast halls and corridors. The palace's ki could sense an individual's intent, and any rebel wishing to do my father harm would never reach my father's rooms but would be led in circles throughout the castle until caught by the guards stationed everywhere. To fight against a living structure such as the Ivory Palace was suicide.

The only option, then, was to draw the emperor out and ambush him. Unfortunately, my father's paranoia had left him a hermit within the walls of Zoutenotou, the palace's proper name. I could count on my hand the number of times he had dared venture to take one step outside the palace walls.

My mother was the one who traveled the empire, doing her best to tend to the needs of the people, making them love her more and more and my father less and less. I never mistook her actions as anything having to do with love and kindness. She was a shrewd woman, understanding the voice and will of the people she ruled. Her motives were self-serving. She wanted to be the one the people turned to if ever the samurai rebels succeeded in imprisoning my father.

The war consisted of my father's soldiers tracking and hunting down anyone suspected of involvement with the rebels, and he waged full-fledged battles with organized rebel troops. My father lost countless good men to the rebels and forced any male of sixteen years or older to join his soldiers for a minimum of five years. If they survived, they were allowed to start their own families and lead their own lives.

I often wondered how much longer my father hoped to rule as emperor without the other major kami getting involved. His behavior threatened the lives of innocent humans, and he was more than responsible for thousands of deaths. His hands were saturated in the blood of the innocent, yet the kami and their First Parents remained indifferent and silent.

It couldn't continue on much longer. There had to be a way to stop it. For some time now, I had pondered the possibility that once I united with my betrothed and left the empire to fulfill my duties as The Healer that the other kami would step in and relieve my father from his duties as emperor. Then the people would be safe.

I also wondered if perhaps I could end it all now by escaping Kagami and joining the other humans in the main areas of Japan. Without my presence, my father would no longer be a necessary ruler of the empire, and perhaps it would be given to my mother, once she became a full kami. The gift of immortality was promised to her by my father on their wedding night. He had yet to deliver said promise, and I honestly doubted he ever would, but perhaps my mother could appeal to other major kami for the gift promised to her. It certainly wasn't an unthinkable request.

I didn't necessarily understand the process of a human becoming a kami with the help of another kami, though I knew it was called an ascension, but I felt uncomfortable with the idea that my ascension as a full kami was scheduled on my eighteenth birthday, the day I would meet my betrothed, Katsu, and be united with him by the god of love and marriage.

I couldn't think of anything in the world I wanted to avoid more than that ceremony. My future husband would no doubt be just as pigheaded, domineering, and abusive as my father. Male kami were completely evil if my father's behavior was any kind of indication.

For months now, I had thought of nothing but planning some form of escape. However, after having talked with Daiki, I no longer felt positive that leaving the empire was the best solution.

Staying and fighting my father for power over the empire held a certain amount of appeal, and would benefit thousands of people. I simply didn't know where to start.

I glanced at the shift in the rising sun and hurried my steps, cursing myself for becoming lost in my musings and, as a result, slowing my pace.

I had nearly made it halfway through the forested path when I heard more scuffling and then an ominous sounding thunk cracking against the bark of a tree where my head had just passed. I stopped short and lifted my hand to the bark, wondering what could have possibly made such a sound.

My fingers touched the bark of the banyan tree and then slowly traveled a few inches lower until they came in contact with the cool feel of metal, jagged and edged with the sides moving out in a V pattern. I let my thumb and finger feel the two points at the top of the V and brought them together, almost touching before my fingers ran into the base of a small, metal shaft protruding from the V.

If I had possessed any sense at all, I would have recognized what had hit the tree and assumed that the weapon had been meant for me, but the idea that someone had shot an arrow at me purposely was almost too inconceivable to comprehend. Assassination attempts were always hazards for an imperial princess, but no one knew I was out here and most likely had no idea who I was. Therefore, it was reasonable to assume that there was a logical explanation for the black arrow protruding from the dark flesh of the tree.

It had to have been an accident, a hunter attempting to catch some local game and feed his family. I tried to pull the arrow from the tree, but when I wrapped my hand around it, I felt my skin begin to burn. I let out a hushed gasp and withdrew immediately. The slow rise of dawn made it only slightly easier to see the arrow. I studied the shaft, but couldn't understand why it would have burned my skin. Then I looked to where the metal had embedded itself within the heart of one of the tree's many curved prop roots. Black lines were spiraling outward from the point of impact and quickly singing the bark, leaving scorched patterns in its wake.

I backed up quickly and shook my head. "Impossible!"

Weapons forged in the land of the dead were common tales amongst villagers and royalty alike, but they, along with their large, cat-like wielders were merely myths meant to frighten children into obedience.

I knew better.

I knew enough about the land of the dead to know that there were kami, once good and obedient, who had turned against our First Parents and aligned themselves with the demon god Amatsu. Their souls were corrupted, and the evil they so desperately wished to inflict upon the world of the living soon changed them into ugly abominations called nekomata… Amatsu's skilled assassins.

Kenji had pounded every facet of the land of the dead, its history, its inhabitants, the god that ruled over it and their weapons into my head time and time again. I had to learn about these weapons and these assassins because I was The Healer, the one meant to heal the veil between the living and the dead, thus preventing Amatsu from crossing over and making the world of the living his permanent home.

I was the threat, the proverbial thorn in this demon god's side, and I had been warned by my overbearing father countless times that an attempt on my life by one or more of Amatsu's assassins before I united with Katsu and became a full kami was inevitable.

There had never been a single assassination attempt throughout my entire life, and I had begun to wonder if perhaps my father had made it all up to scare me into submission and keep me a prisoner within the walls of the palace.

The scorched scarring of the tree dispelled any and all previous doubts. I took another frightened step back and felt something scald me sharply against the top of my left ear. I heard another thunk and saw the second arrow embedded within the tree.

Then the whole tree went up in flames, an alarming sight considering the many prop roots it possessed. The heat exploded in my face, throwing me to the ground. My right wrist buckled under my weight as I tried to get into a standing position. I managed to get up, but threw myself to the ground when I saw something large and ominous out of the corner of my eye. Another arrow, a different tree…all meant for me. This forest was filled with banyan trees. I would be surrounded by fire within minutes if I didn't find a way to move faster.

I grasped the scorched terrain with my hands and quickly pulled myself to a standing position as I heard the padding of soft, stealthy footsteps creep up behind me. When I turned around and beheld the thing that hunted me, I could scarcely believe what my own eyes revealed.

Not fifteen feet away stood a huge monster, something that looked like a cross between a human and a large, black panther. This creature was all muscle and sinew, covered in a layer of scraggly black hair. Its feet and hands were capped with claws that looked like enlarged, curved fangs or talons even. He wore strange straps of some type of animal skin to keep his large sword secured at his side. The sharp blade gleamed wickedly in the breaking sunlight. His muzzle was ugly and scarred, no doubt from countless battles within the ranks of his own assassin brothers, and he had two large tails undulating up and down behind him. I couldn't have fled from this monstrous apparition even if I'd had the presence of mind to do so.

"You don't wish to flee from me, Princess?" His mouth looked unnatural, trying to form the words of my native tongue. "I expected more of a chase from you."

I thought for sure the nekomata would end me right then and there. Instead, he took several predatory steps forward until his grotesque features were merely inches from my own. He pointed one long talon to my left temple and brought it slowly down my face, applying just enough pressure to draw blood. I had heard that the effects of fear could paralyze one so completely that no power of will in any measure could make one react to the most basic instinct a human might have, that of survival.

My fear held my feet firmly in place.

The nekomata's green slits monitored my face as I felt the cut he administered slowly heal before his eyes. Surface wounds, such as scrapes and cuts were easily remedied by my ki.

The nekomata made an ugly, satisfied sounding grunt, as if what he had suspected had been confirmed, and pulled his sword from its sheath.

"I will make this quick, though I love the thought of spending hours torturing a soul with the ability to heal. My brothers are more interested in eliminating this problem as quickly as possible." He lifted his sword high above his head. "And since I am merely a slave to the will of my companions," he took one step forward, "I must comply."

The nekomata let out a strange cry, and I knew my life was about to end, but I couldn't close my eyes. Just before the nekomata brought his sword to bear against me, he stiffened sharply, his eyes flickering wide with pain. His hands slackened, and the sword he'd intended to end my life with fell to the blackened floor between us. He crumpled forward, with black blood foaming at his mouth and the front of his chest.

And then he died.

I stared at the grotesque, lifeless figure on the ground. My eyes shot upward, terrified anew as I heard the sound of a twig break, ringing loudly in the silent wake of the nekomata's violent death.

I couldn't have been more surprised with what I saw. Left standing behind the beast was a handsome stranger with an unhappy look on his face.

The man was about six feet tall, well-muscled with dark hair to his square chin and dark, stormy eyes framed by the kind of brows and cheekbones only a god could have possessed. The hatred in his eyes made me feel as if I had just traded one enemy for another, until I realized his hate-filled glance was directed at the large, lifeless beast in between us.

He finally lifted his eyes to mine, and I saw a slow softening of his features as he took me in. He didn't hide his interest but took his time studying me intently. It was an uncomfortable feeling, as if I had been placed on display at some vendor's market, waiting to be sold to the highest bidder. I wanted to break the silence but still hadn't gathered enough of my wits to form a complete sentence.

He finally broke it for me. "Are you okay?"

I nodded, still not daring to speak, barely able to look him in the eye.

He waited, continuing to stare at me, but he was confused. He seemed to be vacillating between anger and recognition.

"Are you from this area?"

I swallowed hard. "The village."

"The village. What were you doing in the forest?"

"Ah…I…was gathering figs for breakfast."

"This far into the forest? Surely you could have found some closer to your home or to the path, at least?"

"Well…I was being hunted by that monstrosity and must have come much farther than I thought." This was not good. I needed to end this conversation as soon as possible and return to the palace before my father discovered I was missing.

"Yes, and that brings me to my next question," he said, placing his sword point down into the earth and then leaning on it. His posture was that of one feeling casual, but his tensed muscles and strained features told a different story. This man was always prepared for battle, a warrior by the look of his sword and sheath. "Why was an assassin from the underworld wasting his time with an insignificant peasant girl?"

His obvious slight didn't offend me in the least. I welcomed being mistaken for a peasant, relished it with all my heart. It made my job of healing others significantly easier. Having powers, being royalty or simply being different was something I couldn't afford to have anyone outside of the palace discover.

"I couldn't say, only that I may have interrupted him while he was pursuing his real purpose."

The warrior quirked a confused eyebrow at me.

"He wasn't hunting you? He didn't make contact first?"

"No," I lied easily. "That is, not until I managed to stumbled across his prone form. Maybe he was sleeping?"

"Nekomata never sleep. They can't. They can, however, lie in wait for what they are stalking to make its way over to them." He eyed me shrewdly. "I don't believe you."

I felt my heart deflate. I was never going to get home in time with my identity intact.

He made his way over to me, stepping over the nekomata and placing his large frame right in front of my small one. Instinctively, I backed up a step and then stopped, realizing the movement was futile. I kept my eyes fixed on the forest floor but sucked in a sharp breath as he lifted my chin with his finger. Now he was forcing me to look up at him. I couldn't help but feel slightly resentful toward him for that.

"Your manner, your dress, and your bearing indicate that you are far above a mere peasant's class, and nekomata are sent by the demon god for one thing and one thing only." The handsome warrior gently grabbed my right hand with his left and lifted it to his heart. "The Healer," he whispered softly. "He was trying to kill the one meant to heal the veil."

I shook my head defensively and tried to pull my hand from his, but he brought it to his lips and kissed the back of it.

I felt a shock go through me at this overbearing man's bold and callous behavior. My father would have had him executed immediately.

"You will release me at once...please." It was difficult to assert myself with a man. I simply wasn't used to it.

The young warrior merely leveled me with a suggestive glance and then quirked his lips in amusement and turned my hand over, laying a kiss on the soft pulse at my wrist. He couldn't have failed to notice how my heart rate sped up at this inappropriate contact.

I forcefully pulled away. "How dare you? You may have saved

my life, but that hardly gives you the right to handle me in such an inappropriate manner." I used the only threat I could think of that might be powerful enough to stop the young warrior's idea of conquest. "I am betrothed to someone else, and…and he will no doubt kill you for touching me." I had no intention of following through with my union to Masaru Katsu, but he didn't have to know that.

The young warrior didn't look at all frightened. If anything he looked happier with news of my union.

"Your devotion to a man you have never before met does you credit, young princess, but I'm not overly concerned about my demise at the hands of your betrothed."

I inched backward, getting ready to flee the moment he attempted to touch me again. "And why is that?"

"Because, my dear, I *am* your betrothed. I am a kami, a warrior god and keeper of the Grass Cutter Sword."

I looked up in horror as he inched closer and placed both his hands at my waist, pulling me to him.

"I am Katsu."

3

I shook my head several times, trying to take in this bizarre and rather unwelcome twist of fate. This man—couldn't be Katsu. He wasn't anything like I'd imagined. I had expected the man to be large and intimidating to be sure, but I hadn't once considered the possibility that he might be beautiful to look upon or that I would be attracted to him in any way. I had pictured someone somber and remote; someone unwilling to address me unless it was absolutely necessary, but this man looked at me like I was the only thing he would ever want to look upon the rest of his life.

I fairly squirmed under the intensity of his gaze.

Katsu's eyebrows narrowed ever so slightly. "Are you not happy to see me, Princess?"

My mouth opened in surprise at this unexpected question. Why would he care about my feelings? I clamped my mouth shut when I noticed him staring at it hungrily. I'd never before been kissed, but I knew what desire looked like.

Oh dear! This first meeting wasn't anything like I'd thought it would be.

I cleared my throat with some difficulty, realizing that he had wrapped an arm around my waist during my awkward silence. "Forgive me, sir, but I was under the impression that the warrior god wouldn't make an appearance until my eighteenth birthday." I lowered my eyes to his chest when his smoldering gaze became too much for me. "I was told our union wasn't to be finalized until then. So you see, I…wasn't expecting you."

"I see. I guess your father wouldn't have been forthcoming with that information considering my reasons for arriving early."

I felt curious as to what those reasons might be, but knew it would be terribly inappropriate to ask. I waited for him to continue, and when he didn't, I raised my head.

When my eyes met his, I felt the full force of his emotions. Even if I hadn't been an empath I would have had to have been carved of granite to not feel the alarming mix of emotions this warrior god was experiencing. I sensed shock, fear, joy, and affection. Those feelings of affection seemed to center solely around me. I could almost sense him replaying the last few minutes of our encounter. The moment he considered what might have happened to me if he hadn't arrived when he did, made his arms around me tighten ever so slightly and a fierce protectiveness settled in, an emotion so all-encompassing I felt my body shake and my knees begin to weaken.

"You're trembling, Princess. Did that monster hurt you before I came to your aid?"

I shook my head and tried to push away from his iron-clad grip, but I may as well have been pressing against stone.

"Tell me where you are hurt," he demanded.

"Truthfully, I fear the only thing causing me to tremble so is the proximity of our persons and your arms around me." I stared resolutely at his chest as I felt heat slip up the back of my neck and wash over my face. "I'm…not used to such close physical contact with…a man."

I sensed his amusement and satisfaction, though he reluctantly released me. Once freed from his overpowering presence, I stepped back as quickly as I could and inhaled deeply.

"Better?"

"Much." I nodded but didn't miss the narrowing of his eyes or the way they continued to analyze every inch of me.

"Now then, Princess, I'm afraid I must demand you tell me what on earth you were doing out in the forest without a single guard to protect you."

I was certain Katsu was accustomed to throwing out demands and expecting unquestioning compliance. I sighed inwardly, wishing with all my heart that for once in my life I could be the one making the demands and ordering members of the opposite sex around. I also had to scramble mentally to come up with a convincing lie. I was certain if Katsu learned of my involvement with the village and its people, he would put a stop to it—and quite possibly physically punish me as a result. It was certainly no less than my father would have done.

"I left the palace through no fault of my own." I paused, continuing to grasp for some fabrication that might be believable to this imposing kami. "I received a summons from my father by one of his guards requesting that I meet with him immediately. It was quite early in the morning, but my father has summoned me early before, so I didn't think it out of the ordinary." I thought I saw Katsu grimace at that last remark but continued spinning my lie. "No sooner had I left my chambers and walked the length of the hallway, when a cloth was placed over my mouth...and I...remember very little after that. I awoke propped up against a tree, and after gaining my bearings I began making my way back to the palace until...that thing," I pointed to the black monster on the ground, "attacked me."

"And I saved you."

My eyes darted to his, and I felt heat stain my cheeks. "Yes, you saved me."

I took in Katsu's features and noted the way his eyes focused in on me as his feelings of affection for me increased. Strange. I had assumed that an arranged marriage between the warrior god and myself would never hold any affection. He'd taken to me immediately, but I couldn't for the life of me understand why. I held a title and powers that were of little use to me unless I was using them for the good of others. It wasn't much for him to go on.

I supposed I should have been grateful that he had decided to like me, but other thoughts intruded—thoughts of the young soldier I'd met in Daiki's tavern, and how much I wished at that exact moment that he had been the one to save me instead of the man I was betrothed to. A terribly ungrateful thought to have, but a thought, and a feeling, I found impossible to dismiss.

"So someone within the palace walls is a traitor to this empire. I can't say I'm surprised. The emperor has played the fool with his games of intrigue and—" he cut off abruptly.

I sincerely wished for him to elaborate on his political views concerning my father. It never would have occurred to me that Katsu might have a bone to pick with him. I had always assumed he was only interested in the veil and the part he played in keeping balance on the Earth.

There were many things I didn't fully comprehend, but my future was still being decided for me. I couldn't play along anymore without the knowledge necessary to understand whether my destiny was certain or if plotting out my own path might be the best course of action. I determined right then and there that regardless of my intentions to escape my union with Katsu, I would do all I could to learn from him what he knew of my father's plans for the empire.

"I'm interested in the timing, however," he continued. "Why would an assassination attempt occur the day I send word of my arrival?"

His question chilled me. Why indeed?

"It was fortuitous that you happened upon the attempt on my life on your way to the palace, sir."

"It was fate, Princess, plain and simple. You and I are meant to be. Not even a well-planned attempt on your life will ever have the power to separate two people destined for one another."

I swallowed a large lump in my throat and wondered at the tears forming. I was touched by his remarks, and in truth almost craved the loving attention. It wasn't what I was used to. I reached up to swipe at the corners of my eyes before he noted the moisture there, but I could tell by the strengthening of his emotions for me that he noticed and was fighting to keep his distance as per my request.

"Why do you persist in calling me sir?" he asked, effectively changing the subject.

"This is our first meeting. I suppose I assumed things would be a little more formal."

"I think after saving you from a human sized cat it's a little late for formalities." He gave me a mischievous grin. "Besides, this is hardly our first meeting."

I knew what he referred to but felt uncomfortable to admit it. The whole experience had left me reeling, knowing I had been found wanting in some way.

"You were presented to me at our betrothal ceremony when you were fifteen," he continued, "but I wore a traditional mask. You did not see my face at the time, and *your* face was covered in that traditional white makeup that barely allows a man to actually get a glimpse of his intended. I apologize for not recognizing you much sooner."

I remembered the lavish party my father had thrown to announce my betrothal to Katsu. In other words, the day I turned fifteen was the day I was eligible for marriage, and Katsu was present at the ceremony. I had no way of knowing what he looked like beneath the traditional betrothal mask. I wasn't allowed to see him, but he was allowed to look upon me, inspect me as if I was an animal paraded before an audience. It had been humiliating to say the least, and even more so when Katsu never claimed me after the ceremony, as was expected.

Father had never gone into full detail in explaining the reasons behind it. He merely stated that Katsu had found me completely unsuitable, and I would need more training before I could take my rightful place at his side. I'd never wanted to be at his side, but the criticism stung nonetheless. I had waited for some kind of scheduled training or preparation to take place, but nothing other than the increase of abuse to my power through my father's interrogation techniques occurred. I had been left wondering if perhaps my future husband had found me repulsive. I had hoped he would never return after that humiliating day of rejection.

Yet here he stood, and I was not ready for him. I was not ready for anything other than escape.

"You left. I assumed that would be the last we would see of you for quite some time."

He looked surprised. "We're betrothed. Why would you have assumed such a thing?"

"My father led me to believe you were not happy with…with me." I felt uncomfortable having to explain myself to a man I barely knew.

I felt Katsu's anger flash, but he did his best to reign it in. "Your father is a very accomplished liar and a skilled manipulator. I would have stayed to train you, but he felt you were not ready. He insisted it would be better for me to return when you were eighteen and your powers more fully developed."

Now *I* felt angry. "My powers were fully developed many years ago, long before my fifteenth birthday. Why would he send you away? Why would he lie to you when all he has ever prepared me for is our inevitable union?"

"Why indeed." Katsu looked as if he wanted to ask me something, but I could sense his indecision. He felt protective and concerned for my delicate sensibilities. He would have been surprised at the kind of gory experiences I'd been privy to.

"We should return you to the palace. I am sure your absence has created quite a stir."

"Yes. No doubt the guards at my door will be punished. I would not wish any harm to come to them."

Katsu approached me slowly. "May I accompany you home then, Princess?"

The question was rhetorical. I doubted he expected me to refuse him.

"You may."

Katsu delicately took my arm in his and began leading me in the direction of the palace. I swallowed hard. I was not looking forward to the punishment my father would have in store for me, whether he believed my outlandish lie or not.

∞∞∞

"Princess Mikomi, your father wishes to speak with you," my maid, Aiko, said as she glided into my bedroom.

Anger, trepidation, and fear coursed through my body, a familiar reaction to any amount of time I was sentenced to spend with my father, Emperor Fukurokuju. When I looked up from the piece of parchment paper I was scribbling away on, however, my features revealed nothing. I was a docile puppet and duty bound to honor any summons my father made. I despised it more than I could have possibly described. It was a wonder I was able to conceal my real thoughts in regards to the prison my life had long become.

Upon arriving at the palace, the guards had been instructed to escort me back to my room and await my father's inquiries. Katsu had been escorted by other guards after he demanded an audience with my father. The guards, though used to orders coming from the emperor, knew better than to argue with a kami. I'd been writing poetry for the better part of an hour in an attempt to calm my nerves while waiting for Aiko to bring me word.

I felt quite ill imagining the several different scenarios this audience with him would bring about. Naturally, he would wish to be made aware of the attempt on my life this morning, but if that was all he wished for he could have been given that information from Katsu and avoided my presence altogether.

He never desired to see me unless his motives were darker in nature. I hadn't been made to torture anyone in quite some time, but war and intrigue were a part of an emperor's everyday concern. According to my father, pulling traitorous secrets from prisoners of war, or from the poor and seditious deserters, was an unfortunate necessity if the Empire was to survive and thrive.

"Princess, did you not hear what I said?" Aiko rounded the corner of my chair and smartly took the writing utensil from my already stilled hands.

I wanted to snatch it from her and express to her exactly what was in my heart and mind without that nagging thought of duty, decorum or remembering one's place and role in the universe. I didn't want to behave appropriately. I didn't care to pretend I was willing to obey when every particle of my being wished to rebel. There were so many shockingly truthful things I could have flung at her with enough force and volume to shake the ivory rafters of my room, so many grievances she had already patiently sat through and listened to because that's what she had done since I'd been a child. Instead, I stood up achingly slowly, the only form of resistance I dared show, and moved to the mirror to check my appearance as she came behind me and adjusted the large decorative bow at my back.

I studied my reflection in the mirror and noted my hair was perfectly coiffed. I only ever wore the decorative headdress for important occasions or meetings with my father. It was heavy and cumbersome, much like the rest of my attire. My olive skin was smooth and unblemished and my brown eyes were a dark amber color, though they held very little life in them. Aiko had managed to fix the mess my late night excursion had reduced me to. I was a reflection of everything my parents wanted me to be. I looked for any signs of discontent in my expression; something that might betray the careful façade I wore day after day.

"Please stop all of this fussing, Aiko." I covered my frustration by smoothing my silk blue kimono. "I'm sure I look presentable enough."

Aiko tsked softly, just as she had for seventeen years and stepped away.

"I wish you would concern yourself more with your appearance, mistress," she said in a disapproving voice.

"Why? During the few times my father allowed me to leave the palace, my face was draped in yards of black silk. Whom do I have to impress?"

"You know just as well as I do that your veil is for your own protection. There are plenty of rabble out there who would love nothing more than to take credit for the death of The Healer. I was referring to your appearance for your father's sake. He doesn't usually send for you for mundane tasks."

"He doesn't usually send for me at all." I felt no pain with this remark. I had learned long ago that my "gift" for healing was the only reason my father held any interest in me. I may have been the child of prophecy—I tried not to feel scorn at the much hated title—but it didn't make me any more important to him than most daughters are to their fathers, regardless of what I was destined to accomplish.

I considered the prophecy and all that Katsu and I were meant to achieve—becoming the only thing standing in the way of Amatsu, demon god and lord of the underworld. I couldn't think of anything I wanted to do less, and up until my attack this morning, I'd found it difficult to accept that such a prophecy existed. If I turned it into a harmless legend, then it had no power over me.

It seemed as if this alleged prophecy benefited my father in some specific way by linking me to Katsu, but for the life of me I couldn't understand what it was he would have to gain since he had everything. All I did know for certain was that I was capable of healing people who had been injured or were suffering from illnesses, and I was strictly forbidden to use those powers unless directed by my father.

He claimed I needed to save my gift and only use it for healing the veil, but he rarely hesitated to abuse my powers to heal his generals, torture his enemies or extract information from his allies with promises of health and prosperity. I hated the hypocrisy. I hated this palace, but most of all I hated him.

"Mistress, you had better answer your father's summons quickly. He has never been a patient man." Aiko interrupted my dark musings.

"He's not a man, Aiko. He's a god."

I turned my back on the docile reflection in the mirror, too sickened by it to look another moment longer, and quickly walked out the darkened cedar door.

∞∞∞

I waited for my father's servant to fetch me in the summoning room, a highly decorative formal sitting area where people were made to feel intimidated by the painted portraits of important ancestors from my mother's side of the family. All men, of course. The paintings were detailed, enhancing the vibrant colors of their *Hakama*, a pleated garment worn over their clothing, which was meant to illustrate their station and wealth. The more embellishments upon their robes, the higher their station.

I supposed it would have been intimidating to have painted portraits of my father's ancestry peppering the walls, but the only beings he claimed for parentage were the original creators of all kami everywhere, and any image painted of them would never have done them sufficient justice. Precious few kami could claim the privilege of laying eyes upon them.

I sighed heavily. I knew I should have felt more awe and respect for the gods of this universe, but all I truly felt was disgust. They were immortal, nothing more. They may have possessed incredible powers for keeping the world in balance, but I found that many of them never used those powers in accordance with the laws that their First Parents supposedly governed them with.

Take my father, for instance. He was a protector of life and longevity, yet all I witnessed from him was repression and tyranny, killing those who would willing speak up or fight against the deplorable living conditions everyone but the royal family were subjected to.

As someone half immortal, I too had powers gifted to me but was forbidden to use them the way I saw fit. I wanted to help.

I wanted to heal. I wanted control over my life and the lives of those I could protect.

My angry musings were interrupted by the arrival of my father. His presence was highly unusual. I was always greeted by his adviser and brought to wherever it was he was located.

I immediately bowed from the waist and kept my eyes on the floor out of deference and respect. My anger all the while was simmering just below the surface. I felt him lift my chin and grant me permission to stand. I kept my eyes lowered until he snapped his fingers, signaling that I was allowed to look upon him. His robes were covered in threaded gold embellishments. Never willing to understate his position, he wore nothing but the finest clothing created by the most talented seamstresses in the empire. He appeared extremely excited—highly unusual for him.

I startled when he wrapped his arms around me and embraced me for the first time in my entire life. I stiffened in surprise, uncertain and anxious. I wondered if he wished for me to return this affection with that of my own.

I nearly brought my arms about his bulky robes, but he was already pulling away, placing hands on both my shoulders, and bestowing upon me one of his rare smiles.

"You will meet him this evening, my child. Your engagement ceremony will bring joy and happiness to our people. Of this I am certain. I am proud of you, young daughter. Fulfill your duty and your destiny."

I looked at him blankly for a few moments. My engagement ceremony? Hadn't that happened two years ago? Betrothals and engagements were basically the same thing. Why were we repeating the process?

His uncharacteristic behavior, coupled with the unexpected announcement of another ceremony, left me feeling slow and speechless. Had he not been made aware of the assassination attempt on my life and my subsequent meeting with Katsu?

"I thought the ceremony took place when I was fifteen."

My father's happiness melted away as he looked at me sharply.

I had spoken without permission. I bent my head quickly and lowered my eyes to the floor. "Forgive me, Father."

He let out an unhappy grunt.

"That frivolous occasion was more of a coming out party. Katsu could look upon you and decide if he wished to go through with it. Not that he had a choice in the long run, but traditions must be upheld."

In other words, I truly *had* been paraded around like an animal. Such a pity for Katsu, he didn't have the luxury of choosing his own bride like most men did.

"The engagement ceremony will take place tonight. This will allow you to train with Katsu unchaperoned. He will teach you how to harness your powers and combine them with the Grass Cutter Sword in order to heal the veil when the time comes. If you have questions, ask them now."

I wanted to ask him why he had sent Katsu away and refused to allow him to train me until now. Instead, I lifted my head but kept my focus on the floor. "How much time does the warrior god feel we will need for training?"

"He wishes to train you until your eighteenth birthday, six months from now. In any event you will do all he requires of you and more in order to be ready for your future together. Is that understood?"

I nodded.

I felt a little easier, knowing I still had a few months to figure another way out. I hadn't minded my first meeting with Katsu. Honestly, I was surprised by his kind attitude and protective feelings toward me, but after speaking with Daiki, I couldn't help but feel that I was meant to make a difference in some other way. If I could stay here and help the suffering of my people, just as Daiki had mentioned, then maybe joining forces with the rebels was the only way to bring about the overthrow of my father. It was a dangerous idea, but it was also another option, and one that I could make for myself.

"Excellent. Now, there is another matter most urgent and pressing for which I need your particular skill set."

I wasn't surprised that no mention of my near death with the nekomata was brought up. My father had most likely had all of his questions answered by Katsu. Nor was I surprised that my father didn't appear worried or overly concerned about my well-being, though you'd think he would have shown some consideration since his one trump card allowing him to remain in power had almost been assassinated.

I continued to remain leery of his behavior, however. He was happy to the point of being near giddy. Clearly, he'd accomplished something important, and that knowledge worried me.

"One of my generals has been wounded in battle. He has important information needing to be relayed to me and my other officers, but he is unconscious and incapable of sharing this information. I need you to come and heal him immediately. Lives may hang in the balance."

I was sure lives *did* hang in the balance but that he cared very little for whom those lives belonged to or if in fact those lives were saved. I did nothing to acknowledge my agreement. It would have done little good if I had agreed with him or not. The idea that I might refuse him would have been so foreign to him as to never have crossed his mind. I had no choice. I never did. I nodded my head with feigned acquiescence.

"You will follow me to the healing room."

The mention of the healing room triggered a wave of anxiety. The room was little more than a secret chamber beneath the palace where various forms of torture were used to extract information. It didn't matter to my father who the subject was or what side he was on. If there was information worth gleaning, he would use every avenue available.

He turned and walked quickly toward the back door, never once doubting my attendance directly behind him. I would play the part I had played until it was no longer necessary for me to do so, and I would play it just as convincingly as if my life depended on it...which I was sure it did.

He turned and made his way to the back of the long, rectangular room. His study was little more than a front for what lay directly behind the massive back wall laden with samurai adornments. He pulled roughly on the front of a solid gold sword firmly attached to the ivory wall, activating a mechanism within that unhinged a hidden door to our immediate right, slowly swinging it forward. The opening of the wall revealed a stone staircase descending toward a gaping maw of darkness.

As a little girl I'd had nightmare after nightmare of descending these very steps. Aiko would wake me and stay by my side for the rest of the night, never telling either one of my parents how terrified I was. She knew my father would only punish me for such cowardice and my mother would show very little, if any, concern for the impact such a place might have on a child's subconscious.

I followed my father down the stone steps, noting, as I usually did, that the palace's ki felt different in this particular area. More remote and less watchful. It made me wonder if it had abandoned this area of itself due to the way in which my father disrespectfully abused it.

We must have traveled fifteen feet before the staircase leveled out onto a black cobblestone floor with moss covered walls. It smelled of mildew, death, and decay. Not many made it out of this hole with their lives.

After traveling another twenty feet or so, we turned left into a small room where three of my father's servants surrounded a table with a young man lying unconscious atop its wooden surface.

I noted the blood oozing out of a gaping wound that traversed the entire breadth of his broad chest and shuddered at the pain such a wound must be causing him. I waited for my father's permission to approach the young soldier and moved forward when he motioned his hand toward the table.

The servants quickly dispersed at my approach, pushing into the shadows and dark recesses of the room. None of them wished to have any accidental contact with me. To touch a royal princess, even by accident, would have meant immediate execution. I hardly noticed, being used to such treatment by male servants.

I tried not to look at my subjects' faces so as not to get attached in any way. I didn't want to know them or their identity, and I didn't want to feel anything for them or their current, and I might add hopeless, situation.

I placed my hands on either side of the young man's head and closed my eyes, connecting with his ki immediately. The wound in his chest would be easy enough to repair. I sent images and instructions to his spirit to teach it how to accomplish such a feat in such a rapid amount of time.

Any other injuries present were in no way life-threatening, and I knew my father would not wish me to expend any unnecessary power on trivial wounds, but I couldn't prevent myself from addressing his broken wrist on the right side. I sensed from his ki that this was the hand he used to fight with, and if he could not hold his sword he would be considered unfit for his post and bring shame and dishonor to his family, providing he actually left this room alive. I hurried with my task, not wishing to raise any suspicion from my father, and then backed slowly away from the young soldier with my head bent and eyes to the floor.

The soldier sputtered and coughed up some left over blood from the wound he had received and then opened his eyes. I wasn't allowed to pay attention to the things that came after, but I wasn't sure why my father thought I would be able to block everything out when I stood in the same room. Immediately dismissing me didn't mean I ceased to exist.

I sank into the shadows and watched as the soldier surveyed his surroundings with a shrewd eye. He didn't appear to be afraid like most soldiers upon finding themselves placed in this room. Instead, he let out a low, deliberate laugh and slowly sat up. He didn't need to look at my father to know he was there. I sensed he felt very little fear, satisfied with his circumstances.

I was convinced he'd gone mad.

"Emperor Fukurokuju, this is quite the honor. I must have done something terribly heroic on the battlefield to have been brought here instead of the regular healing area."

I was astounded at his sarcastic tone and frank manner. The disrespect and unveiled hatred he exhibited toward my father was so foreign to me it nearly had me coughing and sputtering to try and distract everyone from this man's egregious error. There were many who hated my father, myself included, but I'd never witnessed anyone brave enough to show it.

I waited for my father's explosive response, but it never came. Instead, he surprised me by letting out a boisterous laugh.

"Isamu, I see you are no longer keeping up this tiring façade. Tell me, how long is it that you've worked with those samurai insurgents? Have you gathered sufficient intel to dispose of me and my thousands of loyal subjects?"

I nearly let out a disjointed laugh. I couldn't think of one living being in my father's kingdom who would have considered themselves loyal to him. Then I realized what he was accusing this man of. He was a rebel; a samurai insurgent.

This young man would never again see the light of day. I wanted to curl up into a ball on the floor and disappear into oblivion, knowing full well what would be required of me within a few moments.

"Oh, we've done much better than that, but why share such information and spoil the fun that awaits you? I think silence at this point is a more satisfying option." The man spoke with an easy assurance that didn't fit with the dire circumstances he found himself in. He knew he was going to die, yet he didn't seem to care.

My father approached him, his pace slow and deliberate.

"I think, young Isamu, you will find that willingly sharing what you know will be a less painful option than the methods I will use to ferret out what little you *claim* to know."

The soldier glared at him and bared his teeth.

"I am aware of your methods and do not fear your torture."

My father stared at him for a few more seconds. A happy look lit his eyes; a morbid expression considering the circumstances, but I knew that look far too well.

It was time.

"Daughter!" my father barked.

I jumped and hurried to collect my composure. Walking swiftly to the table, I placed my hands on either side of his head and prepared myself for the unpleasant part of my gift. I wasn't sure what possessed me to do it; I'd certainly never allowed myself this liberty before, but I looked right into the man's eyes and acknowledged that he did, in fact, exist. He stared back at me with no hint of fear or hatred on his part; just a strange kind of intensity that made me feel as if he were lending me some of his strength for the task that lay ahead of me. I closed my eyes and tried to steady my hands as I connected with him again.

I was immediately hit with a loud voice calling out my name.

"Princess, can you hear me?"

I felt a wave of shock ripple through my entire body. The soldier was communicating with me. In all my life this had never before happened.

When my father wanted information he would force me to connect with a person and command their ki to give up every detail of their life and transfer it to mine in order to extract any and all pertinent information that would help my father in winning this insufferable war. Anything that might give him an advantage was fair game.

The process wasn't painful for either myself or my subject, but once their memories were transferred to me, my father wouldn't allow me to give them back and the person was left with nothing; no memory of their life, their loved ones or their sense of self. They were stripped of everything, becoming mere shells of what they used to be, and their ki almost always terminated itself within minutes afterward. It mistook the loss of self as irreparable damage to the brain, and death seemed like a logical conclusion to come to.

That part was painful, for both of us. I always felt their ki searching frantically for some signal from the brain, some sign that it was still functioning properly. It would wait for me to share insightful information, and when nothing was given it would give up and rip away from the body.

It had to be the worst kind of invasion a person could ever experience. It made me vomit every time.

"Princess, we haven't much time. Can you hear me?"

I mentally shook myself and responded.

"Yes, I can hear you, but how is this possible? I've never had anyone communicate with me before?"

"There is no time for me to explain. I must get this message to you. Akane, the woman you met last night in the street, the one you healed, you remember her?"

I thought of the woman I had quickly healed as I headed into the woods on my way back to the palace. I knew it had been a mistake to heal her like that. I'd given my identity away. I could only hope this woman had not revealed to the village that Daiki's medicine friend was in fact, The Healer.

"I remember. How would you know about her?"

"I am her first in command. She feels we can trust you with our cause, with our mission to undermine your father and free our people from his tyranny. Was she wrong in believing this?"

My mind was reeling from this information. He had called the woman Akane. Daiki had mentioned she was the leader of the samurai insurgents.

"Your commander is correct. I have no desire to continue living under my father's rule. I had been planning on leaving the empire sooner rather than later." I couldn't believe I was relating my plans, but my guard had completely lowered.

"We need you here. If you leave now all of our planning will come to nothing. Are you willing to reconsider?"

I kept my eyes closed and tried to keep my body still. I knew my father couldn't hear this conversation, but having it right under his nose with his eyes studying me made me feel as if he knew everything.

"You need to begin slumping forward ever so slightly. Your body, under normal circumstances, would be weakening from the memory transfer."

"Ah, yes, I had heard mention of your father corrupting your gift

in such a manner. It's for this reason I allowed my true sympathies to be discovered. We needed to speak with you."

He slumped forward a little and let out a soft moan.

"Don't overdo it. This part isn't supposed to hurt." He stopped moaning and slumped further down. I had to rest his head back on the table before I could continue my discussion with him. *"You were prepared to die in order to communicate with me? I could easily refuse your request, and then what have you accomplished?"*

"True, but Akane and I both felt that our current predicament warranted taking such risks?"

"What predicament?"

"Our time is running out. If you wish to join our cause, leave your window unlocked tonight. Further instruction will await you."

"It is impossible for you to breach the palace wall and enter through my window without kami blood running through your veins."

"We know, and we have found a solution to the problem."

I nearly raised my eyebrows at this, but remembered to keep my face still at the last second.

"Fine. I will honor your request, but that doesn't mean I will join your cause. I am, however, willing to hear you out."

His relief was palpable and transferred through our link with surprising force.

"I have just one more request, Princess."

"Yes?"

"Please, when you receive my memories don't share any information that would compromise our plans."

"I will have to tell the emperor something."

"Feed him false information. Tell him we plan on attacking his soldiers he recently sent toward the north. That would help our cause tremendously."

I wanted to ask how, but knew we didn't have much more time left. My father had forced me to perform this particular procedure so many times previously, he was now familiar with how long it normally took.

I was loath to do it. This young soldier had been willing to sacrifice his very life merely to pass along a request from his superiors, and I admired his honor and courage. I couldn't imagine what they thought they could accomplish against an immortal kami such as my father, but they were willing to fight for what they believed in. I'd never fought against my father. I'd merely planned on running away. I felt shame course through me.

"I will tell him what you ask, but perhaps there is a way to return you to your commander with spirit intact."

"How?" I felt his hope burning small and steady, as if he were afraid to believe he could possibly survive the outcome of this situation.

"I will instruct your body to slow your breaths and your heartbeats for one hour. You will become unconscious and appear dead to all who look at you. Your body will be taken and placed in a cart and driven several miles from here where it will be dumped into a mass grave site reserved for the poor and seditious traitors of my father. They won't burn your body to release your spirit to the gods or even bury you out of respect for the dead. My father has none, and will most certainly not pretend to have any for a traitor in his army."

"Then when I awaken I will be free, and your father will assume I am dead."

I felt his hope heighten as he realized this plan could work. I hurried to caution him.

"This plan is not without risk. They may be very harsh with your body. You might awaken with broken bones or severe lacerations."

"I'll take that over certain death, Princess. Thank you. I knew The Healer could be nothing like King Fukurokuju."

I may not have been like my father, but I certainly wasn't planning on being The Healer for much longer. That title had haunted me my entire life. I wanted nothing more to do with it or what it signified.

"Hold perfectly still as I communicate with your spirit. May you have luck follow you, soldier."

I felt his gratitude as I began to instruct his spirit to slow his breathing and heartbeats for one hour. I sincerely hoped it would be enough time for him to reach the grave site and then escape. My hands shook as I tried to keep my anxiety under control. I'd never before defied my father right under his nose like this. If we were caught…well, I couldn't die, but death was preferable to the punishments I was sure my father would sentence me to.

Once I finished, I pulled my hands away from the young man's head and opened my eyes. His body lay perfectly still. I marveled at how believable his fake death appeared. His skin had taken on a cool waxy appearance, and there was no discerning any kind of rise or fall from his chest. Anyone looking at him never would have imagined he still lived.

"Daughter," my father yelled.

I nearly jumped at his jarring tone. I backed away from the solider with eyes to the floor and head bowed. I was so tired of behaving in such a subservient manner. For once, I wanted to look a man in the eye and not feel as if I was doing something wrong.

"It is done, then?"

I nodded my head.

"Very good. Come. I will allow you a few minutes to regain your strength, and then you must report to me everything you managed to glean from this traitorous snake." He turned swiftly and left the room. I was once again expected to follow, and follow I did. Just like an obedient daughter would.

I didn't have far to walk, nor did I have much time with which to recuperate, but I wasn't as tired as I normally would have been. I was quite giddy, actually. Hopefully I had just managed to save someone's life; a welcome change to what my gift was usually used for.

I followed my father into a dark room adjacent to the one we'd come from. It was just as lifeless and hollow as the rest of the place. In the middle was another wooden table with two rickety chairs. I perched myself precariously on one side with my father on the other. My back was stiff, my spine straight and, as always, my head and eyes were lowered.

There were several pieces of parchment paper with a writing quill sitting in the center of the table. My father could have had a number of servants scribe word for word what I dictated, but he preferred to do it himself with only the two of us in the room. It was the only occasion I was ever alone for more than a few moments with my father, and it was never pleasant.

Sometimes I would imagine our conversations differently, with him asking what my thoughts and feelings were on deep matters such as life, having a family or conversations where we talked of nothing that really mattered, but enjoyed one another's company either way. Sometimes I wished he would ask me how I felt about his ridiculous prophecy or the idea that I was betrothed to a deity I had never before met.

It was a silly wish, I guess. Fathers didn't do that with their daughters, even if their daughter was considered royalty and The Healer, no less. I was a commodity; a pawn just like any other female in our society. It was a nauseating realization to come to, but it hit me square in the face day after day. If I had an opportunity to change all that, at least for myself, then it was time to be brave and try. So there I sat, preparing to lie to my father, a deity, for the first time in my entire life. It was so frightening, it was almost exhilarating.

"Report," he commanded.

"No family," I responded swiftly. I was sure the young man did have family, but I didn't have that information, and my father had a nasty habit of slaughtering relatives of anyone he deemed untrustworthy. "His parents died during an epidemic when he was two, and he was raised and trained in a small monastery several miles from here."

My father scribbled away as I continued to let lie after lie roll off my tongue. At first my voice was shaky, but it grew stronger the longer I wove the young man's false history. Strange how a small act of defiance could leave me feeling so empowered.

"Any information on their main base of operation?"

For years my father had forced me to search the minds of his victims, looking for any shred of information that might reveal the location of the rebels' main camp. Unfortunately, most members of the rebels were led there blindfolded and departed the same way. I could never get a read on the direction they had taken.

"No. He was blindfolded," I lied.

I hadn't actually searched his memories, but he probably did have some knowledge considering his ranking within the rebel army. I was happy I hadn't actually absorbed any memories. The location of the rebel base was not information I wished to have, and I certainly never wanted my father to have it.

"Anything else?"

"The samurai rebels are planning an attack against your armies in the North. The ones you recently deployed."

"How many men?"

"I'm not sure, Father. I saw a whirlwind of faces, but no distinct thought that revealed numbers or the amount of supplies available to them."

My father's scribbling stopped. I stilled, wishing I had simply lied and made some kind of number up. His hand shot out much faster than I was prepared for, knocking me from my chair and leveling me to the floor. I shook my head and raised my fingers to my mouth. It had filled with a salty, coppery liquid.

He had split my lip again.

As a daughter of an immortal being I had been blessed with the ability to heal myself. My body corrected any injury almost immediately following its occurrence; a trait my father exploited. He could beat me as much as he wanted and no one would ever know because there was never any physical proof. The damage healed within minutes.

I had, of course, attempted to find support and solace in the arms of my mother. She told me it was my fault. An honorable daughter never behaved in a way that would demand physical punishment unless she had no honor at all. I found it wholly ironic that my father could beat me to the point of death with no one to answer to, but if anyone else accidentally touched me, besides my maid, they would lose their life.

My father waited for me to pull myself together and reposition myself on the chair. I'd learned long ago never to cry. It merely made the beatings worse.

"Are you sure of the information now?" I felt his glare bleeding into the top of my bowed head.

I wasn't sure what possessed me to answer him the way I did. Maybe it was the idea that someone had just deceived him without him being the wiser or the idea that others out there were capable of defying my father to the point that it might actually be a worry or a threat to him. Maybe it was the young soldier's courage or the confidence he and his commander had in me without having ever taken a true measure of my character or my heart. Or maybe, just maybe I had finally decided that being beaten to death was preferable to another moment spent living under the same palace roof as Emperor Fukurokuju.

I lifted my head and met his eyes for the first time without being given permission. "I cannot give you information that does not exist within the soldier's memories, and beating me as if you were a spoiled child throwing a tantrum will do nothing to change that fact."

His brief look of astonishment was a look I knew I would treasure for the rest of my life—however short that may be. I waited, resigned to my fate and the brutal beating that was sure to follow my outburst, but it never came. Instead, my father eyed me thoughtfully and then let out a slow, deliberate chuckle.

"All this time, I wondered if my daughter, The Healer, had any kind of backbone." His eyes narrowed, and he considered me for a few more hair-raising seconds. "It would seem you might be worthy of your destiny after all." He stood up quickly, and I hurried to follow, feeling a bit unsteady at his uncharacteristic reaction to my uncharacteristic outburst. "You may go, daughter. I will see you tonight at table. I expect you to do all you can to make a good impression on your betrothed. I fear Katsu is not happy to be strapped to a woman for the rest of his life, but you just might be worth all of this."

My father's praise was more nerve-wracking than his beatings. I wasn't used to his approving gaze or the idea that I had somehow pleased him. I was angry that his praise made me want to please him more—win him over and prove to him I was a daughter worth loving. He was a monster, yet I continued to crave his love.

The idea that Katsu might hate this arrangement as much as I did was news to me. He hadn't given me that impression in the forest. Was it possible I wasn't the only one frustrated with the inability to choose my own fate? Was it possible I could convince him to dissolve the betrothal and give me some semblance of a normal life without repercussions from my parents?

It was too much to contemplate at the moment. I nodded to my father, bowed from the waist and backed out of the room, never turning my back on him until I was out of his presence and hurrying down the dark, cavernous hall.

There was much to accomplish before nightfall came, but first there was someone I needed to visit, an individual in my life who loved and accepted me for who I was, and not who I was destined to become.

My younger brother, Prince Saigo.

My brother's rooms were situated in the northern wing of the palace, but I knew he was most likely with his tutor this early in the morning. Prince Saigo was considered the heir to all of the wealth my father possessed and received the best education and samurai training money could buy. He would soon reach his sixteenth year, and I could not help but be proud of the strong, capable young man he had become.

Reaching his door I tapped twice. I heard him bark, "Enter," in his best, most authoritative man-voice. I withheld an amused smile as I opened the door and entered his study room.

"Princess, to what do we owe the honor?" Kenji said, my brother's wizened old history tutor. He had stood up and bowed respectfully.

"Please, Kenji, you know how that silly behavior irks me."

I looked over at my brother and gave him a wink. He smiled at me and then stood and bowed from his waist as well. His clothing was less formal, with a simple brown kimono wrapping around his muscular frame. The sleeves were short and narrow, unlike the longer more cumbersome sleeves sewn on women's robes.

"Nonsense, sister," he joined in, "we must insist on treating you like the noble, genteel princess you are."

I waved my hand at him dismissively, closed the door behind me and sat down at their table. "You two are impossible."

They began to chuckle as they returned to their seats. I felt as if I could always relax when my brother and Kenji were with me, providing no one else was present. In closed quarters like these we were able to push the ridiculous rules of etiquette and formality aside while enjoying one another's company. Titles, royalty, positions of authority...these were of little consequence when it was just the three of us.

I was feeling better already.

"I'm glad you've come to rescue me, dear sister. Kenji's recitation of the history of our First Parents has been particularly torturous this morning, especially considering how nice a day it is."

"You're the worst pupil I've ever been unlucky enough to be strapped with. Your inability to focus has far surpassed that of your sister's. It's a wonder you two have learned anything at all." Kenji shook his gnarled fist at Saigo.

My brother and I both laughed at his pitiful attempts to be stern or cross with us. We knew he cared for both of us very much. This playful banter was exactly the thing I'd been desperate for.

Kenji gave a tired sigh and straightened out his frail limbs beneath the table. He winced in pain, and I carefully studied him.

"You're having joint pain again, Kenji. Why didn't you summon me?"

He raised a pacifying hand and grunted as I stood up and crossed behind him.

"One does not simply summon The Healer to their quarters to relieve joint pain. One does not summon The Healer for anything unless they want your father to chop their head off."

I bit my lip in anger at my father's ridiculous edict. I wasn't allowed to use my healing powers to help anyone truly in need. He had this silly notion that healing others' aches and pains would lessen my ability to ascend to full immortality and become a kami when the time came. It was pure nonsense and yet another way he was able to control every aspect of my life. The hypocrite held no qualms about using my powers when it came to healing his commanders or torturing his enemies.

I placed my hands on either side of Kenji's head and connected with his ki immediately. It was easy to do so. Kenji knew he could trust me. I felt a sharp jarring pain wash over me and pinpointed the source of it on his left side close to his hip. It appeared that he had a small crack in the hip bone close to the joint. It was small, but a crack was a crack, and it was causing him an enormous amount of pain, throwing off the balance of energy within his body, leading to an eventual infection and fever. I instructed his ki to heal the crack and correct the balance of energy flowing through his body. Once I was certain the healing would take effect, I released his head and stepped back.

"Kenji, how in the world did you manage to injure your hip like that? Did you fall down again?" I could feel frustration creep into my voice as I thought about his stubborn refusal to enlist a manservant to assist in dressing him. My father would have given him anything he asked for, considering his status as the royal historian, but Kenji was prideful and refused the help he so desperately needed.

"Of course not. I'm quite offended at your lowered opinion of my level of grace and coordination."

Saigo snorted in a most unprincely manner. "Grace and coordination? Kenji, you're an excellent tutor, but the gods help us all if ever you manage to get a sword in those wrinkled old hands of yours."

"Saigo!" I said, shocked at his forthright manner.

Kenji threw his head back and laughed heartily. "You children are good for me. Never a dull moment, I must say." He turned and took my hand in his, planting a grateful kiss on the top. "Thank you, my dear. I didn't realize how badly I hurt until the hurt was made better. You take too many risks for an old nobody like me."

I squeezed his hand and sat back down. "I wouldn't have to if you would employ a little help when it comes to dressing yourself." We both let out a dissatisfied grunt.

"Can you imagine a man at my age having someone dress me?"

"Mortifying thought." Saigo laughed.

I threw a piece of parchment paper at my brother and leaned back in my chair.

He smiled and then studied me thoughtfully. "What's on your mind, big sister? I'm sure your visit holds purpose."

I let out a heavy sigh. "Father has just informed me that I will be having a large dinner with Katsu tonight."

Saigo leaned forward, alarm transforming his boyish features. "So soon? I had thought you wouldn't be made to meet him until your eighteenth birthday."

"Apparently, the engagement ceremony will take place tonight. Father has arranged it sooner rather than later so I might make a favorable impression upon the warrior god."

Saigo looked puzzled. "How uncharacteristically generous of him."

"He is hoping it will cement the warrior god's commitment to the match. Father hinted that Katsu wasn't thrilled at the prospect of being forced to marry."

"He's not happy about being forced to marry *you* or just being married in general?" Kenji asked.

I shrugged my shoulders. "Does it matter? Either way, Father seems to think he isn't sold on this betrothal. He wishes for me to spend time with him and convince him otherwise, and to start my training as soon as possible."

"Well, that would make more sense. Father always has his own agenda when it comes to managing yours." Saigo gave me a sympathetic smile. "I don't like this. I thought we would have more time to plan your escape from this hellish situation."

I nodded. I too had hoped I would have more time to escape this prison I'd lived in for so many years. There was much Saigo knew about my current predicament, including my father's abuse of my powers. He didn't know about the abuse to my own person. I couldn't let him know about that when there was nothing he could do to protect me from it.

"What father doesn't realize is that I've already made a favorable impression on Katsu quite by accident."

"How so?"

I then related the events of the night and early morning, starting with Hatsumi's predicament, the woman I had healed and finishing up with Katsu's efforts in saving me from a nekomata.

"I could tell you were in pain at table last night," Saigo said. "I had no idea it would be Hatsumi's time. The baby's coming was too early."

"True, but she carried her son longer than any others she'd conceived. We were fortunate to get this far."

Kenji patted me on the back. "I'm proud of you, child. It's a wonderful thing you've done for that family. I know how much it has meant for all of you."

I smiled, rubbing my tired eyes. "Yes, she and her son will do well."

"Now we have Katsu to deal with," Saigo said, looking unhappy. "Why is Father under the impression that Katsu doesn't want to marry you when the warrior god himself made reference to your betrothal?"

"The more alarming question to ask would center around the assassination attempt. Did you just happen to run into the nekomata on his way to the palace to kill you or had he been there already and gone searching for you once he realized you weren't there?" Kenji asked.

"How would he have known to look for me in the forest?" I wondered.

"Nekomata have a strong sense of smell. They are perfect assassins in every sense of the word. You were fortunate to have Katsu arrive when he did. I wish you would consider taking someone like Saigo or myself when Daiki summons you to the village."

"You know why that is impossible. You two are highly recognizable, and the fewer people who know about my late night excursions the less likely my father is to find out about them. Plus, I hardly had time last night to organize an escort. Hatsumi's pain was too intense."

"It did seem as if your anxiety grew, and then Father summoned you to his receiving room. Bad luck, I must say." Saigo looked as if he'd eaten something sour. "Back to Kenji's question, however—we have to wonder if someone in the palace knew your whereabouts and sent the nekomata after you."

We sat silent, contemplating that frightening thought.

"I agree that your sister's safety is a real concern. Katsu may be your only hope in keeping you safe, child. I know you wish to leave, but you must consider the prophecy," Kenji began.

"Kenji, you and I both know the prophecy is merely a legend," Saigo said.

"Then how do you explain the princess's gift for healing?"

"She has an immortal father who happens to be the god of health and longevity. It isn't that hard to put two and two together." Saigo gave me a happy grin as if that answer discharged me of any responsibilities I might have as The Healer.

"She fits the prophecy's stipulations on every point," Kenji argued. "She is female, a half kami born of a god and an empress. She has healing powers and can use them to heal the veil between our world and the next."

"Ah, yes, this notoriously elusive veil. Tell me, Kenji, how do we know she is capable of healing it if she can't even see it?"

"Excellent point." I smiled. Saigo was always so clever, and always trying to find ways to prove the prophecy wrong.

"That's where Katsu comes in. He will train her on all of that. It's probably another reason why your father has arranged tonight's meeting a few months before your birthday." Kenji rubbed his hands together and then pinched the bridge of his nose. "Of course, I would love nothing more than to help you escape from that damned prophecy's abysmal future. Nothing is worse than arranged marriages, and who really wants to heal a veil between the living and the dead for the rest of eternity?"

"Also an excellent point." I grabbed both their hands and squeezed tight. "Perhaps there is a loophole. Shall we pore over the prophecy again?"

"Yes. Any plan at this point is better than no plan at all." Kenji stood up and walked over to some large shelves on the far side of the room. He pulled out a scroll, a copy of the original prophecy. The real prophecy was framed in glass and held at a Shinto shrine that paid homage to the god of love and marriage. I thought it an odd place to house the original prophecy, but the monks in residence preserved all sorts of ancient writings, so I supposed the prophecy was in good hands.

It had been written in the original formal language of our First Parents, a language very few kami spoke today. It had been translated into a variation of Japanese that most everyone in my country used now. Who knew how much of the translation was actually accurate?

After all, languages are always evolving, much like people and their ever lowering levels of character.

Laying the prophecy on the table, Saigo unrolled its scratchy exterior and flattened it with a few books. Then he read the awful words, a selection of words I knew by heart.

> *Once strong and firm the veil grows thin*
> *Amatsu, with his vengeful heart*
> *Will rend in two and tear apart*
> *The earth and all therein*
>
> *One warrior god will not suffice*
> *His sword cannot undo this fate*
> *Unless he meets his true soul mate*
> *And love unite, but for a price*
>
> *For only she, half mortal born,*
> *Can heal the one that's turned to stone*
> *A kami father, a royal throne*
> *Where mother sits, a kingdom torn*
>
> *Her gift to heal is only part*
> *Of when and where she must become*
> *The Healer, but to heal the one*
> *Death she must overcome*

I closed my eyes and felt the weight of the prophecy sink my spirits.

"Okay, so clearly the warrior god is Katsu, the kami who was charged with maintaining the strength of the veil. He can't keep the veil strong without a mate by his side, but it can't be just anyone. It has to be his soul mate." Saigo paused for a moment considering. "Perhaps we can prove you aren't his soul mate, sister."

"Of course she is, child." Kenji shook his head. "The prophecy spells out exactly who she is. Half mortal, born of a god and a royal mother, she can heal...is any of this sounding like someone we know?" Kenji reached across the table and smacked Saigo lightly across his head.

"But maybe there is another princess out there with the same problems." Saigo insisted.

I had to laugh outright at the way he labeled my parentage and gift. They were problems, indeed.

"I still don't like the 'Death she must overcome' part." Saigo clicked his tongue against his teeth, a nervous habit of his.

"You know the prophecy is referring to my mortal side. I can't become The Healer completely if I haven't transitioned into a full kami by the time Katsu and I begin to heal the veil. If I haven't overcome my mortal side, then I will die working alongside the warrior god." I sighed. "Although, I can't help but embrace that idea. Death seems like a welcome relief and a great escape plan all rolled into one. If only I were the suicidal type."

"Yes, how terribly unfortunate to value one's life over impending servitude," Kenji said dryly.

"What does the prophecy mean when it says 'when and where she must become The Healer'? Isn't she considered The Healer already?"

Saigo had asked this question hundreds of times before, and I always gave him the same answer. "I'm not The Healer completely until I'm a full kami, genius." It was my turn to reach over and smack him lightly across the head. "As far as the 'where' is concerned, I'm assuming it is talking about the exact location where the veil is the weakest."

"That's the problem, sister. There's quite a bit of assuming going on where your future is concerned. I can't help but think we are missing something important here." He clicked his tongue against his teeth again, and then blew out a heavy sigh. "What if the scholars who translated this were wrong?"

"I would have to agree with Saigo," Kenji said. "The prophecy is obscure at best and, at worst, open to interpretation. It's the only reason I've been willing to support this mad escape plan of yours—against my better judgment, I might add." He wagged his bony finger at me and then winked.

Warmth filled my heart at the clear concern he was willing to show for my welfare. It was certainly more emotion than I ever received from my father, the nurturing paternal kind of emotion anyway. I was often the recipient of a myriad of other more unpleasant emotions from the emperor. Kenji had been my tutor for many years, and if I truly wanted to be honest with myself, he'd been much more of a father than my current one had. I valued his opinion on most matters, which was why I decided to reveal the most recent events of my day with him still present.

"My escape plan may have hit a snag or two," I said evenly.

"Did one of Father's spies find something incriminating?" Saigo was instantly on his feet.

I put up a placating hand and motioned for him to sit down.

"No, nothing like that. Father had me interrogate one of his generals this morning." I paused in my narrative when Saigo let out an unhappy grunt. He hated our father's abuse of my power. He didn't know the extent of it, though. I never told him what the end result of transferring a person's memories actually produced. The world was ugly, made uglier by the existence of the emperor, and I would protect my brother from as much of the ugliness as I possibly could. "Apparently, Father believed the man to be aligned with the samurai insurgents and wanted as much intelligence on the matter as he could get."

"You say one of his generals was called into question?" Kenji asked.

I nodded.

"That's very strange for a man of such high rank to never be discovered a traitor until now."

"It would seem he wanted to be discovered in order to get close to me. I think it must have been his plan all along."

"He tried to assassinate you?" Saigo asked hoarsely.

I placed my hand on his to reassure him. "No, he wanted to pass a message along to me." I noted the looks of confusion on my companions' faces and decided to start from the beginning, sharing everything that had transpired, referring to the woman I had healed on the road and then delving into the risky business of defying my father and hopefully saving the soldier's life. There was heavy silence for several seconds after my narrative. Kenji spoke first.

"I cannot believe you took such a risk with a complete stranger. What happens if he awakens before his body is disposed of?"

"I suppose we must pray the young soldier is a good actor, and it would seem he must be if he was able to work his way up to the position of general in my father's army, all the while working for his enemies."

"This is insane. There's no way I'm going to stand by and allow you to keep your window unfastened so some samurai general can sneak into your quarters." Saigo shook his head in bewilderment. "And furthermore, who ever heard of a female commander?"

"Saigo, there are female warriors in Father's armies."

"Yes, but those women are kami warriors."

"Who's to say this commander isn't?" Kenji asked.

I felt surprised by his suggestion. "Do you really think there are kami out there fighting against my father?"

Kenji gave a furtive look around the room. I thought it was silly that he was looking for spies now, after how candid we'd been, discussing my intentions to allow a traitorous general to enter my bedroom window and my intentions to leave the palace for good.

"If there were spies in my quarters, Kenji, I'm fairly certain they would have raised an alarm and charged us with sedition by now." Saigo quirked a mocking eyebrow at our cautious tutor.

Kenji shook his head. "You children take too many chances, and we must be vigilant always. Your father's spies are everywhere. Now, as to the issue of whether or not there are kami willing to fight against him, there's no question Emperor Fukurokuju is an evil deity. The only reason he's been able to hold his power and authority over the empire this long is simply because he was the kami chosen by our First Parents to father The Healer."

I winced.

"I'm sorry, child, I know how tiresome that title is for you. Anyway, now that your birthright is nearing its fulfillment, many people, including kami, are ready for Emperor Fukurokuju and his wife Chinatsu to step down. It's a kami's job to keep the world in balance by overseeing one specific task."

"Yes, I suppose Father has been quite remiss in his duties as the god of health and longevity, what with people starving to death, suffering from incurable disease and being butchered left and right." Saigo's disgust mirrored my own.

"You're quite right, young prince. The emperor has traded his priorities as a kami for greed and power. He was given the opportunity to rule with Chinatsu for The Healer's sake, but it would seem he has lost sight of what is really at stake here, that being the healing of the veil."

"If there really is one, and I'm not convinced there is. I honestly believe it's just one of Father's tricks, using me as some kind of secret weapon, some bargaining chip with the warrior god Katsu."

"Be that as it may, I'm not sure how much longer the gods will allow your father to continue. I sometimes wonder if he will eventually share the same fate as the demon god Amatsu-Mikaboshi."

"One can only hope," Saigo said. "Such a happy thought, really."

"Saigo." I slapped his hand. "After all, he is *still* your father."

"*Our* father," he amended, "and what a shame it is to call such a man family."

I agreed with him wholeheartedly of course, but I had very good reason to. My brother, on the other hand, had never received so much as a slap on the wrist from my father and could do no wrong. He was the pride and joy of the Empire, a man, after all—not a woman like me, a helpless female.

I supposed many could have looked upon our different situations and wondered how we could be so close and not resent one another. The idea would never have crossed our thoughts. I could never wish a single beating to fall upon Saigo's fragile emotions, and I would take punishment after punishment to protect him from a similar fate.

Saigo's dissatisfaction and hatred with the emperor stemmed from his disgust with the abuse of my power, my father's indifferent attitude toward me and the suffering Saigo had witnessed when making his rounds in the neighboring villages. He saw the pain of our people and knew something could and should be done to prevent it, but our father remained stubbornly deaf to their cries for help.

"Back to the real issue here, I agree with Saigo. You simply cannot allow the leader of the samurai insurgents to enter your quarters without someone there to protect you in case the scenario should play out badly. What if they are merely wishing to kill you?" Kenji leveled a questioning look at me.

He always taught my brother and me to consider every possible path no matter the subject we were studying. The several different paths that could result with any reckless behavior on my part needed to be considered also.

"I'm The Healer." I nearly choked on the title. "If they kill me, they kill their savior."

"Maybe they think the prophecy is simply a tool being used to subject them to poverty and enslavement much like you do. It might make them feel more inclined to kill you. With The Healer out of the way, is there really any reason for Emperor Fukurokuju to be in power?"

I felt my jaw drop at this rather frank, yet accurate, assessment. If even The Healer herself didn't believe in the prophecy, it stood to reason that others had come to the same conclusion, especially if those others had a desperate enough reason to want the emperor thrown out of power. I was no longer certain that I had made the right decision in letting that soldier go free.

"It might be worth the risk," I argued. I was loath to give up my opportunity, slight as it might seem, to receive help from my father's enemies. "If they don't wish to assassinate me, then maybe they can use me to help save this empire. I may not believe in healing the veil, but I do believe in saving our people."

Saigo nodded at me and gave me an approving smile. "I will help you then. Tonight when you leave your window unfastened, I will stay hidden within the room and protect you, just in case their intentions are not as honorable as they have stated."

"Of course, I'll be there too," Kenji added. "Life has been a bit dull lately. This old mule could use a little excitement."

I grinned at both of them and took one of their hands in each of my own. "You two mean the world to me, so no risk taking."

"Nonsense, sister. If someone wounds me, I'll simply beg you to heal me on the spot. I would prefer that you allow any and all scars to show through, though. I have it on good authority that some ladies find the wounds of battle rather attractive on a young man."

"You're only sixteen, Saigo. I better not hear of any females looking at your scars," I warned.

"You need not fear on that count, Princess." Kenji smiled. "For *I* have it on good authority that a female is more attracted to a man capable of growing a full beard."

Saigo raised a free hand to his smooth face and sighed in defeat.

My tutor and I let out happy chuckles. I supposed if I was going to face a possible assassination attempt, it was wise to do it with two of the most important people in my life.

∞∞∞∞

After visiting my brother and Kenji, I returned to my rooms only to find Aiko impatiently waiting for me. Apparently, she had heard of the last minute engagement ceremony and felt it necessary to prepare me for the event a good seven hours early. In her defense, the process of dressing and styling my hair took up an insufferably long period of time, but I had hoped to cut the time short by donning one of my specially designed wigs for the occasion.

Unfortunately, Aiko was itching to get her hands on my long, black tresses. My hair fell below my waist, a status symbol of beauty and nobility for any imperial princess. I found the length terribly annoying and would have cut several inches off if my maid and my mother had allowed it.

She sat me down on a brown lacquered chair next to my bed and hauled over a large bowl filled with wax. I sighed. There would be no avoiding this unfortunate situation.

"Aiko, I would rather not wash and rewash my hair in order to free it from this terrible wax you're planning on using."

She stopped the hand reaching for the waxing brush, a thin wooden comb she would use to evenly pull the wax through my hair.

"This is your engagement ceremony, Princess. Your wigs will never do for such a special occasion as this."

I stuck my tongue out at her in a very unladylike manner. "You simply wish to show off your impressive hairdressing skills."

She gave me a wicked wink, reached for the wooden comb, dipped it in the wax and proceeded with her cruel torture.

The wax helped the hair hold its elaborate form, a necessary evil in Aiko's eyes, but I would have rather spent my last hours of freedom jumping into the eel infested moat surrounding the palace or enduring a twelve hour lecture on the development of rice farms in the neighboring villages—anything but this nonsensical preparation for an engagement with which I never intended to follow through.

She started with the lower parts of my hair above my neck and ran wax through them, all the while humming to herself. I sighed heavily, resigned to my fate at this point. Once she sectioned and tied different parts of my hair in the design and shape she wanted, she moved on to the top part of my head around my crown and hairline.

Despite my impatience, the process was quite soothing, and I soon found my mind reviewing the last twenty-four hours. A memory of startling blue eyes, light hair, and fair skin made my own face flush as my heart rate picked up.

By the gods, it wasn't as if he was actually present, but just the mere thought of Musubi brought heat to my cheeks. I found myself wanting to know more about the enigmatic stranger and to understand the affect he had on me. But when would I ever see him again? The thought saddened me more than I cared to admit.

My attention was brought back to the present as Aiko unintentionally jerked my hair while running more wax through a section of hair toward my crown. She then threaded my hair through a large, gold lacquered *kushi*, laying it to rest along the crown of my head.

The comb had been a gift from my mother on my fifteenth birthday, and it might have meant something to me if gifting it to her only daughter had actually meant something to *her*. It was half-moon shaped, and the handle was flat, bearing intricate mother-of-pearl detailing, inlaid in a floral pattern.

Two other smaller combs with the same detailed designs were placed along the sides of my head. Aiko took the lower layers, twisting the tied hair into an elaborate chignon and holding everything in place with gold lacquered *kojai*, inlaid with the same mother-of-pearl design as the combs.

The process took an agonizing four hours to perform, and by the end of it my legs and hands itched to be doing something other than wasting so much time with something as silly as my own hair.

When Aiko had finished, she handed me a hand mirror made from jade and allowed me a peek. I may have felt ridiculous, but I knew I didn't look ridiculous. Beautiful gold ribbons, layered with mother-of-pearl designs complemented the combs and hairsticks. It was truly magnificent…and magnificently heavy.

I was then prodded, poked, and squeezed into the most stunning silk *furisode.* The base cover was a silky, dark blue with a white flowing pattern that adorned the long flowing sleeves, hem, and neckline. In short, I appeared to be the epitome of what every Japanese princess should look like.

Aiko continued fussing with my hair and clothing long after she had finished. "Are you not excited to dine with your betrothed, Princess?"

We hadn't spoken much during our preparations, so I was surprised by her question.

"Of course I am, Aiko. Why would you ask such a thing?"

"You simply do not behave like a young girl waiting to meet the man she will soon marry. You aren't frightened, are you?"

I mentally berated myself for letting my calm façade slip.

"I'm not frightened in the least. What an absurd notion. I'm sure Katsu is a very fair and honorable man."

"Yes, he will be a kind master, I am certain." Aiko hesitated for a second and then spoke again. "However, if for some reason he is not, I hope you would come to me when your nightmares start again." She rested her hand on my shoulder and squeezed it gently.

It was the kind of gentle, comforting contact I craved. I had to swallow hard several times before the lump in my throat disappeared and I was able to speak again.

"Thank you, Aiko. I'm sure it will all work out just fine."

My maid nodded and continued the last finishing touches on my hair. Aiko did her best to take on my personal demons as if they were her own. She had no power to shield me from my parents, and it hadn't taken long before the nightmares set in. I always had terrible dreams after any punishments I received at the hand of my father. Aiko would rock me to sleep whenever they came. In the beginning I would scream so loudly she was afraid someone might hear and my punishments would become much worse. She gave me herbs to ease the dreams and calm my nerves.

I hadn't had a single nightmare for many months now and hoped they were gone for good.

"All right, mistress. You are ready for this evening's feast. I will ask the gods to pour upon you many blessings this night, for your future and also for your happiness."

"And what if my future lies somewhere else, Aiko?" I hadn't meant to ask her that, but my mouth had been faster than my forethought as of late.

Aiko gave me a very serious look before answering. "Then I shall do everything in my power to put you on the path toward the future that is right for you."

A small look of understanding passed between us, and I knew I could count on her for what the next few months might require.

I turned my back to the mirror and allowed Aiko to lead me out of my rooms and through the many hallways and court-yards the palace boasted. We neared the great hall where my father usually held any large gatherings. Visiting kami from my father's militia would be present tonight to witness this most anticipated event.

I felt a very pressing need to vomit what little I held in my stomach, though that would most likely prove impossible given my attire. Kimonos, silk or otherwise, were not very forgiving when it came to freedom of movement.

We arrived at the double doors. I could hear the loud murmurings of the large group visiting amongst themselves, no doubt waiting for my grand entrance. I hoped I could pull a regal and graceful gait off in my flimsy *geta* platform sandals and folds of silk.

"Ready?"

I nodded to my maid, and she motioned the guards on either

side to open the giant, carved doors.

As they opened and the guard on my left announced my arrival, I heard the muffled sounds of conversation die down. Soon all became silent.

"Her Imperial Highness, Princess Mikomi, the Savior of our people, The Healer."

I placed my hands within the opposite sleeves of my kimono, and drew them in front of me. With my head bent slightly forward and my eyes lowered, I traversed the long path to the other side of the room where my father stood.

Once I finally arrived at my destination, I bent low to the waist out of deference to the emperor and waited for his permission to rise. Instead of hearing the rough, barking command I was accustomed to, I felt a strong hand gently grasp my chin and lift me. I was soon standing in an upright position, staring into quizzical brown eyes.

I felt my breath hitch at this unexpected departure from tradition. My father was the one who gave me permission to rise, and no one was allowed to touch me. I might have sent my father a questioning glance, but the look of wonder those beautiful eyes were giving me had completely arrested my attention. Katsu drank me in just as he had this morning. I felt lightheaded at the thought that anything about me might be pleasing to him.

"Katsu, I am honored to present to you my daughter and your betrothed, The Healer, Princess Mikomi." The room roared with a thunderous applause, but I barely noticed. I stepped back, and the hand Katsu had held under my chin dropped to his side. He looked at me with curious interest, and I realized I must have appeared to him like a scared little child. It was not behavior fitting an imperial princess. I straightened my spine and lifted my chin, meeting him eye for eye, giving him a calm, almost challenging look.

He hadn't given me permission to do so, and at first I wondered if he would be angered by my obvious defiance and lack of respect, but he seemed to be delighted by it. He smiled approvingly and nodded at me as if I'd just pleasantly surprised him. He lifted his hand to me, beckoning me to take hold of it. I was still having a hard time coming to terms with this public, physical contact that was generally forbidden by my father, but I accepted the hand he offered and allowed him to draw me to him.

"Princess Mikomi," he said loud enough for the whole room to hear, "it is my honor to finally meet the woman who was chosen by our First Parents to stand united by my side for eternity. I accept this union wholeheartedly, and will willingly devote my life to protecting the veil with you by my side."

I supposed explaining we had already met during an attempt on my life was probably something he and my father would keep quiet about.

He never once took his eyes from my face. My whole body was becoming uncomfortably warm with the unwanted attention. I was very much used to remaining invisible. There was no hiding from Katsu's probing gaze. The room grew quiet again, and Katsu continued to look at me, waiting for me to speak. I cleared my throat as quietly as I could, but from the amused twitch I saw on Katsu's lips I could tell he had heard and could see through my calm façade. Was he laughing at me? I struggled to find the words necessary to end this very public meeting, but the nervousness I felt was beginning to overrule my thoughts.

I finally managed a small kind of bow from my knees instead of my hips since he was too close to me to perform such a deep bow. Apparently, that was all that was needed because the room broke out into loud applause again, and soon whatever festivities that had occurred before my arrival resumed. I breathed out a silent sigh. I remained facing Katsu merely because he continued to hold my hand, studying me.

He took a small step forward, lowering his head toward mine. "Princess, do you wish to eat or would you be more comfortable on the terrace? It is quite warm in this room."

I nodded gratefully and wondered at his noticing my mild distress. I was not used to such consideration from a powerful man, kami or otherwise.

"If you will meet me on that terrace just outside this room, I will go retrieve something cool for you to drink."

"Thank you. That is most kind of you."

He gave me a slight bow and moved past me. I quickly retreated to the landing on my left just past my father's usual seat. Once outside, my breathing came easier. The rainy season had started, and I could see storm clouds gathering in the distance, but for now the sky withheld its torrential shards, and a cool breeze ruffled the silky folds of my clothing.

The night sky filled with lanterns of various shapes and colors, honoring the special meeting that would mark the union of The Healer and the warrior god Katsu. I felt quite disconnected with the excitement and the festivities. To me, it seemed surreal—some fantastical farce I couldn't possibly be a part of. I ached to magically sprout wings and sore right off the palace roof, leaving my gilded cage far behind me. The heavy stomp of booted feet interrupted my brief daydream.

"Could you think of nothing respectable to say in return to Katsu's most gracious speech?"

I turned around quickly, recognizing the angry voice of my father. He didn't give me even one moment to defend myself before his ready fist lifted and fell heavily against my left cheek, splitting the skin across my cheekbone. I felt blood begin to drip down the side of my face.

"Fukurokuju, what is the meaning of this?"

I had gripped the hand rail behind me to keep myself upright but couldn't look up to see who had spoken, though I had a pretty good idea. Humiliation and shame overwhelmed me with thoughts of my betrothed witnessing such a degrading moment.

"Why, Katsu, I was merely teaching the princess a lesson in respect. Her lack of decorum will never happen again."

The wooziness I suffered after being struck began to subside as my body commenced the healing process. I knew the cut and bruise on my cheek would disappear within minutes.

"Teaching? Is that what you call such callous abuse?"

I looked up sharply, surprised that Katsu would have the courage to stand up to my father. He glared at the emperor, clearly agitated by what he had seen.

"You forget yourself, Katsu."

"I forget nothing. Do not put on airs with me and pretend that you have any kind of power over me when you were assigned this empire only a few decades ago. Before that, you maintained your role as any other kami does. Do not expect me to bow down to you as would a lowly human."

My mouth hung open in a most unseemly manner, but it could not be helped. I had never heard anyone address my father in anger. I'd never before met anyone who wasn't afraid to do so.

Katsu pointed a finger at my father's chest. "If you ever lay a hand on my future wife again, Fukurokuju, so help me, I will find the nearest sword forged from the land of the dead and shove it through your cold, unfeeling heart."

I could see the emperor's body trembling in anger, and I was certain he would call out his guards and demand Katsu's head. Instead, he balled his fists at his sides and quickly walked past Katsu, heading back into the great hall.

I remained where I was, with my hand still nursing my left cheek, dumbfounded. What had just happened? Katsu moved with lightning speed to my side, wrapped one arm around my waist and pulled me to him. He grabbed the hand I had placed against my cheek and lowered it.

"How badly did he hurt you?" His voice dripped with barely controlled anger. He took my face in his hands and studied it.

All of this physical contact was beginning to overwhelm me. The only males who had ever been close enough to care for me had been my brother, Daiki, and Kenji, and they had never embraced me like this.

"I'm fine...I tend to...I heal quickly." I was breathless and flustered and could barely form enough thoughts in my head, let alone construct a complete sentence with Katsu holding my face like I was a porcelain doll and looking at me as if I mattered.

"Whether your wound heals quickly or not is irrelevant. Physical violence on your person should never be tolerated. How many times has this happened?"

"Once or twice," I stated.

Katsu hissed under his breath. "All your life then." I marveled that he had seen through my lie. "And each time your body healed quickly so no one was the wiser. Your father is an ass."

I laughed at that. I couldn't help myself. I'd spent so many years hiding the abuse I'd suffered at the hands of my father, and now someone finally knew. I continued to laugh, and then suddenly I began to cry. Deep, gut-wrenching sobs shook my body so badly I could barely keep upright. Katsu pulled me close to him and held me with my head tucked under his chin.

I'd never met anyone like him before. Most of the men I knew had very little time for their wives and even less patience for any emotional expression. Crying simply wasn't done, and here I stood crying like a baby while he held me as if it was completely acceptable and not some show of weakness.

"I'm sorry," I managed, once my crying subsided a little. "I'm never like this. I don't usually cry. I apologize for the scene I've made."

"Stop. If anyone had backhanded me as hard as I saw the emperor backhand you, I would have cried on the spot."

I giggled but kept my head down. I still felt unsure about what behaviors were appropriate around my future husband. I didn't know what he would allow. "You would never cry, I'm sure. You're simply saying that to make me feel better."

"Well, that might be true, but I certainly would have *wanted* to cry."

I chuckled again and looked up, meeting Katsu's eyes and giving him a shy smile.

Katsu placed a soothing hand to my left cheek. "I didn't get a chance to grab that drink for you. When I saw your father pass me, the look in his eyes gave me pause. I'm very happy I listened to my instincts and followed him back."

"I'm not really thirsty any longer."

He eyed me worriedly. "You still have some blood here. Let's go down to the gardens, away from the prying eyes of that great gathering in there and get you all cleaned up."

"Yes, thank you. I don't like to be in crowded rooms. It…I feel very self-conscious."

"A princess who dislikes being the center of attention? Now that is a surprise."

Was he teasing me? I glanced at his features and beheld his wide smile. I smiled back and looked at the floor again as he grabbed my hand and led me into the crowded great hall and out the way I had originally come.

Katsu's kind behavior had me completely baffled. I had been prepared to suffer through this night in silence, willing to bear this forced meeting because I knew I wasn't going to have to continue pretending that I agreed with my fate and the expectations that had been drummed into my head all my life. I'd never considered that I might actually have an ally in the man I was destined to marry. I'd certainly never expected him to champion me against my own father.

It took some time, but we soon left the palace and entered the gardens circling the palace in the back. Katsu led me to an ivory bench nestled next to a silvery, oval shaped pond filled with colorful fish.

I loved these gardens, they were extensive and elaborate in their landscaping. The outer wall of the garden was lined with bushes, trimmed to perfection. As you wandered past the pond you could follow a trickling flow of water that led to a grouping of whimsical looking statues made up of female kami who represented peace, prosperity, and good fortune. The trickling water spouted up through the statues, creating a beautiful waterfall.

Cherry trees of varying shapes and sizes were placed strategically throughout the expansive space, along with several other trees and flowers, but my favorite were the white cherry blossoms, snow blossoms, and azaleas. Where trees and flowers were absent, the soft earth was covered in lush grasses of the brightest greens, interrupted only by small rock formations and sand patterns.

Yes, these gardens were a peaceful place of refuge whenever I needed moments for myself. I was happy to share this place with Katsu but nervous to be with him unchaperoned. I sat meekly and waited. He walked over to the pond and ripped a strip of cloth from the undergarment of his black silk kimono.

"Oh, no," I said before I could stop myself. I slapped a hand over my mouth and then tried to make my person as small as possible when Katsu looked at me questioningly.

"We need to wipe that blood from your face."

"Yes, but we have plenty of linen within the palace. There's no reason you should ruin your clothing for my sake."

Katsu knelt down by the pond and wet the strip of fabric, bringing it up and wringing it out. He then walked over to where I nervously waited and positioned himself next to me. When he lifted the wet cloth toward my face, I instinctively leaned back and put my hands up in a defensive gesture.

I felt silly the minute I did so, but my nerves were completely frayed by my father's behavior and Katsu's unexpected kindness. I felt terribly unbalanced emotionally and could no longer keep my reactions in check.

Katsu lowered his hand the minute I backed away.

"Mikomi, I hope you understand that I do not think it appropriate for a man to hurt a woman. I would never hit you. Do you believe me?"

I honestly wasn't sure if I did or not. I didn't really know Katsu, but he had protected me from my father, and I saw no reason to be afraid of him until he gave me one.

"I believe you. I'm just very used to far different treatment." I relaxed my body and sat forward.

Katsu's eyes looked a bit stormy as he lifted his hand again and brought the wet cloth to my face. He gently wiped away the blood.

"If your father cannot be trusted to keep his temper in check, then I will demand that you and I are married on the spot and take you away where I can protect you."

"Oh, no." I raised my hand and grabbed his arm. It was a very brazen move on my part. We were not yet familiar enough with each other for that kind of physical contact, and yet I had to remind myself that he had held me while I cried not fifteen minutes earlier.

Katsu quirked an eyebrow at me. "I take it the idea of marrying me displeases you. Perhaps I am not handsome enough?"

His assumption horrified me, worrying I had offended him, especially after the kind way he had treated me. The thought of marrying him wasn't as repulsive to me as it had been, but if he took me with him tonight as his bride, I would never have that meeting with the general of the samurai insurgents.

I hesitated for a moment. Then, gathering my courage, I scooted closer to him and grasped his hand with both of mine. I gauged his reaction to the physical contact I had initiated, but he didn't seem displeased. Encouraged by his warm, teasing smile, I answered his question.

"That's not what I meant. You are wonderfully handsome." When Katsu gave me a wide smile, I realized how frank I had just been. "I mean...of course you are fine to look upon...I just...I think that perhaps—"

Katsu began chuckling quietly. He placed his other hand on top of both of mine and squeezed them. "I am merely being playful, Princess. I like the way your beautiful brown eyes grow large and wide when you think you've said or done something wrong. It's quite endearing."

He thought my eyes were beautiful? I felt them grow wide all over again, and Katsu laughed out loud this time.

"There is much for you to learn before we are wed, and I would like to spend time getting to know my future wife. In other words, I promise not to marry you and whisk you away from the palace until you are ready."

I smiled and nodded. Then I looked down at our entwined hands and felt my body warm at the realization that he was rubbing his thumb softly against the inside of my wrist. I let out a shaky breath and slowly pulled my hands out of his. I could tell he wanted to hold them longer, but he let me go. Another surprise. He wasn't going to force my affections. I might have tried relaxing, but the need he felt for me was playing on my own need for his attention.

"Is there anything you would like to know about me at this moment?" I asked. I looked up quickly but couldn't hold eye contact with him and lowered my gaze to my hands resting lightly on my lap.

"Were you afraid to meet me?"

I swallowed hard. I had been expecting a less personal question, but I knew I could answer him honestly without any fear of punishment.

"Yes. I had heard that you were not pleased with this arrangement."

"That's very true. I've been told for thousands of years that you were my destiny. I had no choice in the matter, and I had no idea when you would be born. I guess I rebelled at the thought of someone choosing my bride for me."

I marveled that our feelings about the betrothal could be the same. It had never occurred to me that Katsu might resent this situation as much as I did. Then I felt a little sad, wondering if he still felt that way.

"I understand." I tried to keep the disappointment from my voice. I didn't necessarily want to go through with this marriage, but I was warming up to this warrior god who had protected me against my biggest enemy, treating me like a person instead of a pawn or even a prop. At the very least, I realized, I wanted his friendship. I didn't want him to resent me because of what I represented.

"And you? How did you feel about the match?'

I felt my eyes go wide and heard him chuckle again. It surprised me that he would be interested in my opinion.

"I suppose...I was not happy to be given little choice in the matter. It is difficult to consider a life with someone you've never met."

"Yes it is. To be perfectly honest, I was determined to hate you. Isn't it amazing how quickly one's feelings can change?"

I met his gaze to measure his sincerity. "You don't hate me, then?" I waited with my breath caught in the back of my throat. When had this kami's opinion of me become so important?

Katsu smiled. "No, Mikomi, I don't hate you. I feel quite the opposite."

His warm look seemed to heat my cheeks with its intensity. He lifted his hand to my face and rubbed his thumb softly over my healed cheekbone. If I had been standing I most certainly would have needed assistance remaining upright. Katsu was not the reserved, menacing warrior god I had so often pictured in my mind. He was sympathetic, understanding, communicative, and surprisingly affectionate. Men simply didn't behave this way, let alone deities, but then maybe I was so used to my father's behavior that my perceptions were skewed.

I needed to say something in return, but his soft caress and the warm way in which he gazed at me made my thoughts stutter and scatter. I opened my mouth to speak, but the loud snap of a branch echoing in the still night air distracted me from anything I might have said. Katsu was on his feet with his hand resting upon the hilt of his sword. I stood up as well and looked toward the opposite side of the pond where the noise had originated.

"It might have been a bird or small cat," I offered quietly, but Katsu didn't relax his position.

I looked across the pond again and thought I saw a dark shadow moving forward. After a few more steps the shadow moved into the moonlight. I gasped and grabbed Katsu's arm.

"Well, Princess, you were half correct. It's certainly a cat."

The figure standing before us was a copy of the large assassin that had tried to kill me this morning, a black panther with the musculature of a man. Its dark mane hung loosely around his head and ears, much like a lion's, and his snout was made more gruesome by the sharp pointing fangs that descended on either side. It wore a black leather vest, leaving its arms and chest exposed. Its waist was encircled about with a belt holding various weapons and a gleaming sword, all black in color and wickedly sharp. Its feet and hands ended in sharp claws the length of small curved daggers, and its tail looked as if it had been split into two, flicking sharply back and forth behind it.

"Hand over the child, most honorable Katsu, and I will leave you uninjured," it hissed and mocked at the same time.

Katsu withdrew his sword from its sheath and pulled me behind him. "You'll not touch a hair on my betrothed's head. I suggest you leave as quickly as you came before I have to dispense with you and your two friends hiding in the shadows."

My heart jumped to my throat. There were three altogether? I was sure that Katsu was an accomplished fighter due to the nature of his gifts, but how could one kami stand against three monsters?

A low growl seemed to vibrate from the black beast's chest. "So be it."

The cat-like thing propelled itself forward and jumped, sailing across the length of the pond while pulling out its sword. The sharp, metal end was pointed directly at Katsu's chest. Katsu roughly pushed me to the ground. I barely had a chance to look up in time to see the two clash swords.

"Guards," Katsu yelled, "come quickly. The princess is under attack."

I waited for a response from the guards who usually stood at every door in the palace, but no one ventured out to the gardens.

I heard a low growl to my right and saw another shadow stealthily creep toward me.

"Silly kami, do you truly believe we would not have dispensed with your flimsy palace guards?"

The shadow rushed at me from the dark depths of the choked foliage. I rolled to my left and backward, hoping to arrive at a standing position before that abomination could grab me, but my bulky clothing hindered my movements.

A black, hairy arm slithered its way around my waist and

pulled me to my feet. I reacted instinctively and slammed my wedged shoe down on top of his unprotected foot. I was rewarded with a shrill howl and its grip around my waist slackened, giving me enough freedom to break away. I turned to face it as it came at me again and could do nothing to protect myself as its heavy fist landed on my face. It was the second time in less than an hour that my face had been the target of someone's anger.

As I felt the warm blood gushing down the side of my cheek something within me seemed to break. I had tired of the pain and the beatings, furious at having no control over what happened to me physically. But most of all, I was no longer interested in meekly bowing my head and submitting myself to whatever punishment someone else decided to administer.

Instead of running away from the great black cat, I ran forward to meet it.

"Mikomi, get back." I heard Katsu yell, but I paid him little heed.

As the cat reached out and grabbed me roughly by the arms, I placed my hands on its chest and connected with its ki. It surprised me such a creature had one, but it was twisted and misshapen much like its deformed body. I imagined searing, burning pain starting at the chest and spreading out over the rest of the body. Its ki complied quickly, and soon the nekomata released me, writhing in agony on the grass.

A sharp sword swooped downward and plunged into its chest, making a sick gurgling sound. I withdrew and watched in numb silence as Katsu dislodged his sword from the beast's chest and then decapitated it. Bile surged up the back of my throat, and I slapped a hand across my mouth, horrified to be witness to such violence, but more upset with the part that I had played. I had never willingly used my gift to give pain to anyone, and even though I was defending myself, I couldn't help but feel as if I had violated my own moral code.

I looked to my left and saw that Katsu had already dispensed with the first cat that had attacked us, but I couldn't see the third attacker anywhere. I was certain Katsu had said there were three of them.

"Princess, your face is bleeding again. Were you stabbed by one of their swords?" He looked completely panicked at the thought. He stepped over the dead body separating us and reached for me. In that moment I heard another branch snap behind him and a vicious looking nekomata materialized in the moonlight.

"Katsu," I yelled.

The warrior god turned quickly and raised his sword as his opponent brought down a shiny black blade. He was able to block it and shoved the cat backward, but not before its claws lashed out, cutting across Katsu's face. I screamed as I watched blood spurt to the ground. I feared his injury might slow him down, but Katsu lifted his sword and began slashing and stabbing faster than my eyes could follow.

The cat seemed equal to the task, but the quick slashes Katsu continually delivered began drawing more and more blood, and the monstrous cat's movements began to slow. Katsu saw he was gaining the upper hand and turned a sharp circle to his right, slicing his blade across the cat's throat and severing its head from its body.

I stood in stunned silence as I studied the gory mess surrounding us. The blood I could handle. It was the three decapitated bodies with their heads several feet from them that made me grateful I hadn't had a meal in some time.

I felt a warm hand grab mine.

"Mikomi, show me where you were injured."

I looked up and nearly fainted at the sight of Katsu. He had three gashes that ran the length of his left cheek, barely missing his eye. They were oozing blood and some strange black substance.

"Your face!" I reached forward, but Katsu blocked my advances.

"I will heal soon enough. I need to know if any of the nekomata stabbed you with their weapons."

"No, I am well, but you clearly are not. You must let me heal you."

"As I stated before, Princess, it isn't necessary. My body will heal itself, eventually."

"But I can do it much faster and take away any discomfort you might be feeling in the process."

I grabbed his hand as he started to protest and led him to the bench we had previously used. I urged him to sit down while he protested, and then I placed both my hands on either side of his head. Once connected, I instructed his ki to clean out the wounds and mend them without any scarring. The black substance seemed to be resisting the process, but with a little more instruction, Katsu's ki was able to overcome whatever infection had set in.

Once I was satisfied with the healing taking place, I opened my eyes and studied Katsu's face. There were pink lines where there used to be large open gashes, but those disappeared within minutes, leaving his face just as beautiful as it had been the first time I laid eyes upon him.

"Good. It's almost finished. Do you feel any pain?"

Katsu smiled and softly shook his head, then he lifted his hands and rested them on both of mine. I hadn't realized that I was still holding either side of his face until he was touching me. He drew one hand away from his face and pulled it to his lips where he gave the inside of my wrist a soft, tender kiss. I felt a slow blush creep up my cheeks and was grateful for the low lamplight. My hands began to shake, and I withdrew from his intimate affections.

He must have misinterpreted his effect on me for that of fatigue. "I should never have let you heal me. It's put too much strain on you after what you've just endured."

He rested an arm around my waist to support me, treating me like some fragile porcelain doll. I had healed much worse many times over and had never once suffered enough strain to keep me from remaining in a sitting position, but I had very little control over my movements in his presence.

"Why have there been two attempts on my life in less than twenty-four hours?" I asked.

"You must understand how badly Amatsu wishes you dead. When you and I are married and succeed in healing the veil, Amatsu will no longer have a chance at freeing himself from the land of the dead. He'll be trapped there forever. I'm guessing he has somehow been informed of my arrival and has upped whatever plans he's had for ending your existence."

"Why tonight with so many people here?"

"Perhaps he thought the celebrating would distract everyone long enough to send assassins through, though how he managed to send three is very surprising. He usually only has power enough to send one."

"Why would he send three?"

"Now that you and I have officially met, we are that much closer to foiling his plans. He wanted you dead tonight. He knows his plans are going to fail."

I didn't want to hear any of this. I didn't want to believe that there was actually a demon god out there willing to send assassins to kill me, because that meant the veil between the living and the dead truly existed, and it was failing. What would happen if I shirked my duty and refused to join Katsu? How many lives would I endanger if this prophecy was accurate and I refused to accept my fate?

I pushed these thoughts from my mind and decided there had to be some other explanation for the nekomata's presence. I couldn't bear the thought of accepting a destiny I'd mentally spurned for most of my life. I just wanted my freedom and a chance to live my life on my own terms. Even with Katsu, kind and protective by my side, I desperately wanted to escape. Then I realized what he had just done for me.

I turned to him and grabbed hold of his arm.

"You risked your life to protect me. You could have been killed, Katsu."

"You are The Healer, Mikomi, of course I would risk my life to save yours."

His explanation made me feel worse. The Healer. My title would always be larger than myself. If my supposed role in this universe hadn't been so important, would he have fought for me still? Would I matter to him in the way I wanted to matter to a man fated to share life with me for eternity? Wouldn't it be a glorious thing to be known only as Mikomi and nothing else?

I'd never pondered much upon the subject of love. My previous idea of paradise had been an escape plan involving a life filled with obscurity and solitude where no one knew anything about me. I would never marry or have children. I simply wanted to be alone without anyone demanding anything from me. Having my betrothed sitting next to me and realizing that I could actually grow to care for him had changed everything.

I didn't want to be loved for my title or my gift. Having either of these things left one with responsibilities burdensome enough to weigh down the strongest of men, but the world's safety had been placed on the shoulders of a frail looking princess of seventeen. I didn't want someone to look at me and see only the girl of prophecy, but I feared that was all Katsu saw.

"Of course you would," I finally responded. "And it is honorable and noble of you to take your duty so seriously. Thank you for your dedication to your duty."

Katsu gave me a puzzled look. I wondered if he could sense my agitation. Fortunately for me, we were interrupted by shouting outside the garden gates, and several guards ran through.

"Honorable Katsu, we were informed that you and the princess were under attack and needed our assistance," a young soldier who gave a respectable bow from the waist said.

I noticed Katsu studying him thoughtfully. "You may rise soldier, but please tell me, who informed you of our distress and why didn't you come sooner? The attack began and ended several minutes ago."

The soldier looked as if he might be sick. He had failed in his duty to keep us safe, and that type of failure demanded the ultimate punishment.

"There was a kitchen maid in the corridor who notified one of my men, but we came immediately thereafter."

"I wonder why it took the maid so long to inform anyone of our dangerous situation. Can you find this maid and bring her to me for questioning?"

The soldier looked relieved and bowed again. It wasn't his head on the chopping block this time.

"I also need two of your men to accompany the princess back to her quarters and guard her doors for the rest of the night."

I panicked, wondering how I would ever be able to receive the message from the samurai commander if I had two guards listening outside my door. I wanted to argue but had not been given permission to speak. Undermining his orders would have been terribly rude and disrespectful, so I remained silent by biting the insides of my cheeks.

"Is the princess injured?" one of the guards asked, directing his comment to Katsu and completely ignoring me.

"I believe she sustained a small cut to the face, but it has healed since then," said Katsu. "Return the princess to her rooms immediately, and I will help take up the search for the missing maid."

Katsu left my side without a backward glance. I knew it wasn't seemly to speak with me in front of the guards, but I expected some kind of farewell from him instead of being summarily dismissed. Disappointed with myself for feeling anything for him, I continued biting the inside of my cheeks. My betrothed gave orders like a seasoned general, expecting immediate obedience, accustomed to getting his own way. I should have known better than to think he might be a different kind of deity.

5

Two guards flanked me on either side and silently escorted me to my quarters. They weren't allowed to speak with me, let alone touch me, but I found myself wishing to interrogate them about the maid who had sounded the alarm, too late to be of help to anyone.

I entered my room and closed the doors firmly behind me.

"Sister." I heard a soft whisper. I spun around quickly and clamped a hand over my mouth. Saigo stuck his head out from behind my mirror and gave me a mischievous grin.

"Saigo, what on earth are you doing here?"

"Did you forget about our pact to protect you from a possible assassination attempt?" Kenji whispered as he walked out of my large bathing room.

"I think it a little late for that, considering three more nekomata just tried to kill me and my betrothed."

"What are you talking about?" Saigo asked.

I quickly explained to them my meeting with Katsu and the three nekomata that had attacked us in the garden. I left out the part where he had defended me against my father. I still didn't want Saigo knowing about the abuse I had suffered all these years.

"Incredible," Kenji said. "The demon god must be getting very nervous to have sent out four of his assassins in one day. I've heard it takes quite a bit of power for him to send any assassins through the veil, let alone four. He would be virtually powerless as of this moment."

"What a shame we can't enter the land of the dead and take advantage of his weakness." Saigo enthusiastically brandished his sword.

"Saigo," I said in a stern voice, "I never want to hear of you making plans to enter the land of the dead. Do you understand me?"

"Nonsense, sister. Did you misplace your desire for intrigue and adventure?"

"It vanished in the wake of the decapitated nekomata."

"That would have been truly exciting. Why do you always get to have all the fun?"

"Fun?" Kenji shook his head. "Your sister was almost murdered by the most deadly assassins of all creation, and you think she was having a party in the midst of it?"

"Knowing Katsu was present makes it a less perilous situation. I've heard the warrior god is fierce and merciless. How did you two get on, by the way?"

Saigo's abrupt change in subject had me snorting in a very unladylike manner.

"We got on just fine. He clearly felt it was an honor to have the chance to risk his life to save The Healer." I'd meant it sarcastically, but Saigo didn't catch on.

"Yes, these days who wouldn't? You're quite famous, you know."

I tsked loudly at my brother. "What is the hour, anyway? I'm rather anxious to get this meeting over and done with."

"We have about an hour before it is time to meet this commander," Kenji said.

I heard a brisk knock on the door.

"Princess," Aiko called from the other side.

"You two need to hide, quick," I whispered.

Saigo and Kenji hurriedly dove into my bathing room and shut the door tight just as Aiko came scurrying in.

"I'm sorry to not have been here sooner, but I thought you would be out much later with your father and your betrothed."

She didn't seem too alarmed, and I wondered if the news of the assassination attempt had been covered up. I probed her emotions, but she merely felt flustered, no doubt disturbed at the thought of keeping me waiting.

"It's fine, Aiko. I simply tired much sooner than expected and was allowed to return to my room."

"I'll fetch your sleeping gown and help you prepare for bed."

"I'd rather sleep naked," I mumbled. I felt smothered by so many layers and yards of fabric. My thin, cotton gown for sleeping was infinitely better than a ceremonial kimono, but the sudden stifled and boxed-in feeling that descended upon me made me wish I could be free of everything, including sleeping gowns.

"What was that, mistress?"

"Nothing. Thank you, Aiko."

As my maid rummaged in my closet for something suitable to sleep in, I checked the lock on the window and saw that it was secure. As soon as Aiko left the room I could unfasten the window and then wait.

She returned swiftly and began unwrapping the endless amounts of silk surrounding my body. Once that monumental feat had been accomplished, she brought the sleeping gown over my undergarments. She then lifted the thin cover upon my matted bed and bade me goodnight. The moment my door closed, I anxiously sat up while Saigo and Kenji ran out of the bathing room.

I went to the window and unfastened the latch, but I dared not open it even a crack lest some guard from the outside see it and report it.

"How much longer, Kenji?" I asked.

Kenji screwed on his spectacles and eyed a strange looking contraption hanging on his sash. I still couldn't understand how he managed to read the hour from it.

"I believe we have less than thirty minutes."

"So, now what?" Saigo whispered impatiently.

"Now we wait. No falling asleep, young man."

"You're in more danger of dozing than I am, *old* man."

I smiled at their playful banter and settled myself on my bed, anxiously awaiting the commander's arrival.

My eyes flew open as I heard a soft tap at my window. I turned my head and noted that I was in my bed and must have dozed a bit. The candles had been doused, and the only light spilling into the room came from the full moon through the cracks in my window. I watched as it swung open slowly and a lithe, decidedly female figure nimbly climbed in, closing the window behind her.

"Princess." I heard her whisper.

"Yes," I whispered back. "I am here."

The figure crept slowly over to my bed and then sat down beside me. I wasn't afraid, even though I probably had good reason to be. I thought I found it more fascinating that someone was actually sneaking into my room without my father's knowledge. I nearly let out a wicked laugh.

The figure struck something sharp and the room filled with a soft light. She set her candle inside a ceramic holder and placed it upon the night stand next to my bed. I looked upon the true form of the general for the first time.

She was strikingly beautiful with stunning red hair that could have rivaled the shade of the setting sun, and her coloring resembled that of Musubi's. I couldn't account for her parentage, but I was fairly certain she hadn't been born in Japan. Her clothing appeared dark and nondescript. A man's fitted robe and small trousers hugged her slender form.

The idea that this woman led men into battle baffled me. She seemed so slight. I felt an unwelcome wave of jealousy momentarily overcome me, thinking how often I would have liked to have asserted myself and ordered a few men here and there. I may have been a princess, but I was still just a woman.

She sat down on the bed next to me and gave me a respectful bow. I gave one in return. Though etiquette dictated I wait for her to speak, I worried about the soldier I had tried to save.

"General Akane, I must know how your soldier fared. I tried to save him, but I have no idea if he was able to escape before the guards realized he still lived."

The female commander's eyes shone brightly.

"He lives, your highness. I will forever be in your debt for saving my…soldier's life, and mine, to be perfectly honest with you. It was good of you to stop and heal me when you didn't have to."

I noticed her hesitation when she referred to the young man I had saved, and I noted some strong emotions climbing to the surface, emotions she worked hard to push away. She must have loved him very much. It astonished me, her willingness to allow him to sacrifice his life simply to pass on a message, considering her strong feelings for him. The general seemed to have read my thoughts.

"It wasn't my idea that he be discovered and captured. I needed a volunteer within the emperor's ranks, and he blew his cover, revealing his true loyalties before I knew what was happening." Akane gave me another slight bow. "You will never know the joy I felt when I saw him entering our camp after hearing he'd been taken to the palace to be tortured."

"I am truly happy the ruse worked, and he was able to survive his ordeal. I worried I might have failed him and had no way of knowing until now. Thank you for putting my mind at ease."

"It is I who must thank you. I never dreamed that you would risk yourself at that moment to save another's life. It fuels my confidence that perhaps I might persuade you to use your gifts to accomplish even more good."

She paused for a moment, and I nodded she should continue.

"Princess, my name is Akane. I have come to you hoping you might consider helping our cause. The people in this land cannot survive much longer under your father's rule. There is no food for the villages because the soldiers take what isn't theirs and destroy the rice fields we have worked so long to cultivate. The emperor will not listen to reason and cannot be made to understand the severity of the situation or the fact that soon all who live within the empire will succumb to this famine brought on by the emperor's maltreatment if current practices do not change." She hesitated.

"Therefore, your only option is to fight," I said.

"Yes, Princess. Regrettably it is the only thing we feel we can do, and we have been doing it for quite some time."

"What is it that you want me to do?"

"There are two things I would wish for you to consider. First, I have no doctors, but I cannot afford to lose any more men. Simply put, I need The Healer."

I thought about that for a moment, letting the idea sink in. I had always wanted to use my gift to help and serve people, yet it was mostly used to torture and kill. Helping to heal soldiers who were battling against my father seemed like a dream come true for me, but even as the thought crossed my mind I realized how impossible it would be.

"I would like to join your cause and help you, but the minute I am missing, my father will hunt me down and destroy anyone who stands in his way. I would be more of a liability than I would a help."

Akane shook her head. "With respect, highness, I disagree, and I have already thought this scenario through. We do not wish for you to join us in the field permanently. You would still live in the palace, but we would send you messages whenever we might need your help."

"I would still be required to sneak away from the palace which is impossible to do. I am never allowed to leave the palace walls. My visits to the village to heal people are a difficult undertaking."

"We have recently placed guards within the palace to accompany you to our meetings. The two men outside your door even now are part of our group."

I raised my eyebrows in surprise.

"All right. Well, that takes care of the guards. Now how will I explain all of these outings to my father?"

"I think I can help with that, Princess," Kenji said as he walked out of the bathing room.

Akane sprang to her feet. I barely had time to register the sword in her hand before she was upon Kenji. Kenji surprised me by deftly deflecting her thrust with his cane and circling round toward my bed.

"Akane, all is well. This is my tutor, Kenji."

"I specifically requested that you be alone," Akane hissed.

"You didn't really think we were going to let my sister talk to the general of the samurai insurgents without our protection, did you?"

Akane spun around quickly only to be met with the sharp end of Saigo's sword.

"Saigo, put the sword down. Akane means me no harm."

"Oh, I know. I was just getting ready to defend myself in case she threw that sword at me in the same manner she did with Kenji. Lucky you had that cane with you, old man, or we'd be preparing your body for cremation."

"I never throw a sword," Akane scoffed, "and I highly doubt you'd be capable of defending yourself against a warrior like myself."

Saigo lowered his sword to the ground, and by the small light of the candle I could have sworn he was smiling at her.

"Do you think you could teach me to fight like your samurai insurgents?"

I thought I could hear Akane chuckling.

"Saigo, under no circumstances will you ever fight with the samurai insurgents," I whispered. He sighed heavily and came to sit down on the bed beside me.

"You're really no fun sometimes. You're aware of this, right?"

"You said you might have a suggestion, old man?" Akane asked.

"My name is Kenji, and yes, I think I might be able to convince the emperor that her highness's training for healing the veil would best be served by studying books written about the veil, and it just so happens that these books are not found within the palace walls."

"I didn't know there were specific books written about the veil," I said.

"Oh, there aren't, but I doubt Emperor Fukurokuju will know that."

I looked to Akane to see what she thought of the idea.

She nodded. "This could work. We send you messages letting you know when and where we need your help, and your friend Kenji gets you out of the palace with the emperor's permission."

"I have one stipulation," I said.

"And what is that?"

"No one can know who I am. As far as your soldiers are concerned, I am simply a woman of medicine and nothing more. I don't want anyone aware of my title or my position."

"I think that is a good idea. However, the fact that you are a single woman will cause problems amongst the soldiers. If we don't want any of them pursuing a possible interest in you, and in the process uncovering your identity, it would be best if you were said to be married," Akane said. "The emperor's spies are everywhere, even within the ranks of my samurai."

I shivered at the thought. I hated the guards that were constantly keeping watch over me, but I was aware that father had his spies following my every move. We would have to be very careful.

"Does that mean you are agreeing to this plan, Mikomi? I thought we were going to get you out of here as soon as possible," Saigo said.

Akane walked over to the bed and raised a questioning brow.

I considered how dangerous it would be to join sides with the samurai insurgents against my father, but in the end, I didn't really care. My plan for escape, born from a desire to change my current circumstances, had guided me to this exact moment. This path achieved that for me and afforded me the opportunity to help and heal many others in the process.

I also loved the idea that a woman was running the show.

This commander was proficient with the sword, and her situation intrigued me. I wanted to know more about her, and if I were being honest with myself, I wanted to feel as if a woman could have some kind of control over the events happening within her life. It looked as if Akane had somehow managed to be her own person, her own master. I wanted to know what she knew. I wanted the confidence she carried with every step she took and every gesture she made. If freedom was my main desire, I couldn't think of a better figure to emulate.

"Yes, I will do what you ask, Akane. There is one thing I would ask for in return, however."

"Name it," she said without blinking.

I leaned forward and eagerly took hold of her hand.

"Please teach me how to fight like you. I'm not eager to hurt anyone, but I would like to learn how to defend myself."

Akane looked at the hand I had placed on hers and her mouth seemed to drop in awe. She may have been a seasoned soldier, but it must have been a bit disconcerting to have royalty behave so informally. When one considered how she arrived in my room, it seemed silly to think that simple hand contact might surprise her.

She covered my hand with her other one.

"Princess, you will have my soldiers with you defending you at all times, and I will defend you with my life."

I was so touched by her bold declaration that I almost let go of my wish to learn, but defending myself was one more step toward becoming like Akane and gaining my own personal freedom. I couldn't let the opportunity pass me by without at least fighting for it.

"Akane, I have no doubt that you and your soldiers are more than capable of protecting me, and I am very grateful for your willingness to sacrifice your life on my behalf, but I never want it to come to that. I want the knowledge necessary to protect myself if the need should ever arise, and what if I need to protect someone else?"

"I think it a good idea, child," Kenji said. "Heaven knows neither your brother nor I will prove effective in defending you. We may not even be present at times, and I would feel easier about this dangerous escapade knowing you can take care of yourself."

I heard Saigo make a disgruntled noise in the back of his throat. I knew he would worry about me, but it couldn't be helped. Things needed to change, and the people in our empire had suffered long enough. I didn't know if I wanted to follow an obscure prophecy and heal an invisible veil, but I *did* know that I could be The Healer in a more tangible, life-giving way. I could save my people, and if I could help the insurgents gain any kind of favorable ground over my father, then I would gladly abandon all of my own selfish plans of escape and join their cause.

Akane continued to stare at me intently. Then she nodded. "I have someone in mind who might be able to train you. He has fought on our side for quite some time and is one of the best warriors we have. Still, though I trust him with my own life, it will be important to keep your identity a secret."

"Thank you," I breathed happily.

"It is I who must thank you, Princess—"

"Mikomi," I corrected.

"Mikomi."

"You said there was something else you needed from me?"

"Yes, you have access to all of the information the emperor holds, concerning his movements and sources of supplies. I hoped that perhaps you could use this access to acquire information we might need from time to time, but only so long as you are not endangered in the process. Information is leverage, and any leverage we can gain over the emperor will help our cause tremendously."

I stood up and then paced the room, considering her proposal. I had never used my ability to transfer memories with people who weren't being interrogated by my father, but I wondered if I could somehow manage it around his visitors without them being the wiser. Then I wouldn't be left with the difficult task of sneaking into my father's rooms unless absolutely necessary. "I would be happy to do all I can in acquiring whatever information you might require."

"Excellent." Akane gave me a grateful look. "I will discuss your training with the man I told you about and contact you with details for our first meeting."

Akane looked as if she might leave, and a sudden thought emerged.

"I must ask you—how on earth did you manage to breach the palace walls? You're not a kami, are you?"

Akane reached inside her shirt and pulled out a small vial of red liquid linked to a strap around her neck. "Kami blood," she stated. "I wasn't certain it would work, but we needed to find some way of reaching you. Glad it functioned as I'd hoped."

I shook my head at her reckless behavior. If it hadn't worked, an internal alarm would have resonated within the palace walls, leaving Akane with the difficult task of escaping a barrage of imperial guards. "Where did you get kami blood?"

"We have a few kami on our side anxious to see the end of King Fukurokuju's reign. It wasn't too hard to convince them to help."

"How will you be able to send me a message? Surely you won't risk the life of another soldier." I worried I wouldn't be able to save another one despite the success of the first.

"I have my ways…Mikomi. You'll learn this soon enough."

I felt her preparing to leave again and panicked, worried I might never see her again. It was strange to have found a friend in Akane so quickly. I spoke rapidly in order to prevent her from leaving just yet.

"Akane, what is the name of this warrior who will train me?"

"All in good time, Princess," she whispered.

And then she was gone.

My father rarely summoned me to eat with him and Mother. They never seemed to care much for my presence, and my charming conversation wasn't something that motivated them to have anything to do with me, considering I wasn't allowed to speak unless spoken to. Yet here I sat, on a golden, tasseled cushion covered in red silk with Father to my right at the head of a chestnut brown table resting just above our knees. My mother sat on the other end and Saigo across from me.

My brother sneaked a questioning look at me and then stared down at his plate before father could notice. I stole furtive glances at my mother. I rarely saw her, and despite her ambivalence toward me I still loved her and wished to please her in some small way. Besides, I'd had enough of looking at my father.

"I've brought you all here today for two specific reasons," my father bellowed.

I sensed a headache coming on and wanted to rub the sides of my temples. It seemed the only volume my father ever used was thunderously loud.

I hadn't slept well either. After tossing and turning the first few hours of the night, Aiko had entered my rooms and given me a sleeping draught. I hadn't needed them for quite some time, not since my nightmares had subsided, but Aiko was always prepared.

The sleeping draught had been a strong one this time. If Aiko hadn't tried to wake me this morning with such dogged determination—and a half pitcher full of cold water— I never would have pulled out of my deep sleep.

My father resumed his speech. "The first being this—the warrior god Katsu was most pleased with you, Mikomi. He mentioned that you were agreeable, strong, and indispensable in the fight against the nekomata…though I'm sure he embellished that last bit."

I gripped my eating sticks tightly within my fist and refrained from mentioning that I had healed said warrior god's pretty little face. I supposed it shouldn't have irked me that my father glossed over my involvement in the attempt on my life, but I was tired of having my role and my abilities so minimized.

I was also quite concerned about the pain I had caused that nekomata. I had never before attempted to simulate the kind of pain that one might feel if their body had been burned. I wasn't sure how I'd managed it either and hoped to never have it happen again.

The only thing I could attribute my reaction to was the terror I felt in the nekomata's presence and the overpowering need to defend myself, hence my desire to be trained in the art of the sword. I held no illusions that I might possess the presence of mind to defend myself like that again. More worrisome still, the possibility that I would never position myself close enough to an enemy before being cut down.

"The attempt on your life within the palace walls has me very concerned. It should not have been possible for the nekomata to enter the palace. This leads me to believe we might have a traitor amongst us. Someone willing to risk their very life in order to do the demon god's bidding."

I doubted my father was concerned in the way a normal father should be. If I died he lost his empire.

"Chinatsu," my father continued, "I know the attack on our daughter has been quite hard on your nerves. Perhaps you would like to finish your meal and retire to your room early this morning?"

He made it seem like a question, but everyone present knew my mother had just received a veiled command. I looked at my mother, but her eyes were downcast. She hadn't said a word to me since I'd arrived for this little family meeting, and I highly doubted she had felt any real fear of losing her daughter when she was notified of the attempt on my life. I longed to hear her tell my father she was well enough to finish her meal…stand up to him…but she sat demure and quiet. She then nodded her head and raised herself to a standing position, leaving the room with her attendants following her and never once looking back.

By the gods, sometimes I hated that woman. I knew I shouldn't judge her for not standing up for herself. I had only just begun my own kind of rebellion against the man I called father, but for once I would have loved a kind word or some show of motherly concern, especially since I'd almost been killed the previous night.

The servants quickly cleared her side of the table and added a clean, porcelain plate and eating sticks.

I glanced toward Saigo, wondering if he had noticed the extra place being set.

"Father, is someone joining us for this meal?" he asked.

"Indeed I am, young Saigo," said a strong voice.

I didn't have to look up to know that Katsu had just entered the room. I kept my eyes lowered to the food on my plate and nearly squirmed self-consciously as he sat himself down to my left. I could feel his eyes on me, and wished I could be anywhere else but in his presence.

He had protected me from my father and saved my life the previous night, and perhaps we might have shared a small yet brief connection, but once we were no longer alone he had proven himself to be just like any other male I'd ever met.

I was only as important as my gifts made me to be. Only as important as the title of The Healer allowed me to be. I could have been any woman at all and it wouldn't have mattered to Katsu so long as I was capable of healing the veil.

I knew it was only logical for him to think and feel this way, but I wanted him to care just a little more about me and a little less about my abilities.

"Katsu," my father said with barely suppressed rage.

He no doubt remembered the threat Katsu had made against him while defending me. I might have enjoyed my father's anger if I hadn't felt so out of sorts.

"Fukurokuju," the warrior god responded.

I thought I heard Saigo gasp under his breath a little. It was considered disrespectful to address my father as anything less than emperor, and calling him by his first name in such an informal manner showed a lack of concern for my father's station and title. I realized, however, that Katsu knew my father long before he was ever made emperor.

My father bristled and then fisted his hands on either side of his plate, attempting to keep his anger in check. He never controlled his anger in my presence, but now he somehow managed to pull himself together enough to speak.

"Mikomi, Katsu will begin your training today. Though your gifts are quite powerful, they have only ever been used a few times to heal injuries needing your special skills."

I nearly choked at the bold-faced lie.

"It will be important then that Katsu train you to control your powers and focus them on strengthening the line between our world and the dead. It will be tedious work, but I am sure you will be up to the challenge. You've never disappointed me before."

The show he was putting on would have been laughable if I hadn't felt so anxious. This was really happening. I had known all of my life that one day I would have to train for this, but keeping myself in denial, convincing myself that this was all superstitious nonsense had been the only way I could cope with the pressure placed upon my shoulders, and now that the moment had arrived, I wanted to continue considering the prophecy a mere fairy tale.

I needed to do everything I could to help the samurai rebels against the emperor. I longed for much more than the life Katsu and my father planned for me.

"We will begin this afternoon," Katsu said, directing the comment toward my father. "I trust that will not interfere with any of your current interrogation plans?"

I felt my eyes go wide at his mocking comment. I had to bite my lip to keep from laughing outright. He knew my father had been abusing my powers, and held no qualms in airing out the offense. It was so refreshing to see my father squirm for once, even if I could only watch from lowered lids.

My father stood up abruptly, muttering something about not being hungry anymore, and left with his attendants following him.

I kept my eyes on my plate and remained silent. I wasn't sure what I was supposed to do, but based on Katsu's behavior last night I thought it better to remain perfectly prim and proper since my brother and several servants were present.

"What in the world was that all about?" Saigo said, breaking the uneasy silence. "I haven't seen Father that upset since...well let's be honest...since yesterday, really."

I let out an involuntary giggle and threw my hand over my mouth to stifle it. I raised my eyes to Saigo's, who wiggled his eyebrows wickedly. My giggles continued, but I couldn't stop them this time, especially since Saigo had joined me. I heard someone else chuckling as well and turned surprised eyes on my betrothed. He wore only a half grin on his full lips, but it reached his dark eyes, making me think that perhaps he wasn't quite so stoic in public as I feared he would be.

"I believe I may have said something a trifle upsetting," Katsu said. "Wouldn't you agree, Mikomi?"

"You mean about Father using my sister's powers to torture, scar, and kill for information?" This time Saigo was not laughing, and my laughter died rather quickly.

I reached across the table for my brother's hand.

"It's all right, Saigo. I think now that Katsu is here, there will be no more interrogations for me."

"Absolutely not," Katsu agreed firmly. "I wish I'd been apprised of your circumstances long ago. If I hadn't stayed away, I could have done something about it."

I said nothing. I saw no reason to blame him for the actions of my father, but I did wish that someone, perhaps even myself, had stood up to him long before now.

"Why did it take you so long to meet my sister?" Saigo asked.

"Saigo, that really is none of our business," I interjected.

"Your father made it clear that her powers had not developed fully, but in truth I stayed away for personal reasons," Katsu answered, surprising both Saigo and myself. "Sometimes there are decisions made in this life that can never be undone, and you spend centuries trying to cope with the consequences."

I could sense his pain, though I tried not to. For whatever reason, Katsu had let his guard down and despair rolled off of him in waves. It was nearly all-consuming, and I couldn't help but reach my hand toward his in an effort to comfort him. The minute I touched him, he blinked once and seemed to come back to the present. He moved his hand from mine and began eating his meal.

Disheartened, I leaned back and kept my eyes on my plate, not feeling the least bit hungry anymore. I couldn't understand how Katsu could be so kind and caring with me one moment and then abrupt and dismissive the next. It was disconcerting to say the least, but in the end I guessed it shouldn't have mattered. I had no intention of healing an imaginary veil, and I wasn't about to marry a man out of duty or honor or even for convenience's sake.

Akane had given me another avenue of escape, a different path to follow, and I intended to follow it wherever it might take me.

Saigo dropped his eating sticks with a loud clatter. "Well, I must bid you both a happy goodbye. If I arrive late for my studies again, Kenji will no doubt use that ridiculous cane on me."

I gave my brother a soft smile and watched him as he made his exit. I envied him, really. What I wouldn't give to make my own exit and choose when it happened.

"Are you not hungry?" Katsu asked.

"I'm afraid the events of last evening have affected my appetite. Perhaps you would excuse me?" I prepared myself to leave, believing he would no doubt be happy dining in solitude, but before I could make my escape, his firm, warm hand gently descended upon mine. I was frustrated that he had stopped me and somewhat elated that he had initiated contact this time. My jarring emotions couldn't seem to make up their minds.

"I would wish for you to stay. Perhaps we can begin to know one another more thoroughly before our training session this afternoon."

His voice was commanding, but his eyes were kind. I allowed my body to relax a bit and nodded my assent. Feeling anxious and somewhat rebellious, I determined to ask him something supremely unimportant.

"What might your favorite color be?"

Katsu gave me a strange look. "Green."

I waited.

He smiled.

I continued to wait.

Finally he laughed and said, "What might *your* favorite color be?"

"Blue. You see, we're getting to know each other already."

Katsu chuckled again, and though I hated to admit it, I enjoyed putting a smile on his face. Anything to wipe away the grief I had sensed just moments earlier.

"If you could have any wish fulfilled, what would it be and why?" he asked.

I felt my small smile slip away. I could never tell him what I truly wished. I could never discuss how desperately I wished to be loved for the right reasons, to have a future guided by my own choices and my own mistakes, to have children of my own instead of becoming a full kami, never able to bear children if I was going to heal the veil. No. I couldn't tell Katsu any of these things.

And so I lied.

"I wish to serve my people and perform my duties as needed."

"Agreed. That would be my wish as well. I believe we are getting to know one another fairly well and finding we have so very much in common."

His hand continued to rest atop mine, and he squeezed it gently.

"Yes," I said with as much forced cheerfulness as I could muster. "I believe we are."

∞∞∞

The guards escorting me back to my rooms after breakfast were the same guards that had been at my door the night before. I realized with an excited jolt that I was surrounded by members of the samurai insurgents—a thrilling realization to come to. Just before I opened the door to my rooms I felt a hand slide into mine and then it was gone, leaving a small piece of parchment in its stead. I did my very best to avoid reacting to the quick contact. I closed the door behind me and then jumped for my bed, unfolding the note and reading it as quickly as possible.

Meet me just before dusk at the Yanbaru ruins.
Burn this letter immediately.

The Yanbaru ruins were in the opposite direction of the village and the small forest separating it from the palace. At one time it had been a place of learning and growth for enlightened humans and kami. It had been destroyed many years ago by the emperor in response to the uprising of the rebels.

The only parts of Yanbaru my father hadn't destroyed were the holy relics, statues of our First Parents, and a Shinto temple dedicated to the god of love and marriage. The monks that dwelled within had been able to use their own magical powers to protect the temple and shrine. Not even my father dared to destroy another kami's place of worship. Not unless he wished to declare war against his own kami brothers.

I had not spent much time in that particular area. I wasn't interested in looking at the destruction my father had wreaked upon a place that had once held so much potential for helping those that dwelled within the Kagami Empire. I tended to avoid the shrine and temple due to the god that it served.

According to history and tradition, Musubi-no-kami was the god who was given dominion over the hearts and unions of the inhabitants of this earth. Humans in this empire could travel to the shrine and find The Holy Cherry Tree, a relic of magical properties used by the god of love and marriage, to bind soul mates together forever. One only needed travel to The Holy Cherry Tree, declare their choice of bride and ask for Musubi's blessing in the form of a single white cherry blossom. If this particular kami found the match acceptable, the blossom would fall from the branches of the tree and be used in the wedding ceremony, binding the participants to one another for eternity.

One might think it a romantic notion, but I knew better. The brides in question never had a choice, and though it was rumored that there were many occasions where the god denied his blessings upon certain unions, I had a difficult time believing it. Musubi-no-kami may have been a god, but he was also male and probably cared very little for the wants and needs of the women involved. Their fate could be sealed with one single blossom, just as mine could.

I'd never before met this particular kami, and if I were being honest with myself, I had very little desire to. Part of his duty and honor involved giving my union to Katsu his blessing by performing the marriage ceremony himself. I disliked the idea of yet another kami gaining power over my decisions and forcing me into a marriage I wasn't ready to accept. As a result, I never ventured toward the ruins, the Shinto temple or The Holy Cherry Tree.

Though I held some reservations about the area in which Akane and I would meet, I felt my whole body tingle in anticipation of tonight's meeting. It was a step in the right direction. I walked over to my nightstand and opened a drawer decorated in finely carved floral patterns. I pulled out two fire stones and sat the piece of parchment on the stand. After striking the stones together and igniting the small bit of parchment, I watched as the ends blackened and curled in upon themselves, burning away any trace or sign of this new beginning.

I was in control now, and it felt just as liberating as I'd hoped. I needed to get a message to Kenji. My guards were not allowed to let me leave my rooms unless summoned—new security measures due to the attack last night—but I had a feeling these particular guards would allow me to visit my brother's tutoring session for a word with Kenji.

I opened my door softly.

"If I am to keep my commitments for this evening it will be necessary for me to visit my brother and his tutor first," I whispered. I hoped my wording was obscure enough to avoid raising any alarms if the area held a spy or two but pointed enough for them to understand my meaning. One guard nodded and pulled the door wide. I stepped forward and began walking meekly down the hall with a guard on either side. I found it wholly ironic that for the first time in my whole life I felt more secure with two rebels surrounding me than I ever did with the palace guards.

After several twists and turns throughout the great expanse of the palace, we soon reached the door to my brother's quarters, and the guard knocked lightly.

"Her highness wishes to visit her brother," one of the guards said only loud enough for my brother and Kenji to hear through the door. It opened up quickly, and I stepped in just as fast. I noticed that Kenji stood behind the door with a surprised look on his face. I waited until the door closed behind me, certain we were not being listened to.

"Why on earth are you being accompanied by your guards, Mikomi?"

"Apparently, Katsu insisted my security was lacking, and now I have guards following me everywhere. Fortunately for us they are on our side."

Saigo clapped happily.

"This is all so exciting. Nothing like a bit of intrigue to liven up any tutoring session—eh, Kenji?"

Kenji sat down at the table with a sigh. "I'll probably be dead long before you learn anything of real value."

I might have joined in the banter, but I wasn't there for my own amusement, and I needed to enlist Kenji's help before my tutoring session with Katsu.

"Kenji, I have received a message from Akane. She wishes to meet me at the Yanbaru ruins this evening."

"And so it begins," Saigo intoned dramatically.

"Can you discuss my need to further study the veil with father as soon as possible?"

"It isn't much notice, but your father rarely turns down an audience with me. I will send the request immediately, and with any luck he'll be too distracted to see through this fabrication."

"Thank you, Kenji."

Kenji left the room, and I sat down at the table next to Saigo. I placed my shaking hands in my lap and decided to help my brother with his studies.

"You'd better continue your reading. Kenji will come back and be very disappointed if you've fallen too far behind."

"You're just afraid Kenji will blame you for distracting me." We both laughed softly, and then our moods grew serious.

"You will be careful out there, won't you?"

"I will be on high alert, and if anything happens to me I can always heal quickly."

"I hope that wasn't you trying to comfort me? Because you're quite terrible at it."

I gave him what I hoped was a reassuring smile. "I'll be careful. Now, let's focus on something else...like this tutoring session."

I needed to take my mind off my meeting with Akane or I would be driven completely mad with anticipation.

Now, if I could just survive my training session with Katsu.

I'm not sure why I took such care with the state of my dress and appearance. I was merely going along with this farce until I could break away and become my own person, but keeping up appearances seemed important now more than ever. It had nothing to do with the fact that Katsu was quite a handsome individual...for a kami. I smoothed down my black tresses and ran a hand down the length of my silk green kimono. I may have changed into clothing the color of what Katsu had claimed was his favorite.

I entered the gardens with my guards accompanying me and continued ahead without them as they stood watch over the area. The gardens looked especially beautiful in the sunlight, though the sky looked slightly overcast. It was hard to believe that something as ugly as nekomata had ever placed one foot upon these lovely grounds.

I spotted Katsu sitting on the blinding white bench next to the pond. The moment his eyes met mine they seemed to warm ever so subtly. I almost smiled at the idea that he might have been happy to see me, but then his face changed and there was his stoic mask again.

I wasn't sure where the Katsu that had come to my rescue the night before had gone. Where was the Katsu who had defended me against my father? The one who had gently wiped the blood from my face and held me close when we were deep in conversation? He had built an impressive wall around his emotions which prevented me from reading him as easily as others. I couldn't account for his behavior since I couldn't read the emotions driving him, and so I was determined to school mine.

And now here we were, back in the gardens where he and I had had our first real conversation; also the place where I was almost killed…and the place where he promptly forgot about me once the guards had shown up.

My beautiful gardens were now tainted.

Katsu stood as I approached, and I nearly stopped my laborious tread. I had forgotten how very tall he was, and how broad his shoulders were. He wore a warrior's vest of brown leather and brown trousers…nothing like the traditional style of clothing that my father wore, complete with kimono, jacket, and split skirt. I guessed as a warrior god you had to wear what gave you more freedom of movement. I tugged on the confining fabric of my kimono and longed to be a man.

"Mikomi," he said, bowing from the waist.

I bowed and then waited in that same position.

"You may rise, Princess. You needn't be so formal with me."

I refrained from voicing my thoughts and merely rose from my bowing position.

"Tell me what you know about the veil," he commanded.

"Very little, I'm afraid. All I know is what the prophecy has stated."

Katsu looked at me in surprise.

It irked me that my ignorance had become so painfully obvious or that I might care about his regard for me.

"So little, Mikomi? Were you never allowed to touch the veil when healing someone?"

"I…I…never knew I could. I didn't think it possible to access the veil when healing someone."

Katsu took my hand and bid me walk with him on one of the winding paths through the foliage.

"In truth, the veil is all around us because the land of the dead is here, but in a different dimension. You'll be able to sense it the same way that I can once you have had a feel for it during a healing. You will also be capable of noticing where the veil's weaknesses lie based on its texture. When weak, the veil bends easily, like glass under extreme temperatures, but when the veil is at its strongest it will feel like an impenetrable wall. It won't matter if you have to travel halfway around the world to strengthen it...you'll be able to sense where it needs to be fortified once you connect to it."

I nodded and pretended confidence where none was felt. I found it difficult, picturing myself sensing anything other than someone's ki.

"Now, in order to sense the veil you will need someone to practice on."

I felt anxious all of a sudden. "Surely you don't mean to injure yourself so that I might heal you?"

Katsu looked confused for a moment, and then his face cleared.

"No, practicing on my person would be wholly useless. There is no veil to sense when healing a kami."

"I don't understand."

"A kami is immortal, and you cannot gain access to the veil with our ki because the veil is for those people who are meant to die."

I absently plucked an oval-shaped leaf hanging from a tree we were passing and worried it between my hands as I contemplated this new information.

"We will find someone who is mortal for you to practice on."

I grabbed his arm without thinking. He looked down at my hands and back at me, and I dropped them immediately. I could have sworn he had been about to hold my hand in his, but for whatever reason he stopped himself. I thought I saw some intense emotion flash across his face, but then it was gone. It was frustrating. He was extremely adept at shielding his emotions.

"I...I'm sorry...I just wonder if it is safe. I wouldn't want to hurt anyone."

Katsu took another moment to compose himself. Somehow, he had managed to build up a wall that my empathic abilities couldn't penetrate.

"The man you will be practicing on is already very ill and will soon die. There isn't anything you could do that would possibly inflict more damage."

Katsu motioned with a flick of his finger, and two guards materialized out of nowhere, carrying a frail looking man with tattered, soiled clothing. They carefully placed him on the grass before me.

I knelt down by his side and grabbed his hand. He looked at me, but didn't actually see me. The pupils and irises of his eyes were covered with a thin milky substance. His gnarled, bony hand gripped mine with surprising strength. I sensed his fear as he reached out with his other hand. Did he not understand the reason for which he'd been brought here?

"Where did he come from?" I asked, horrified.

"I believe he was found in the village a few miles north of here."

"Where is his family? What is his name?" I could hear the slight rise in my voice and felt tension in my body.

"Does it really matter? He is being of service to The Healer and all of mankind."

I couldn't believe what I was hearing. This poor man had no doubt been kidnapped and brought here without one word of explanation.

"The Healer." I heard the old man mumble. "Where is The Healer?"

"I'm here." I grabbed both his hands in mine and brought them to my face. "I'm right here."

He used his hands to read the curve of my chin and cheeks, the length of my nose and width of my forehead.

"You can heal me?" he asked once he lowered his hands into mine.

"I can try."

I placed my hands on either side of his face to connect with his ki. My heart sank when I saw the extent of his illness and felt certain his fate had already been decided. The one downside to my gift, the one thing I never had any control over, was who would live and who would die. Who could be healed and who could not.

This man had probably been promised a cure for his illness, but he was meant to die.

I broke away from him and sat back.

"If you will give me just one moment please," I said, keeping my rising emotions in check.

I stood up and walked the short distance to Katsu. He raised a questioning eyebrow at me.

"Katsu, please forgive me, but I think there has been some mistake. This man believes I can heal him, but he is meant to die. Was there no one else with minor injuries that I might have healed?"

"I understand your distress, Princess, but I made no mistake. I picked him myself. I too sensed that he was meant to die."

I stared at him, dumbfounded.

"Yes, but he is under the impression that he will be healed."

"I may have allowed him to think you would be capable of healing him. He might have put up a fight, otherwise."

I wasn't sure how I restrained myself from smashing my fist into Katsu's head. I supposed a life schooled in the art of repressing my emotions had served me well.

Katsu finally seemed to take note of my distress and placed his hands on my shoulders in a placating gesture.

"Mikomi, the only way you can sense the veil at first is by attempting to heal someone who is meant to die. What you will find when you start the healing process is—"

"A wall," I mumbled automatically. "A block of some kind."

I knew it well. It was the thing that taunted me every time I fought to heal someone that deserved to live but died anyway. The obstacle I struggled to overcome any time I tried to do something good and right.

Katsu smiled at me as if I had just earned a nice pat on the head for responding with the correct answer.

"Yes, then you have felt it before. The veil is there, preventing you from healing anyone whose soul is ready to pass over. I want you to try healing this man, and once you sense the veil, take special note of how it feels."

"Feels?" I struggled to follow his instructions, worrying about the fate of the sickly, old man.

"Mentally. In a way you are touching it with your own mind… your own ki. Become accustomed to the way it feels, and you will be that much closer to sensing the veil. Connect with him again and focus this time."

I turned around and slowly walked back to my patient. After kneeling down next to him, I gently took his head between my hands, once again connecting to his ki. The pain was awful, worse than it had been the first time. I wasn't sure if his illness had a specific name, but it resided in the lungs and made it very difficult for him to breathe.

I tried to instruct his ki to minimize the size of a large mass lodged within his lungs, but I received no response. I pushed his ki aside and tried to minimize the mass using my own—something I had tried several times before whenever another person was unresponsive. My instructions and suggestions never reached the tiny intelligences within the lungs. Instead, the wall that I had been dreading rose up before me and blocked me at every turn. I pushed against it. The veil felt like a very thin pane of hardened glass. Unyielding and immovable. I tried feeling my way up, down and to the side, seeking an end to the impenetrable wall.

Nothing but cold, hard glass.

Frustrated, I disconnected from the old man and let go.

"I'm sorry, sir," I whispered. "I cannot heal you."

He grabbed my hand and held on tight.

"But you're The Healer. They promised me you would heal me."

I glanced to Katsu, who had the decency to look slightly ashamed of himself. He flicked his fingers again and the two guards who had brought the stranger in, reached down to remove him from the gardens.

The man held fast to my arms and began to cry. One of the guards hit him over the head in an attempt to free me from his grasp.

"No, stop," I commanded, surprising both of Katsu's guards and myself. In the seventeen years I'd lived here within the palace, never once had I given any kind of command nor raised my voice like a man.

"Mikomi, what are you doing?" Katsu asked.

But I wasn't listening. I wouldn't listen to someone who valued life so little and behaved in such an unfeeling manner.

The guards continued to hold the man in their arms while I placed my hands on either side of his head and connected with him. I gave instructions to his ki to heal the damage that time, age, and illness had caused and did my best to take away all of his pain.

When I opened my eyes I was looking into his. They were beautiful and completely healed.

"I cannot give you back your health as you were promised," I said in a shaky voice. I raised my hand to his face and gently held it there. "But I can give you back your sight."

The old man stared at me in wonder as tears slid from his newly healed eyes. I looked at the astonished expression on the guards' faces. "You will return him to his home and make certain he sees his family before he dies."

"Yes, Princess," the guard to my right said.

I couldn't be sure, but I thought I saw a small look of respect on each of their faces before they turned away and left. I stared after them, wishing I could have done more to ease the poor man's burden. There was much I could accomplish if I didn't have to heal the veil.

Katsu cleared his throat. "That was very kind of you...what you did for that man. You didn't have to."

I turned to face him, but I had cooled my anger and schooled my face. He would never know how sickened I felt at his utter lack of feeling.

"May I speak freely?"

"Of course," he said in surprise.

"There are many things we are not forced to do, but perhaps we should do them anyway, whether they are considered duty, destiny or simply a matter of choice. If we have a choice to make then we should choose it. If we have a gift for healing, then we should use it. We should lift people's burdens and make things right." I stepped closer to him and clasped my hands in front of my heart. "There is too much suffering and too much sadness. Just as I have sensed that there is suffering and sadness within you."

His eyes widened at my bold statement. I reached my hand out slowly and softly placed it against his heart.

"I can fix it, Katsu. I can make it right."

He looked at me in wonder and slowly lifted his hand, placing it on top of mine. We stood there like that for a few precious moments—a connection that shattered with the snap of a branch and the approach of more guards. Katsu blinked and stepped back…and the moment was gone.

"Honorable Masaru Katsu, the emperor wishes a word with you."

I glanced at the soldier speaking and thought he looked familiar. He glanced at me so quickly no one would have noticed, but in that moment I wondered if he was another samurai warrior.

"Of course," he said, turning to address me. "Princess, we will begin tomorrow at the same time. I will want to discuss what you learned from our training exercise today."

I barely had time to bow before he was off.

Dismissed again.

I really should have become more accustomed to it by now, but in truth, it hadn't bothered me as much in the past as it had lately. I watched as he strode confidently back the way we had come and then out of my sight.

"Princess, this message arrived earlier from Master Tutor Kenji," the guard said. He bowed from the waist and offered the small piece of parchment to me.

"Thank you," I said, taking it and opening it immediately.

Be ready before dusk for our educational outing. Your personal guards will be accompanying us for your protection.

I smiled. Kenji had been able to convince Father of the necessity of our outings, and from the looks of it had already found a way for us to be accompanied by our allies. He really was terribly good at all of this intrigue and subterfuge. I wasn't well practiced in the art of deceit, but for a cause like this I would willingly become an expert.

I folded the note inside a pocket within my kimono and looked at the guards. "I wish to stay for a few moments in the gardens, please."

The guard who had handed me the note nodded and stepped back. I walked at a normal pace around the winding path and headed straight for a large, copper colored rock that sat next to a wild looking bush with leaves and twigs pointing in every direction. There was another bench, dark green in color, placed next to it. I sat down and then reached forward toward the rock, pretending I had discovered a flower on the ground. I checked the rock for a message from Daiki, but found nothing.

On the one hand I was relieved. No news was good news, but I wished to visit with Hatsumi and check on her baby boy. I would look again for a message from Daiki in seven days. He didn't always leave them, but I knew it was important that I never miss the first day of the week.

Straightening myself into a standing position, I noticed my maid, Aiko, touring the gardens with an older soldier. My curiosity piqued, I took a few steps forward, thinking I might follow them, but then paused, not wishing to intrude. Aiko never mentioned anything about a possible suitor.

I should have expected her inevitable departure. Now that I was to be married off and carted away within the next six months it only made sense that she would do what she could to secure her future.

I fully intended to tease her about it later when I saw her next.

I had a grin on my face as I headed back toward my rebel guards waiting just within the garden gates. My mood lightened at the thought of Aiko finding her own happy ending.

∞∞∞∞

Once again my guards escorted me to my rooms. I almost lost my footing as I closed the door due to the surprise I felt at the strange specter of my mother sitting primly on my bed.

"Mother?"

She looked at me with barely concealed disdain. It was a look I was unfortunately familiar with. That didn't mean it hurt any less to endure.

"I've heard you started your training today," was her opening remark.

"Yes, I just finished."

"I've also been informed that you healed a diseased-ridden man's eyesight, and a peasant at that!"

"That's true. I was hoping to give him the opportunity to see his family before he passed on."

My mother studied me for several seconds. It appeared she was unimpressed with what she saw. I knew I would never be as strikingly beautiful as she, but I wasn't a hopeless case, surely.

"I thought your father and I had impressed upon you the importance of reserving your healing powers. You'll never be immortal if your powers are wasted on filthy peasants and ailing servants."

I assumed she was referring to the maid within the palace whom I had helped during childbirth several weeks ago. I should have known that everything would be reported back to her. Her spies were larger in number and far superior to that of my father's. I would need to be doubly careful now that I had given her reason to be displeased.

"I am sorry for my error. I merely wanted to help them—"

"Don't talk to me about your noble desires or your foolish wishes." She now stood and walked over to me, taking my chin roughly in her hand and squeezing hard. I felt her nails digging into my skin and could have sworn she enjoyed the obvious pain it caused me.

My mother had never shown much love for me, but she had never been cruel like this. I hardly understood what was happening.

"I have sacrificed my life and my happiness, agreeing to a loveless marriage with a vindictive fool so The Healer, the child of prophecy could exist and save the world, and you are jeopardizing your destiny by giving in to your weak, nurturing side. I won't allow it. Do you understand me?"

"Yes, I understand. I...I didn't know you felt that way about Father," I managed to say.

She let go of me and stepped back. "Who doesn't feel that way about your father? This empire has fallen into disarray due to his lust and greed for power. My people suffer at his hand, and he sits high and mighty on his pedestal thinking his good fortune is due entirely to his own prowess. He may be a kami, an entitled deity, but he is emperor because I made it so. I fulfilled my duty and gave birth to The Healer. I married him so you could exist."

A tiny light went off in my head, and pieces of my life's puzzle began clicking into place.

"You resent me for this. You hate me for what it cost you."

I saw tears, real tears, slip down my mother's face.

"I don't hate you, Mikomi. I wish I could feel anything other than despair, but I can't work up enough feeling to like you, let alone love you, and I don't care if that makes sense to you or not. If I ever catch you healing again, I will punish you far worse than your father ever has."

She was suddenly racked with a horrible cough. I'd never heard my mother cough like that before. It startled me into action, and without thinking, I moved to her, hoping to connect with her and find the cause of her ailment, but she shrank from me and threw her hand forward. "Don't you *dare* attempt to use your powers on me!"

"I'm sorry. I only wished to help."

"Then do your duty and become The Healer. That is all anyone needs from you."

My mother wiped the tears from her eyes, straightened her clothing and swiftly walked past me out the door.

There were many things I could handle, and many things that I *had* handled. My father's abuse, my suffocating existence, even a betrothal to a man I didn't love and wasn't sure I could respect, but with all of these hardships I operated under the delusion that despite my mother's indifference there had to be a part of her, a small piece of her that loved me. With that hope shattered I felt displaced, untethered to my emotions or my drive for something better than life as I had always known it.

I wasn't sure how long I stood there with tears streaming down my face before Aiko entered my rooms and laid me upon my bed. I didn't think I slept, but I wasn't certain I was conscious either. The light from the outside world diminished slowly, and all of my hopes and dreams descended with it.

I heard a knock at my door and mechanically rose to open it. Kenji stood with a bright smile on his face, chasing all of my dark thoughts away. My mother didn't love me, but Kenji and my brother did. Maybe I wasn't so unlovable after all.

He bowed at the waist and rose swiftly. "Princess, our *educational* outing awaits us."

I gave him a weak smile, attempting to muster my courage and determination despite my mother's devastating revelations.

There were people who loved me and a life waiting to be lived; a destiny all my own. It was time to move forward and embrace it.

8

The small wrap I held around my shoulders did little to protect me from the growing chill in the air. We waited within the Yanbaru ruins for Akane and her warrior to arrive, but I was beginning to grow impatient.

"Child, if you continue to walk back and forth like that you'll wear out your shoes, and I'll be held accountable for it."

I stopped my frantic pacing and tried holding still.

"It's no good, Kenji," I said as I began pacing again. "I'm nervous, cold…and hungry, now that I think on it. Pacing keeps me grounded."

Kenji said nothing but gave me an amused chuckle. At least one of us was having an enjoyable time.

I couldn't keep my eyes from straying to the Shinto temple rising up beyond the ruins, lighted by large torches, candles, and paper luminaries. I couldn't see The Holy Cherry Tree in the distance, but I knew it was there, mocking me and calling to me all at the same time. I felt myself moving forward, with the temple in the distance as my lighted beacon. For reasons I couldn't quite understand, I felt myself drawn to a place I had avoided all of my life.

"Child, where are you going?"

I heard Kenji and my guards following softly behind me.

It took only a few minutes to clear the ruins and approach The Holy Cherry Tree resting several hundred yards in front of the temple. Though dusk had settled over the earth, the tree let off a golden light all its own. Its bark and limbs were a golden amber hue, sparkling with a light only something as holy and magical as this relic could produce. The white cherry blossoms stood out against the darkened sky, sending off a magnetic aura of promise. The sweet fragrance of the blossoms filled my senses and pulled me forward. The tree was mystical and magnificent, but I knew what it was meant for.

Despite my deep reservations, I allowed myself to be pulled forward, entranced by its beauty and the possibilities it held. I stood only a few feet away from it when I felt a presence standing next to me. I couldn't take my eyes from the ethereal blossoms, however. I struggled to rip my gaze from the hypnotic scene and acknowledge the person standing next to me but failed miserably. I needn't have worried since the stranger broke the silence first.

"Are you here to request a blessing from the god of love and marriage? A little late in the evening for that sort of thing, wouldn't you say?"

I knew that voice. The low timbre of his words effectively broke whatever hold the shrine had over me. I abruptly turned and came face to face with Musubi, the man from Daiki's tavern. I couldn't hide my elation as I felt a slow grin capture my lips. The glow from the tree glinted off his blue eyes, and they seemed to twinkle merrily from their dark depths.

"What are you doing here?" I asked.

"I wondered the same thing of you. Is there some injured soul wandering the ruins looking for a pretty woman of medicine to attend his every need?"

I blushed. "Of course, not. I'm merely…passing through."

He arched a skeptic eyebrow at me. "Passing through? With two warriors and an old man trailing you?" He paused, waiting for me to offer up some explanation, but I remained silent. I couldn't break my promise to Akane and tell him who I was. He continued in another vein. "You don't intend to ask the god of love and marriage for a young man of your own, then? I hear the deity is quite generous with his blessings when pretty young maidens are involved."

"Of course not." My blush became fiercer. "I'm not in the market for a husband at the moment, and even if I had a young man in mind, I certainly wouldn't ask a kami for permission."

Musubi studied me, clearly intrigued. "Really? Why ever not?"

Well, now I'd done it. I couldn't seem to behave properly whenever I found myself in this man's presence. He looked upon me intently, as if my response might matter more than anything else ever possibly could.

"I'd rather leave my fate in my own hands." We were facing one another now. A powerful urge to wrap my arms around him and pull him to me assaulted my senses, and I barely controlled the impulse.

Musubi reached for me. He lightly took hold of my hands and pulled them toward himself, studying them for a moment. His lips turned up at the corners and his smile was kind. "They seem like capable hands to me." He gently rubbed his thumbs within both of my palms.

I couldn't have uttered a single word.

Musubi had woven me under his hypnotic spell as effectively as had the shrine for the god of love and marriage. He lifted a hand to my face, and I held my breath as he brushed soft fingers against my hair and then brought his hand back with a flourish, revealing a beautiful, snow-white cherry blossom. He wove it through the strands of my hair just above my ear and then stepped back, considering me for a moment or two.

"It's a pity you're intent upon choosing for yourself. If circumstances were different, I would kidnap you from this very spot and force you to spend eternity with me." He raised his eyebrows as if challenging me, and then gave me a mischievous grin.

Heat crept up the back of my neck and blossomed outward. I was grateful for the darkened sky and my olive complexion. He took note of my embarrassment and let out a wicked chuckle. I couldn't help but feel delighted by his attentions and had to remind myself that he was merely being playful.

"If I have it my way, you'll be claiming her tonight, and for as long as it takes to win this insufferable war," a woman's voice said from behind us.

I turned quickly to see Akane striding forward with a satisfied grin on her face. I felt so happy to see her I could hardly help myself. I rushed forward and wrapped my arms around her, giving her a very informal greeting. She laughed and hugged me back.

"I knew you wouldn't fail us," she said.

"Of course not. I said I would be here, and here I am."

"This is the woman upon whom you've placed all your hopes and dreams?" Musubi said.

I turned to see that he no longer appeared as happy as he had been before Akane's arrival. He leveled me with a serious look. "Perhaps you might be willing to explain to me who you are and why you're so important to our cause. Akane has been rather tight lipped about it."

His displeasure and stunned astonishment hit me hard, but he reined in his emotions quickly. I looked to his eyes and noted the way their frosty azure depths brazenly took me in. I couldn't seem to focus on anything else except their exotic hue, so foreign to me.

I walked forward and without thinking touched his cheek and then softly rested it against the side of his face. His eyes grew large at the unexpected contact. "Your eyes…I've never seen eyes this color before. Does it hurt?" I hadn't realized I'd spoken out loud until I heard both Akane and Kenji laughing behind us. Musubi merely continued his startled assessment of me.

I didn't feel embarrassed by my strange behavior because standing next to this man and holding his face in my hand felt more right than anything I had ever experienced in my entire life.

He lifted his hand to mine and rested it there.

"And if it did, would you know how to fix it?" he asked.

Everything went very still after that. The warrior and I continued our staring contest until Akane made a loud clearing sound in the back of her throat.

I stepped away quickly, but couldn't keep my eyes from his face.

He took in a deep breath and let it out slowly.

"Well, that was interesting." I heard him mumble under his breath.

"Did you say something, Musubi?" Akane asked.

"Yes. Are you planning on telling me what is so important about this..." he pointed to me, "...woman that you have me leaving my post to train her?"

I bristled at his tone but held my mouth in check.

"Mikomi is a very gifted student of medicine, and we need her to help patch up our men."

Musubi surveyed me again. "Yes, I'm aware of her abilities, having already met her at Daiki's tavern, and I considered having her help our cause but quickly dismissed the idea. It isn't safe for her."

"That's why you're going to train her."

Musubi shook his head. "I don't like this. It is completely inappropriate for a woman her age to be amongst soldiers, unmarried and unchaperoned."

"That's why you will be with her posing as her husband."

My eyebrows rose at this. I hadn't expected Akane to produce a real stand-in husband. I thought we would fabricate a story and that would be that.

"Pretend to be married? To a child? That's absurd!"

I tried not to feel offended by his immediate rejection of the idea.

"It's the only way to successfully pull this off without anyone questioning the legitimacy of our story. The men respect you. If she is posing as your wife they will leave her alone."

Musubi shook his head. I could sense his anxiety on my behalf. "No, Akane. I will not allow this tiny female to endanger herself any further than she already has."

"I'm also a tiny female, and it isn't your call, Musubi. As far as danger goes, nothing will happen to her provided you train her as well as you trained me." She pulled out her sword and swung it expertly to the left, right and down. "It is, after all, what we agreed to."

He gave her a withering look and then landed that look on me. I was grateful for my wrap, considering it was cold enough outside without his glare frosting me completely.

I straightened my spine in an effort to look a little taller. He must have noticed because his amused look made me feel fairly ridiculous.

"She may be small, but I assure you this young lady is quite capable," Kenji offered on my behalf.

I gave him a grateful smile.

"Fine," Musubi said. "But for the record, I think this is a terrible idea, and I doubt very highly that this frail little child will be capable of anything like lifting a sword, let alone wielding one."

"Duly noted," Akane said dryly. "You have exactly five hours before we must return to camp. Use your time wisely, my friend." She stood up and started to leave.

"Just where do you think you're going?" Musubi asked.

"Kenji and I have some educational matters to discuss. We'll only be a few damaged structures away from you, so if you need us simply shout."

I watched as Kenji and Akane strolled side by side around a curve and out of sight.

I turned back to Musubi and cleared my throat. "I understand that you think I won't be able to manage, sir—"

"Musubi."

"Yes, well, I can assure you that despite my appearance I am strong, and I am a good student, but most importantly I can help your wounded men."

Musubi rubbed a hand over his beautiful blue eyes and nodded.

"I believe you can help our men, but forgive me if I doubt your physical capabilities. Akane is a small woman, but she has fire. I can tell by the way you stand that you are used to being ordered around. You're submissive and meek. You'll never last on a battle field."

I saw red and knew my anger was about to boil over, but this time I didn't try to repress it. I didn't try to squelch it. I simply let the hot anger flow. Squaring my shoulders, I marched right up to my pompous teacher and pointed a finger at his chest.

"I swear, if I have one more man in my life telling me what I can and cannot do, I will steal Kenji's indestructible cane and beat you with it."

The slow grin that spread across Musubi's face might have delighted me if I hadn't been so angry with him.

"Young lady, I believe I'm willing to work with that."

"Before you learn to handle a weapon you must learn how to stand," Musubi said.

I narrowed my eyes at him.

"I know how to stand. I'm standing right now."

"I'm not referring to your ability to remain motionless, although you do paint a rather pretty picture in that stunning outfit you're wearing."

I felt my face grow warm and looked at my green kimono, smoothing it out self-consciously. I hadn't even thought about changing into something more suitable, and the high quality of the fabric didn't help my anonymity. I heard Musubi chuckle as if he enjoyed getting me flustered.

"There are eight quadrants that can be used for fighting and you must learn how to stand within these eight quadrants before you can learn anything else."

I nodded, but still felt confused.

Using the pointed end of his sword, Musubi drew two straight lines in the dark earth; one intersecting the other in the middle. He pointed at the place where the two lines met.

"You will stand here and face the line that points to the

north."

I did as I was told.

"These lines are like a compass, pointing north, south, east and west. These are your first four quadrants. Your compass is also made up of sub quadrants."

He drew lines in the middle of each regular quadrant and walked back to face me.

"These are called octants, northwest, northeast, southwest and southeast. If you can consider the space you fight in to be broken up into eight different quadrants you will be able to practice all of your footwork in eight different directions. It is not enough to be able to fight to your north or your south. Nor is it enough to fight on your east side or your west." He paused and pointed to the compass line in between north and west. "Your enemy will not accommodate you by attacking you where you are at your strongest. He will come at you from whatever angle he finds you are weakest. You must, therefore, learn how to stand and how to advance in any quadrant."

I drank in the information he imparted like I was a thirsty child in need of refreshment. I could learn this. I wanted so badly to protect myself.

"Stand with your right foot forward and your left foot back, but your feet need to be pointed a little to your left."

I moved into the position he instructed. He surveyed my stance and nodded.

"Now step forward with your right foot and follow it with your left so you are essentially standing in the same position you were before, you merely advanced forward. This is your north quadrant."

I followed his instructions and looked up. "This is very simple."

Musubi smiled like he was waiting to trap an ignorant animal.

"This has put you in a position where you can pivot and use a strong-side turn."

"A strong-side turn? What does that mean?"

"You pivot and swing your sword to the side that will require the least amount of energy. If your right foot is forward, then you will pivot to your left. Pivoting right with your right foot forward is considered a back-turn or a weak-side turn. You must build strength to lift your sword in that direction, so for now we will have you practice without a sword, pivoting to your strong-side. I want you to use your hands defensively as you would to block an attack. Hold your right arm in front with palm flat, and keep your left arm closer to your chest. As you change directions your arms will change position with you."

I used my arms to balance and pivoted back to my left. I was now facing south.

"Good. Now step forward with your leading foot, which is now your left, and pivot to your strong-side, to your right. This is called *Zango*."

I pivoted left and faced north again.

"This encompasses two directions of movement that you can use when fighting. North and south is one and two. Using your right foot, step to quadrant three which is east, and pivot to your left to quadrant four which is west. Always pivot to your strong-side."

I moved to the right and pivoted to my left, then stepped forward on my left and pivoted to my right, making sure I went from east to west and back again.

"I want you to do this with all four quadrants. Pivot north, then south and then east and west as you did before with no hesitation." Once he was satisfied that I had the right footwork, he continued, "Northeast to quadrant five, then southwest to quadrant six. Then finish up with northwest to seven and southeast to quadrant eight."

It wasn't that difficult, and I easily slid my feet where they needed to be.

"Now, I want you to start from the beginning and do *Hachi Kata*, all eight quadrants, one thousand times."

I dropped my hands and stared at him.

"One thousand times? How will I ever keep track of how many times I've managed a full circle? What if I lose my balance?"

Musubi gave me a wicked grin and chuckled softly.

"If you lose your balance, then you start over. If you lose count, then you start over."

I gave him my best sour face and started at quadrant one. The movement of *Hachi Kata* was actually quite soothing. I wasn't moving very fast—my clothing failed to help me on that count—but I was moving correctly. I found my mind clearing and my ki tuning into my body in a way it never had before. I felt peaceful…and happy. I truly felt happy.

Ouch!

I looked down and saw that I'd managed to stub my toe on a root upturned by my footwork.

"Start over," Musubi said with a pleased smile on his face.

I sighed and began the process all over again, while the handsome warrior sat upon the earth and leaned back against the bark of a tree. Well, he certainly looked comfortable. Removing that satisfied smirk from his face would have been an enjoyable diversion, but I knew he must be testing me. I couldn't fail no matter how many times I had to pivot and step, pivot and step.

I struggled to stay focused, sensing his beautiful eyes watching my every move. I lost count four times and stumbled twice as much. Every time I made a mistake he would happily call out, "Start over." I must have completed a full circle more than the required one thousand times, but Musubi was relentless, and I refused to give up until I had managed to complete the circle one thousand times with no mistakes.

"I did it," I managed to spit out. I folded my arms across my chest and dared him to tell me I hadn't.

He just sat there with a wicked gleam in his eye. "Now do it backward."

"What?"

"There will be moments when your attackers will come from behind, and you will have to defend yourself without hesitation. Instead of stepping forward you step back and pivot. Do that with all eight quadrants. You'll complete the circle one thousand times."

I couldn't believe that this was the way he had trained Akane. I felt like he was trying to prove a point or discourage me from continuing on with this crazy plan of mine. He had no idea how determined and motivated I was to leave my former life behind me. I began the circle again, but moved slower going backward than I did going forward. I gritted my teeth and continued on. Fortunately, I only lost count once and only lost my balance twice.

My arms were tired and sore, but I wasn't about to give up. Finally, I reached my goal, and gave Musubi a challenging look.

His smile only became more pronounced.

"Now combine the two, moving forward and backward, then forward and backward again. One thousand times."

Furious, I resisted the urge to burn him with a scalding remark and bit my tongue, doing what he asked instead. It was much harder than I thought it would be, and I wanted to rip my kimono off, throw it on the ground and scream in frustration. Surely five hours had already passed. I felt like I had been doing this for an eternity.

I pushed the hair out of my face and shoved back the sleeves on my kimono. Formal princess wear was a ridiculous encumbrance. If I had been given any idea the kind of physical exertion I would be facing tonight, I might have dressed in some of Saigo's clothing.

"I had hoped you might finish your first training session before next week. Can't you move any faster?"

"I am having trouble with the movements because my clothing is hindering my footwork."

Musubi stood up from his comfortable place by the tree, gave me an innocent smile and approached me.

"Allow me to fix that for you."

Without giving me a moment's notice or even asking my permission, he quickly ripped my kimono open and unwrapped it from my person, throwing it to the earth. It wasn't tied with all of the extra accoutrements most formal kimonos had, so the removal of my clothing took less than a few moments. I stood, for all the world to see, in my underclothing! Not that they were terribly revealing. The black, cotton leggings covered me all the way to my ankles, and the top covered me all the way to my wrists, but the material was quite form fitting. There was nowhere for me to hide.

I was so shocked by his brazen behavior that I simply stood there staring down at my silk green kimono in a heap on the grass.

"I rather like you like this." I looked up to see him eyeing me from the top of my head to the tips of my toes. "Yes, I do believe your underclothing suits you."

"You are the most despicable…the most…I can't believe you just ripped my dress off!"

"As your teacher, I am here to help you in any way that I can, and if your clothes are bothering you, it is my duty to strip them from your person."

I snorted at this.

He raised his hand to his forehead in mock despair. "I'll admit it is a heavy burden to bear, but for you I bear it willingly, and as your *husband* it would seem I'm the only man alive allowed to do this anyway."

I spluttered something unintelligible. I honestly couldn't form one word, let alone a complete sentence.

"Now that your movements will no longer be so limited, I want you to take it to a higher level and move a bit faster, like this."

Musubi pushed me away from the center of my compass, placing me at the end of the line pointing north. He then moved back to the center. Advancing quickly, he stepped and pivoted, completing a full circle and ending right in front of me with his face mere inches from mine. I didn't dare move an inch and felt myself breathing heavily.

"Eventually your movements will become just as fast. Your attackers will not come at you one by one. They will come two at a time, three at a time, in any direction they choose."

He placed his hands on my waist and pulled me forward.

"Your body must do these movements so often that they become instinctive. You will not have to think," he guided my waist backward, "you will not have to analyze," he pivoted my body around, "you will simply know." He pulled me with my back against his chest, his hands still at my waist.

I had never felt so exposed. The heat from our bodies mingled, and I could have sworn he breathed in the scent of my hair before continuing.

"I want you to add something different to the exercise."

His breath on the back of my neck was making it hard to focus. He slid his hands up the sides of my body and my arms, raising them above my head, then he fisted my two hands together.

"You will do sword movements in order to prevent injury to your body. Raise your imaginary sword above your head with your arms bowed ever so slightly and then swing your arms forward and down to slice at your opponents and block their attacks." He stayed tight to my body and pulled my fists forward and down, then brought my arms up again. Placing his hands on my waist he turned me to face him and my arms shakily dropped to my sides. After one intense moment of staring at one another, I rested my hands on his, hoping to remove them from my waist, but I found that I had only enough strength to apply a small amount of pressure. He responded by holding me tighter.

"You will do this movement with the sword every time you step forward, and then you will pivot."

I nodded automatically. His voice and manner of teaching were hypnotizing my senses and keeping my body on high alert.

"You will complete the circle with the sword movements added...one thousand times."

I nodded again. I would have agreed to anything just to get a little breathing room, a little space between us before the rapid knocking of my heart against my chest gave my emotions away. I wasn't the only one affected, it would seem. Musubi's emotions battled against one another. His anger was a constant, his fear for my well-being was beginning to take precedence, and protectiveness and possessiveness warred with one another for supremacy.

He didn't like what he was feeling, but he didn't let go. He just stood there, considering me. I not only felt his emotions, but saw them playing across his face. I felt my body absorbing them—anger, hatred, pain, confusion, anxiety, fear...and hope. Then his face abruptly changed and the door to his emotions slammed shut.

I had to blink my eyes once or twice to clear my own head. When I looked upon Musubi again, he wore another playful grin on his face, and pulled me even closer.

"I do so like you in these undergarments."

That was enough to snap me out of whatever spell his teaching methods had woven over me. I shoved him away, and he let out a huge laugh. I grumbled and stepped back into the circle, but my chest was still beating hard and my breathing was labored.

He had been right, though I was loath to admit it. I was much faster on my feet without the weight of my kimono, and although it took a while to coordinate the sword movements with my footwork and complete the circle at the same time, my speed gradually began to increase, and I accomplished the task he had set forth.

I looked at him as I finished and thought I saw a small amount of respect light his eyes.

"Now what?" I asked.

"To be perfectly honest with you, I thought you would've fallen down on the ground and quit by now. I didn't think your body would handle all the exertion."

He said it as a compliment, but I could tell he was troubled. I knew my body healed quickly, and I wondered if a normal individual would have been in worse shape. It was just one more thing that might reveal who I was, but it couldn't be helped. I had already accomplished everything he'd asked without even considering the wisdom of doing so. Maybe I should have acted weak and frail, but the thought of Musubi getting the best of me made my teeth grind together.

"I never quit," I responded.

"No, it looks as if you don't." He gave me an appreciative nod.

It was at that moment that Akane and Kenji came to retrieve us. Apparently, our torturously long training session had come to an end. I should have felt exhausted after the physical exertion and bombardment of emotions I had experienced, but I felt exhilarated. I felt as if I could continue training all night long.

"How did your first meeting go? I'm assuming you were able to learn at least one technique?" She quirked an eyebrow at me, but her question was more for Musubi's benefit.

"She is a quick student. I believe we will get on well together," Musubi said.

I looked at him in surprise. He had spoken pleasantly enough, but the stormy set of his eyes were telling a different story. He wasn't going to lose face and give up, but then neither was I. I would learn to fight no matter what the difficulty of our trainings or the clash of our personalities presented. Besides, the thought of never seeing him again was an unacceptable alternative. I didn't wish to contemplate it further.

"I am pleased that this partnership is already a success. Was it necessary to strip her to her underthings, Musubi?"

"A necessary evil, considering the restriction of movement the kimono caused."

Akane nodded. "I'm sure you gave her fair warning before having her clothing removed?"

Musubi grinned. "Why don't you ask her yourself?"

Akane gave me a questioning look, but I merely nodded, too tired to tattle on my handsome trainer.

"Mikomi, my men will escort you and Kenji back to your home."

"Thank you, Akane," Kenji said. "Your hospitality has been greatly appreciated,"

"I will contact you again when your training requires it or your services are needed," she said, directing her comments to me.

"She will need to continue her training on a regular basis,

Akane. She will have to return again tomorrow evening." Musubi folded his arms across his chest and gave me a smug smile. I wondered if he thought I would refuse due to my sore muscles or an inability to steal away from my "well-to-do" family.

"That should be fine, so long as Kenji can convince my... parents that another educational excursion is necessary," I responded quickly.

Musubi didn't look disappointed, but he didn't look pleased either.

"I hope you are prepared to work hard again. I don't plan on being as lenient as I was tonight."

So now he was going to torture me until I willingly ended my own training. He literally had no idea who he was dealing with.

"I look forward to exceeding your expectations," I said. I gave him a smile so sweet he couldn't possibly have failed to notice the insincerity behind it.

"Excellent," Akane said. "I'm sensing a bit of healthy competition. Whom do you think will win this battle of wills, Kenji?"

"My yen is on Mikomi. Her high tolerance for pain is quite possibly the most disturbing thing I've ever witnessed. You don't stand a chance, young warrior."

Musubi gave me a fierce look. The smile that crept across his face was akin to that of some monstrous predator. It sent delightful shivers rushing down my spine.

"We shall see, won't we? Until tomorrow, Mikomi. Unless of course the night's physical activities have left you too incapacitated to stand for any real length of time."

I gave him a withering look, but he merely laughed at me.

"Come, Akane. There is still much to be done."

I watched as Akane waved goodbye and accompanied Musubi across the ruins and out of our sight.

I felt hollow and empty once they were gone. I knew it was ridiculous, but I wasn't sure I would be able to wait until the next evening to see Musubi. I shook my head in frustration and tried to forget about the way he made me feel. It was a fleeting moment—nothing truly serious, nothing that had any real bearing on my future. I would forget about the warrior until I was forced to train with him, and then I would forget about him again.

Simple. Easy.

Yet somewhere deep within, I knew my heart was in serious trouble.

The next morning, Katsu summoned me a little earlier for my practice session. When the guards arrived at my door to retrieve me, I came close to telling them I wasn't interested in learning anything more about the veil and that I refused to meet Katsu anywhere. I was still furious at the callous way he had treated that poor man, and I also wanted to behave a little more like Mikomi, samurai warrior in training, and less like The Healer.

Not to mention the grogginess I felt, having taken another sleeping draught the previous night at the insistence of my maid. Apparently, I had been thrashing about within hours of sleep, and Aiko nearly had to wrestle me to the ground to awaken me. It concerned me that my nightmares were returning, and that I had no recollection of them. The details usually stayed with me.

Once she was able to wake me, I had taken the draught and according to her, slept soundly after that. Afterward, she asked if I could remember any of my nightmares, but I couldn't tell her anything. I couldn't remember what they had been about. I'd felt angry and frustrated, wondering if my nightmares had been brought on by the stress of joining the rebels or enduring Katsu's presence—or both.

To distract myself, I heartily teased Aiko about her new soldier I witnessed her walking with in the gardens. She turned several shades of red and stuttered so badly I had to assure her that

I was happy for her and hoped she would continue seeing him. She still seemed a bit flustered by the subject and left the room in a hurry without helping me dress or even do my hair.

I felt exhausted, irritable, and painfully aware of how helpless I was when it came to grooming myself. How could I possibly save the world when I couldn't figure out how to put on my own kimono?

Needless to say, the last activity I wanted to participate in was another horrifying training with Katsu.

My good sense overcame my frustration, however, and I obediently arrived in the gardens just as Katsu wished. He stood with his hands clasped behind his back and a grim expression on his face.

At first, I feared he knew about my activities from the previous night. But how could he? Unless someone had been following us. I mentally shook myself, knowing I was expecting the worst when I needed to remain as positive as I possibly could. If I behaved nervous or skittish it would make him and anyone else watching me suspicious.

"Katsu," I said, bowing deeply from my waist.

"You may rise, Mikomi. Please, there really is no need to be so formal with me."

I gave him a shy smile and received one in return. He really was quite handsome. I knew I might have been happy with him if I desired to accept the future that had already been chosen for me, but I wasn't my mother, and I couldn't sacrifice my happiness only to become bitter and angry like she had.

"Walk with me," he said, offering me his arm. We walked on in silence for a few moments, and then Katsu spoke again. "I must apologize for the way I handled our first session together. It must have seemed very wrong of me to give that man any hope of being healed when there was none."

It surprised me that he would admit to being wrong. It wasn't something I was used to.

"It pained me to see his hopes shattered," I managed to say. All of a sudden I felt like crying. "I understand that you were trying to help me become more familiar with the veil, but there has to be another way."

Katsu gave me a grim look. "Unfortunately, there isn't. I promise you, however, I will not give anyone false hope. The woman I've brought to the palace this morning understands her illness is incurable but wishes to help you in your training. I personally explained everything in detail to her, and she agrees that nothing is more important than learning how to heal the veil."

I swallowed any protests I might have made as we walked through the gardens into a large clearing. There, sitting on a small, green cushion sat a young woman. She couldn't have been any older than myself, but she appeared to be in pain, and her left leg was swollen red and badly deformed, protruding from underneath her floral patterned skirts.

Katsu continued walking forward, but my feet stopped moving, and I pulled on his arm to stop him. I knew I couldn't heal her, and I was already agonizing over the problem. Didn't he understand how difficult this was for me? Couldn't he tell how badly someone else's suffering affected me? I didn't want to do this again. The first time had been enough.

"Are you all right, Princess?"

I stared into his questioning face and hoped he could read the pleading in mine. His confusion remained. No understanding light seemed to pierce his oblivious musings. All that mattered to him was my training, and I began to understand that the value he placed on another's life was far lower than it should have been.

I wanted to bear my heart to him, explain how I felt about my gift, what I expected from myself, how I wanted to help people, but even before I opened my mouth to speak, I knew he wouldn't agree and would most likely argue. He would say exactly what my mother had said—healing people would prevent me from becoming a full kami. Giving life would eventually take my own.

So I said nothing. I closed my mouth and continued walking forward. I was The Healer, meek, obedient, and submissive.

"Yesterday, when you connected to the old man, were you able to sense the veil?"

"Yes, it felt more substantial this time. Like flat glass or crystal."

"Very good. That's exactly right. The more familiar you are with its texture the easier it will be to sense it everywhere you turn."

We approached the young woman in the chair, and she gave us a sad little smile.

"Hello," I said to her. "Can you tell me your name?"

"I am called Cho, your highness. Please forgive me. If I could stand and bow, I would."

I knelt down next to her chair and placed a calming hand on her shoulder.

"There is no need for that, Cho. I can understand the kind of pain you are in." I could feel it too. The infection in her leg had already spread to her heart. She wouldn't have long to live. "Tell me how you injured your leg."

"I cut it on a knife. It was an accident, and I must not have cleaned it properly."

I sensed she was not telling me the complete truth, but I didn't want to pry if she wasn't comfortable answering.

"You understand that I cannot heal you, then—that I am merely practicing?"

A small tear escaped one eye and traveled down her cheek.

"I understand, Princess. But I believe in you and who you are. If I can help The Healer fulfill her destiny, I will perform whatever duty I must."

I swallowed the lump forming in my throat but found it hard to speak.

"Then let us begin."

I held her head and connected to her.

Princess, can you hear me?

I tried not to let the shock register on my face. It was the second time in less than three days that someone had communicated with me during a healing.

"*Cho?*"

"*Yes, Princess. Akane wished for me to pass a message along to you.*"

I felt confused all over again.

"*Cho, how did she know about my training sessions with Katsu? I never told her.*"

"*You didn't have to. Her spies are everywhere, and since I was a perfect candidate for your practice sessions, she asked if I would perform this one last duty for her and volunteer myself to pass along a message.*"

"*You didn't cut your leg on a knife, did you?*"

"*It was a sword. I was injured in battle and the infection has become too much for my body to handle, but now that you have joined our side, you will save so many before they end up like me.*"

I felt a tear escape and tried to keep my emotions in check.

"*I'm so sorry I couldn't have helped you sooner, Cho.*"

"*It matters not, Princess. What is important is my message for you. Many of our soldiers were ambushed early this morning at a minor camp stationed far into the Yanbaru forest. Somehow, the emperor discovered its location. Akane needs you to meet her at the ruins again as soon as possible.*"

"*I can have that arranged, but please tell me what I can do for you. Do you have family that must be notified?*"

"*I'm an orphan. I don't belong to anyone, but I am happy to give my life for this cause.*"

The pain in her leg was fairly crushing my senses, and it was taking all of the control I possessed to stay connected with her. I began to ease her pain, though she had not asked for it. I couldn't get rid of the infection. Every time I tried, that ridiculous block would throw me back. The feel of it had become more familiar, but my resentment was growing stronger. I spoke to Cho again.

"*Please rest assured that your message has been received and all will be well.*"

"*Thank you, Princess. I...*"

"*Cho? Cho?*"

Her breathing became more labored, and her heart struggled

to pump blood through the valves. I tried instructing her heart to calm its frantic beating. It was overworked and stressed. Everything I attempted continued to be blocked by the veil. The only thing I had been allowed to do was eliminate the pain, but that failed to help her breathe or pump blood through her body. I finally gave up and pulled away from her ki, opening my eyes and wrapping my arms around her.

"Princess," she breathed out softly.

I looked down into her tired eyes and smiled.

"Mikomi," I said. "We are friends now, you and I, so you must call me Mikomi."

She managed a very weak smile, and slowly the breath left her body; her head rested against mine. I pulled her body from her cushion and onto my lap where I could hold her more securely, but she was already gone. She was gone, and I could do nothing to bring her back. I sat there, rocking her in my arms...back and forth...back and forth. I couldn't seem to let her go, though I hadn't even known her. There simply wasn't enough time to know her, and that saddened me more than I could have possibly expressed. Would anyone have been willing to listen either way? Would Katsu?

I didn't want to think on it anymore, so I emptied my mind and heart of any sad thoughts or devastating emotions and continued to rock Cho back and forth in my arms.

I wasn't sure how long Katsu attempted to get my attention, but I didn't register his voice until I felt his hand on my shoulder and Cho's body slipping from my arms. The guards were carrying her away, and I was powerless to stop them. I continued to sit on the ground, rocking back and forth...back and forth.

"Mikomi, you must snap out of this. You must look at me."

I finally latched on to what Katsu was saying and noticed he sat next to me.

"I couldn't save her," I mumbled.

"Princess, I warned you she was meant to die. You cannot take this so personally. You aren't meant to heal anyone, you are meant to heal the veil, and she willingly sacrificed her last minutes to help you accomplish that."

How could he be so heartless? Did he really not feel her pain as I did? Could he not understand that it wasn't about her death —it was about her life, the life she could have had if I had been there to save it? What was the point of having all this power if, in the end, it helped no one?

"Katsu?" I finally asked.

"Yes?"

"Do you ever wish your life could be different? Do you wish you could go back and make a different decision or chart a different course?"

He took my hand in his and kissed the top of it. I was too emotionally spent to feel surprised by the intimate gesture.

"I wish I could go back, yes. There are several choices I would change, and many loved ones I would treat differently, but as far as my destiny is concerned, *that* I wouldn't change. I know my place, and I know who I am."

Maybe that was part of my problem. I had no idea where my place was and no identity that resonated with me.

I leaned my head against his shoulder, too tired to care if it was inappropriate or not, but he pulled me in close and embraced me.

"I know this is difficult for you, Mikomi. You feel things deeply, and you wish to help everyone. You can't bear suffering even in its smallest form. Your compassion does you credit and is one of the things I...I appreciate about you."

I lifted my head to search his face.

"If you know these things, why do you put me in situations that can have no happy ending?"

"I do it to prepare you. I do it because I must, and it breaks my heart to see you struggle, but this is the process we must go through."

He brushed a strand of hair behind my ear and held my eyes with his.

"Perhaps that is enough training for one day," he said.

I gave him a grateful smile, and he called the guards over to accompany me back to my rooms.

As far as he knew, this particular practice was over, but my real training with Musubi had barely begun.

∞∞∞∞

I rushed into the ruins with Kenji a few yards behind. His hip had been bothering him, but he refused to allow me to heal him. He thought I needed to save my strength for whatever Akane might need me to do.

Stubborn man.

I heard a low whistle to my left and turned to see Akane kneeling on the grassy earth surrounded by several soldiers, all with varying injuries. The stench of blood hung thick in the air, and the combined pain of these soldiers overwhelmed my body and chilled my bones. I joined Akane and grasped her hand firmly.

"Which soldier's wounds are the most critical?" I asked.

She looked haggard but gave me a relieved look. "Start with this one next to me. He was stabbed in the stomach and has lost quite a bit of blood. I'll have the next one ready for you."

I knelt down beside the bloodied, unconscious body of a boy not more than sixteen years of age. He reminded me of Saigo, and my chest went tight. I held his head between my hands and connected with him. His stab wound had cracked the sternum and punctured a lung. There was so much tissue damage and blood, I felt certain I would be unable to save him, but I began instructing his ki to knit his sternum together and repair the hole in his lung. Fortunately, the veil wasn't present with this particular healing. The blood that had pooled within needed to be relocated to his circulatory system. I gave several instructions for tissue repair and then helped his body cope with the blood loss. His ki managed to reuse the blood from the internal bleeding, a process his body never would have accepted on its own.

I pulled away from him and noticed that he was breathing easier now, and his face had relaxed. Taking a deep breath, I readied myself for the next possible situation where the veil might come into play. Then I moved on to the next soldier.

The following hour continued in much the same way. I assessed the severity of a person's injuries, gave instructions to their ki and waited until I felt the body had accepted the healing taking place. Every single one of them had life threatening injuries, and every single one of them had been unconscious.

"Here is the last soldier," Akane said. She looked tired and worried, but I hoped my efforts had lightened her load a little.

He was an older man, also unconscious.

"Akane, I can understand why some of these men are not awake. The pain from their wounds was probably too much for some to bear, but not all of them should have fainted from pain or loss of blood."

Akane looked at me sheepishly. "I gave them all a sleeping draught. We must make certain that no one, other than the guards I assigned to you, have any idea who you are. If these soldiers witness your process for healing, they will begin to wonder about your identity, start asking questions, and eventually your involvement with our group will get back to your father."

"Perhaps we should let Musubi know who I am. I sense we can trust him."

Akane looked at the ground and shook her head. "I trust Musubi with my life, and I know that part of his heart is very good." She looked up at me again. "But Mikomi, part of his heart is bad. There is something in his past that haunts him, and he won't let it go, nor will he discuss the matter with me. And out of respect for him, I cannot press him further. I think it best, for safety's sake, that we keep your identity a secret, from him especially."

What Akane said troubled me. I had also sensed that he held tightly to something dark and dangerous, and I wanted to know everything there was to know about the mysterious Musubi. I wanted him to know everything there was to know about me.

It made me feel terribly uncomfortable, to have to lie to him or keep things from him, but I knew Akane understood the situation better than I did. I would respect her wishes and keep my name and title to myself.

"How will you explain these miraculous healings to your soldiers, or to Musubi for that matter? Are there other kami that can do what I can?"

"To some extent there are, and that is exactly the kind of story I will be telling. I have several kami who have joined the cause and are willing to help share a small part of their ki to heal our soldiers."

"They will believe this story?" I wondered.

"They won't have any reason not to."

"I fear that Musubi is not quite so gullible." I placed a hand on Akane's shoulder. "How will you keep him in the dark concerning my involvement?"

"I will make sure he sees you treating some of our men with less serious injuries. Is it possible for you to help them heal slowly or does the healing take place immediately?"

My eyes lit up at what she suggested.

"You mean, I might instruct a bone to heal over a quicker period of time, but not all at once? If they don't heal immediately he won't become suspicious."

"Exactly, he'll simply assume you have some miracle herbs and a healing touch, and the rest of my men will think that as well."

I pulled my hand back and began some nervous pacing. "That could work. I've certainly used this tactic before when healing patients at Daiki's tavern. Are there men in your camp that need these types of services now?"

"Yes, but it is several miles from here, and you have already been healing for over an hour. You are most likely exhausted, and I don't want anyone at the palace to question your whereabouts."

I waved my hand dismissively. "Kenji received permission to tutor me for the rest of the afternoon and evening, and as you are well aware…I have already suffered through my veil training with Katsu."

A tired sadness passed over her face and her shoulders sagged. "How is Cho?"

"She passed away in my arms, but she felt no pain in the end. I was able to take that from her." Akane bent her head down and swallowed hard. I could tell that allowing Cho to come to me, knowing in the end that she would die, had not been an easy decision for her to make. I wondered if they had been close. "How did you know I wouldn't be able to save her? How did you know to send her to me?"

"There are many things I can tell you, Mikomi, but there are many things I cannot."

I understood her meaning and decided to let it go for now. At the moment, there were more pressing matters to attend to.

"What will we do with all of these men?" I wondered.

"I will stay here with them and feed them the story we just discussed while you travel on with Kenji and your guards to our camp. I can meet you there later."

I felt uncomfortable leaving Akane there alone with men who wouldn't be aware enough to help protect her if she were found and attacked by my father's soldiers, but she refused to leave her men behind, and I could only respect her for such a decision.

Kenji and I traveled on with our faithful guards by our side. It occurred to me I didn't know their names as our journey progressed and was about to ask them, but we arrived at the camp, and my intentions to get to know them were forgotten when I took in the scene before me.

The camp had been ransacked. Men were running this way and that, gathering up the few supplies that had not been destroyed by my father's soldiers and saddling them to the horses that stood surprisingly calm and still amidst the chaos. Other men were out attempting to gather the horses that had been lost during the scuffle. The guards led me to a point on the far right side of the camp to a large tent. I kept my eyes lowered as we passed soldier after soldier. I could feel their curious stares and heard them whispering, but nothing more happened, and I hoped to be forgotten as quickly as I passed.

The tent flap opened suddenly and out stepped Musubi, looking worried and anxious. I felt my whole body come alive in his presence and tried to stop the silly grin that threatened to spread across my transparent face. The moment he realized I was there, he appeared relieved and reached his hand out as if to touch me, but then a different emotion crossed his features, one I couldn't recognize, and he quickly pulled back.

I tried using my empathic abilities to get a read on his emotional state, but found myself to be completely cut off. His emotional wall wouldn't give way to my determined probing. He and Katsu seemed to be alike in that respect.

"What in the world took you so long to get here? I thought you and Akane might have had some trouble with the emperor's guards and planned on retrieving you myself."

My body glowed with happiness at the thought that he felt concern for my safety. I also hadn't realized he'd been expecting me.

"I am sorry. Some of the soldier's wounds were more critical than Akane or I had anticipated. I had to be very thorough and careful in their treatment."

Musubi nodded. "How many will live?"

"All of them, I think." I hurried on at Musubi's astonished look. "Akane had enlisted some kami to volunteer a little of their healing abilities to take care of what I couldn't. They were there to help once I managed to do all that I could."

Musubi looked troubled. "That does not sound plausible or even possible. A kami, if they revert too much of their healing power to someone other than themselves is in very real danger of losing their immortality. I know of no kami willing to risk this, even if they divert their powers just once or twice."

"Well, maybe there are kami out there more concerned with others than their own immortality."

"You don't understand, Mikomi. It isn't that kami are unfeeling and don't want to care for the pains and illnesses of others. It isn't their calling. They only have enough healing power to keep themselves immortal. Healing a life-threatening injury could hold serious consequences for themselves and their real calling in life. They keep the Universe balanced and risk that balance when they risk themselves."

I hadn't known much about the cause for a kami's immortality, but I found it very interesting that Musubi seemed to be an expert on the subject.

"I don't understand why Akane failed to inform me about these other kami. She never keeps information from me," he mused.

I tried not to look or feel guilty, knowing full well Akane and I were both keeping secret a very important bit of information concerning myself and my abilities.

Musubi shook his head. "I suppose I will have to consult with her later. In the meantime, there are soldiers in there who are in need of your medicinal services." He pointed toward the opening of the tent. "I will come and collect you within an hour for another training session."

He began to walk away, and without thinking I reached out to grasp his arm. He looked at my hand, and I retrieved it immediately. "Forgive me, I simply wanted to ask...why must we remain here when the emperor's soldiers have already discovered this camp. Isn't it important that we evacuate to a new location before he attacks again?"

"We wounded many of his soldiers in the surprise attack. I do not think they had any idea how many forces we had at our disposal since this is one of the smaller camps. His intelligence, though accurate in our position, must have been lacking in detail. It may have been an ambush, but we killed almost every soldier he sent. I do not think he will attempt another attack today."

I felt saddened at the loss of so many men. Most of my father's soldiers were most likely good men who had no choice but to fight to keep their families fed. It pained me to think so many of them had died for a cause they didn't believe in. Musubi took his leave, and I felt colder without him. Squaring my shoulders, I entered the tent and breathed a sigh of relief. There were only a handful of men who needed my attention, and their wounds would not require quite as much energy as the last round of men had.

Before I was able to enter any further I felt a warm hand on my shoulder and turned, coming face to face with Musubi. His full lips were so close to mine. It would have taken a single step on either of our parts to join our lips together. The abruptness of our close proximity must have startled him also. Whatever he had been about to say became lost as his eyes studied my face in open wonder. He looked at my lips and then back at my eyes. I swallowed hard and fought to keep my heavy breathing in check. He reached a hand up and grabbed a strand of hair near my face that had come loose during the journey over here.

"Did you...want something?" I managed to stutter.

He blinked twice and pulled his hand away as if a viper were trying to strike him. His face drew down an impenetrable mask of indifference.

"Yes, I forgot to mention there are herbs and other medicinal supplies in the corner of the tent. You are to use them as you see fit."

"Yes, thank you."

He nodded, and then his look turned wicked. It was difficult for me to keep up with his different moods and emotions, especially when most of the time I didn't have access to them.

"I quite like this new dress of yours." He drew his mouth closer to my ear, and I took in a sharp breath. "But I still think your undergarments suit you even more."

I placed my hands on my hips and stamped my foot in frustration.

"You have no manners, Musubi. No sense of propriety."

Musubi gave a hearty laugh as he walked out the tent opening. I couldn't help but let out a soft giggle after he vanished.

Though my thoughts remained on Musubi's peculiar behavior and the way he made me feel whenever he was near, I managed to dress several superficial wounds that needed cleaning, and mended broken bones by instructing some of the men's ki to have them completely healed by the end of the week instead of immediately. With any luck, they would all assume their injuries had not been as severe as they might have thought, either that or they would think I was the most skilled physician they had ever come in contact with, and in a way, I guess that would have been accurate.

I had to be stealthy in the way I connected to them. Cradling their head in my hands and closing my eyes would have given me away immediately. Instead, I simply touched their arm as I dressed a wound and connected to them in that way. It was a little more difficult to perform a different task while instructing their ki to heal several injured areas at the same time, but I managed it and secretly congratulated myself on my own ingenuity.

I relieved some of their pain, but since I had slowed down the healing process for many of their injuries I left some of it there so they wouldn't make the mistake of overexerting themselves and possibly causing more damage to their bodies.

The men expressed their gratitude for the service I rendered, meeting my eyes with respect. I supposed if you were fighting alongside women in battle you tended to let go of the ridiculous notion that women weren't worth anything other than birthing babies and looking pretty on your arm. It was refreshing to receive that kind of respect and deference instead of having them pretend I didn't exist when standing right in front of them.

And I was happy, happier and more satisfied with my life than I had ever been before. I had saved several lives today, eased their pain and discomfort. These were the activities my gifts should be used for, and what I was meant to do with my life. I was Mikomi, not some useless princess, and I was *a* healer, not *The* Healer. For me, that distinction meant everything.

As I finished up with the very last soldier—a young man with a dislocated shoulder and broken wrist—he grabbed my hand with his good one, and held fast to it. I looked him in the eye as an equal, and he gave me a grateful smile.

"Thank you. I'm not sure what you did, but the pain is bearable now."

"You are welcome. You will be feeling like yourself again in no time, I assure you."

He smiled and stood, one of the few men capable of getting on his own two feet considering most of the other men had wounds and breaks in their legs. He still held my hand tightly with his own. The small look of gratitude turned to one of interest as he studied me.

"I am surprised that your husband would allow you to travel here, healing soldiers without him present."

I wasn't sure how to respond to his comment.

"Or perhaps, you haven't a husband but are in need of a protector?" He gave me a shy smile.

My confusion cleared as I realized the young man was interested in me on a more personal basis, hinting at a possible courtship. I might have told him I was flattered, but before I could utter a single word, I felt strong arms wrap around my waist.

"Our little healer already has a protector at her disposal, soldier," Musubi said from behind me. He pulled me back against his chest, leaving an unspoken challenge simmering below his words.

The young man looked chagrined. "My apologies, sir. I wasn't aware that this young lady belonged to you."

"She does."

I held my breath at how right those words sounded when spoken from Musubi's lips. He rested his chin upon the top of my head and tightened his arms around me. I couldn't help but allow myself to sink into his embrace. "And now that you know who her husband is, I would appreciate it if you would let any other interested parties aware of her marital status."

The young man nodded. "Of course." He gave me a smile tainted with a hint of regret. "Thank you again for your help. I am glad to have met you."

"And I, you."

He then bowed and quickly made his way out of the tent.

Musubi turned me around to face him the moment the young man had left. His look was stern. "You just *had* to be beautiful. Heaven forbid Akane find a healer suffering from warts, boils or baldness."

I raised my eyebrows at that. "You think I'm beautiful?"

Musubi looked as if he'd just been caught doing something naughty. He took a step back and surveyed the room, refusing to make eye contact with me. "You are very good at this. Quite the little healer." Clearly, he was looking to change the subject as fast as he possibly could. "How did a woman so young become such an expert in the art of medicine, especially one as wealthy and pampered as you?"

I placed my hands on my hips, getting ready to defend myself. He leaned against one of the tent poles with his arms folded across his chest, eyeing me suspiciously.

"Tell me, Musubi, are you capable of giving a compliment without making it sound like an insult?" It amazed me how easily he undermined my usually reserved responses.

He lifted a finger and tapped his chin as if seriously pondering my question.

"No, I can't say that I am." The taunting grin on his face was difficult to resist.

I tried resisting it anyway. "You are one to talk, you know. I don't think you are much older than I am. I'm willing to bet you are no older than three and twenty."

Musubi threw back his head and let out a mirthful laugh.

"You are not much of a fighter, Mikomi, but you are highly entertaining." He wiped a fake tear from his eye and made a great show of shaking it off his finger.

No matter what, I couldn't seem to verbally get the best of him, and for some reason I found that delightful.

"Now that you have finished with your patients, it is time for more training. Are you certain you are not too tired from last evening's exercises?"

I quickly walked to where he leaned against the tent pole,

folding my arms across my chest.

"I am perfectly capable of handling another training session with you. You're really not the taskmaster you seem to think you are. Are you going easy on me because I'm a woman, or are you simply too tired to make any real effort to teach me?"

I knew perfectly well that I was challenging him and would most likely be in over my head because of it, but there was something about his manner and attitude toward me that made me want to prove to him I was much more than what his preconceived notions had painted me to be. I wanted to exceed his expectations. I wanted to impress him, but I also wanted to please him. It was going to get me into trouble, I was sure of it.

Musubi's smile grew wide and wicked. "If you feel I am going easy on you, I'd be only too happy to make our time together infinitely more intense."

"Fine," I said. I was definitely in trouble.

"Then follow me, little healer."

From the tone of his voice, I knew I would soon be paying for my little outburst.

10

"This time, you are going to learn the proper way to hold a samurai sword," he said. He walked over and held out a curved, slender, single edged blade made of wood. I sighed when I noted it was merely a practice sword. If Musubi noticed, he didn't show any sign of it.

We had traveled several hundred yards from the encampment into a clearing of soft grass surrounded by cherry trees. The cool breeze coupled with the fresh fragrance of cherry blossoms spun a magical atmosphere of hope and possibility. I might have considered the location quite romantic if Musubi's mask of indifference hadn't resurfaced once again. He was all business now.

"This sword is called a *katana*. Notice the *nakago*, or hilt, is long enough for both of your hands to hold it at the same time. Your right hand will be placed above your left just under the *tsuba*, the hand-guard."

He demonstrated the proper way to hold it and then handed it to me. I placed my hands in the same position. It made me feel powerful and protected, but wielding a real blade would leave death and destruction in its wake. It was a heavy responsibility to bear.

"Mikomi, if that hilt were someone's throat, you would have strangled them to death by now. You cannot hold your sword as if you are afraid of it."

"Sorry." I loosened my grip and tried relaxing my stiff fingers.

"Better. Now, we must put this around your waist." He reached into a bag on the ground and produced a belt-like sash. After considering me for a few seconds, he walked over and began undoing my kimono again. I dropped my sword and immediately stepped back, holding out a defensive hand.

"What in the world do you think you're doing?"

"I cannot for the life of me understand why you don't come to practice wearing something you can actually move in. The fabric of your sleeves is never ending, and you continually trip all over the folds of your kimono."

"Akane didn't give me much notice, and I was not in a position to change into different clothing when I left my place of residence."

Musubi shook his head. "We will have to rectify that issue for you, but until then," he closed the distance between us, "you will have to make do without it." He pulled me to him and quickly removed my clothing, faster than my spluttering protests could form upon my lips.

Once again, my cotton body suit was exposed for all the world to see. He whipped out the sash and brought it behind me, leaning forward and slightly brushing his cheek against mine. I wasn't sure if he had meant the light contact or not, but my face burned as he abruptly pulled back. He fastened it securely as I struggled to control my body's response to his close proximity.

"I could have removed the clothing myself, you know." I felt like I had to say something to fill the awkward silence.

He rested his hands at my waist, giving me another wicked grin.

"But it's so much more fun when *I* do it." He backed away and picked up the sword I had dropped. He was lucky to have moved so fast. I had come very close to giving his face a much deserved smack.

"Now, you store your *katana* in your *obi,* with the sharpened face turned up. This will facilitate a quick removal and striking motion simultaneously. It's a useful tactic when defending yourself."

The sword hung through the sash on my right side.

"Grasp—do not choke—the hilt with your left hand, then pull it up against your left side and straight out so the end of the sword will hit an opponent in the stomach if they were standing in front of you."

I followed his instructions, and when he was satisfied with my positioning, he continued.

"Step back on your left as you swing your sword in an arc forward to pull it fully out of its *saya*, its sheath, until the pointed end comes to rest against my chest. I will stand in front of you so you can practice that motion a few times. Please, try not to kill me."

"If only," I muttered.

"What was that?"

I sighed heavily and practiced the movements, pulling the hilt to the left, straight out, sweeping it into a forward arc out of its *saya* and pointing it at Musubi's chest. The first time I performed this task, I almost stabbed him in the stomach, to which he chuckled and muttered something about the battlefield being more hazardous to his health with my added presence. I continued to perform the motions until he felt I knew how to hold and unsheathe my *katana* properly.

"There are several different positions you must learn. You are going to step with your right foot forward and lift your sword backward so that the pointed end is at a forty-five degree angle. This is right foot forward, upper position."

I lifted the pointed end of my sword straight up into the air.

"No, straight up is ninety degrees, back a little further and you will have it right."

I adjusted and waited.

"Swing the sword down in front of you at a forty-five degree angle, and you will have right foot lower position. Then step forward with your left in the lead without moving your sword. This is left foot upper."

Once I got the hang of it—it really wasn't that hard—he continued speaking.

"Move the sword out to the side of your head, pointed about fifteen degrees off of the ninety, but not too close to your head because eventually you'll be wearing a helmet of some kind… maybe…although, if I do my job right there will never be a need for you to defend yourself. This is called left foot lead, middle. Then move the handle of the sword to your center, square your shoulders and keep your feet in place. This is left foot forward, lower."

"Do I really need to know the names of all these positions? If I think about the terminology, I'll get so confused, I won't be able to move to them."

"Giving up already, are we?"

I threw him a frustrated glare which only amused him further.

"It's not that difficult to remember once you get used to it, and eventually the names won't matter as the swordplay becomes second nature to you. These different positions are like springboards for your movements. If they are precise, your movements will be also."

I decided I'd better quit whining. I was the one who wanted to learn this, and I had challenged him not thirty minutes earlier to make the process more difficult.

"Now, start from the beginning and move through the sequence of positions slowly and fluidly. This is not a race, and I am not concerned so much with quantity as I am with quality."

I nodded and started from the beginning, allowing my movements to flow smoothly as I hit each position and advanced to the next. Once again, I marveled at how the process soothed me. I was aware of every aspect of my body, the weight of my sword, the small breeze playing through the loosened strands of my hair and the way the wooden blade became an extension of myself. I wasn't sure how long I continued through the positions before my movements became instinctive.

"You seem to have a good handle on this exercise, so let's try something different. I will call out the positions, and you will move to them. I want swiftness and precision. Left foot forward, lower."

And so began an interesting dance of commands and responses, where my ability to follow instructions depended on my focus and mental clarity. I was slow and hesitant at first but became more confident as time progressed.

I wasn't sure at what point Musubi stood before me, calling out positions and mirroring me as I hit them, but I was no longer dancing alone, and the peace I felt as Musubi stood in front of me, maintaining eye contact and performing the same dance I did was something I had never felt before. He called out one last command, and we ended with our blades centered and touching.

We neither moved nor spoke for several seconds, but openly studied one another. I couldn't help but wonder if I had exceeded his expectations. Perhaps he was proud of me, and maybe, just maybe, he believed in me.

"You have an uncanny ability to pick things up faster than most of the students I have worked with. Your form and technique are perfectly accurate. I've never met someone with that kind of mastery over their person."

I knew he meant it as a compliment, but I could see my abilities troubled him, and I was afraid that I had, once again, accomplished something no true mortal would have been capable of. If I didn't temper my abilities, I was going to give myself away. I fought to think of some subject that might distract him.

"What made you decide to join forces with the rebels?" I asked.

Musubi stepped forward and sheathed his sword. I did the same and continued to stand facing him.

"I imagine the same reason you did. I wanted to help those who could not help themselves. I'm also susceptible to lost causes."

I raised an eyebrow. "You think this rebellion is a lost cause?"

Musubi shifted the sword at his hip. "I don't think it, I know it. These rebels cannot possibly win against a deity. They can kill all of the emperor's soldiers if they wish, but as long as Fukurokuju remains in power they will never win, and he will remain in power until The Healer takes her rightful place beside the warrior god Katsu."

He nearly spat Katsu's name like a curse. I could feel his anger like heat leaping from his body. I wondered what it was about Katsu that caused him such anger.

"Why fight if you feel the cause is a hopeless one?"

"Because I fight with an entirely different goal in mind. There is someone else who will pay for the wrongs committed against these people and for a very important life lost." Musubi ground his sword into the stone at his feet. "He'll pay…and eventually, so will she."

His response left me with more questions than answers, but the hot anger rolling off of him in waves began to make me feel uncomfortable and a little afraid as well. I tried to lighten the mood by diverting the subject to something that would cool his anger.

"How did you come across Akane? She mentioned that you were the one to train her."

Musubi's anger evaporated almost immediately, and a small smile lightened his brilliant eyes.

"Akane started life as a starving orphan on the street, which is where I met her several years back. She attempted to steal some food from my bag when she thought I wasn't looking. I caught her red handed and forced her to follow me back home. There was a good woman in the village where I dwelled at the time. She willingly gave shelter to Akane, and I decided to teach her how to defend herself. It never occurred to me that anything would come from her training, but she is the fiercest general I have ever met. I'm quite frightened of her now."

I chuckled at his playfulness, but then I began to feel a bit discomfited as another thought hit me.

"Does that mean you two are lovers?"

Musubi's eyes narrowed. "You know, for a woman you have a strange tendency to ask very personal questions."

"Oh, forgive me," I said, feeling my face go warm all over. Maybe it was the uncharacteristic behavior I had displayed over the past few days or the fact that I had left the palace under false pretenses, or maybe the feel of a sword in my hand had liberated me in some way, but I felt as if I could do anything, be anyone, behave any way that I liked. "You don't have to answer that question."

"Well, I'm afraid I must. Otherwise, you'll always be wondering, and that might make things a bit awkward considering Akane is very much like a sister to me."

I let out the breath I'd been holding. I couldn't begin to understand why, but his answer had meant everything to me. Then I wondered about other girls and became panicked all over again.

"Well, if Akane isn't your wife, then who is? Aren't you afraid to be without her?"

Musubi gave me a look I found difficult to interpret.

"According to Akane, *you* are my wife." He chuckled at my sour look, and then his face grew somber. "There was a woman once, but she passed away several years back."

His anger returned, and the heat from it began to scorch the air with its intensity. I knew only I could feel it, but the emotion seemed to echo throughout the clearing. I wondered how he could survive with such bitterness in his heart.

He didn't look very old. In fact, he looked only a few years older than myself, but he talked as if his loss had happened centuries ago. That was exactly how old and how deep his pain felt to me. Like it had lasted for centuries.

"I'm sorry for your loss. She must have been a very special individual."

Musubi studied his sword and fingered the hilt. "She was."

I felt sad and hopeless. I wasn't sure if I was absorbing his emotions or experiencing my own, but I wished with all my heart that I could help him hold on to the memory of lost love with a sense of joy instead of bitterness.

"You are a very special individual as well, wouldn't you agree, Mikomi?"

Musubi studied my face again, and I wondered what he meant. It didn't sound like a compliment to me. More like an accusation.

"I'm not special. I'm nobody, really."

He shook his head and closed the distance between us in two easy strides. He lightly took hold of my chin.

"You're clearly a well-bred woman of consequence, yet you have an amazing amount of knowledge where medicine is concerned, and you take to the fighting arts as if you had been doing it all your life."

I swallowed hard, but couldn't break eye contact with him.

"I suspect that you are special in more ways than one could count, Mikomi. There is something you and Akane have not told me, but I will not press either one of you about it just yet."

"There is nothing to tell. I'm simply a girl who wishes to help your men. That's all I am."

Musubi lowered his face closer to mine, and drew a finger down the side of my cheek.

"We shall see," he whispered.

∞∞∞

"I want to accompany you the next time you have a meeting with Akane," Saigo said.

"I'm not so sure that's a good idea, young prince," Kenji said. "It is nerve-wracking to have your sister out doing the work she is doing, but to have you there as well without being a fully trained samurai yourself leaves you vulnerable and me anxious. Also, I have no idea how I could convince your father that veil history is something you should be studying along with your sister."

Saigo grunted sourly and folded his arms across his chest. I reached across the table on my left where he sat sulking and gave his hand a sympathetic squeeze.

"Besides, Saigo, I haven't received a message from Akane for almost four days. Circumstances between Father and the rebels have quieted for now."

"Yes, but you get to leave the palace and train every day with a samurai warrior. I'm stuck with our boring staff, and I never have the same sword trainer."

"I cannot believe you would ever find my lessons boring, Saigo," Kenji said, pretending outrage. "There can be nothing more thrilling than the study of historical politics and their effect upon our future."

Saigo made a snoring sound and dropped his head on the table, pretending sleep. I giggled, but soon my thoughts returned to my handsome samurai instructor.

A full three weeks had passed since I'd started my samurai training with Musubi and veil training with Katsu. It made me dread the day one minute and then look forward to it the next. I didn't mind Katsu's company. He was actually becoming a good friend, despite our many differences and his tendency to overlook and undervalue anyone or anything that didn't pertain to what he focused on accomplishing.

I was still unable to sense the veil surrounding me, even though he had been very patient with his instructions and my slow progress. We both wanted to avoid having to bring in any more people who were terminally ill, but each time I failed to sense the veil on my own I would be forced to deal with another dying individual during the next practice session.

It was an agonizing process, and made me feel as if a part of me faded away with each life I failed to save. I'd become so emotionally overwrought by it that I had taken to shutting myself within my rooms to write poetry until it was time to train with Musubi. Poetic verse seemed to be my only outlet for the emotional upheaval my trainings with Katsu produced.

The hours I trained with Musubi were quickly becoming some of the most treasured moments of my life. I knew when I held my *katana* in my hand it was meant to be there. With each new lesson and each new exercise my abilities were growing, and Musubi's curiosity as to my secret with Akane grew as well. Something else seemed to be growing in strength, though I was sure it blossomed solely on my part. With every new day I spent in Musubi's company, my affections for him increased.

There were moments when I sensed he might hold some kind of feeling for me also, and other times when I was sure it was only my imagination. He saw me as a student and a peculiar mystery needing to be solved. His interest in me went no further than that of teacher and student. Even though I was aware that my growing feelings were one-sided, I couldn't put a stop to them, and I couldn't prevent them from gaining ground and overcoming all of my reasoning and logic.

I knew I had left my heart vulnerable and unprotected where Musubi was concerned, but I couldn't have fenced in my emotions and shielded my heart even if I had wanted to, and that was exactly my problem. I would have rather experienced this kind of pain than any other kind that had ever been inflicted upon me because that pain brought with it thoughts of Musubi and a chance to be near him.

I was also anxious to learn as much as I could before my eighteenth birthday. With a little over five months left before the marriage ceremony and my ascension as a full kami, I still had no plans for how I would avoid it, only that I needed to become a master in the art of fighting in order to have any hope of survival for Saigo and myself if we had to leave to avoid the marriage and permanently join the rebels.

With any luck, Akane's plans for taking my father's throne would happen sooner rather than later. Though the details had not been shared with me, I knew I was an integral part in gathering the information she needed. My father hadn't summoned me for one of his "meetings" since Katsu arrived, and though grateful for the reprieve, it couldn't have come at a more inopportune time. Without these meetings, I could be of no benefit to Akane and her goals for usurping my father. I continued to work toward a solution to that problem.

For the last three weeks I had checked for messages from Daiki as well. I didn't receive word from him for the first two weeks and wondered if something had happened to him. Fortunately, I found a communication from him the previous day as I walked the grounds of the garden. His note was brief but stated there was a newly married girl who had conceived three months ago and was in need of my services. In other words, the young lady in question was most likely malnourished and exhibiting early symptoms of a possible miscarriage.

I had left a note in return, letting Daiki know he should set up a meeting with the young girl for the next day. I felt satisfied, knowing that I would have another opportunity to use my powers for good.

So far, my extra activities with the samurai insurgents had not raised any suspicions from my father. The precautions we were taking enabled me to continue training with Musubi and helping the rebels however I could. The only thing that continued to trouble me was my nightmares. According to Aiko, I screamed and thrashed in my sleep every night now. She had taken to routinely giving me my sleeping draughts, hoping to prevent possible spies or other guards in the area from relating my alarming behavior to my father.

I appreciated her concern. My father had been known to beat me for what he called a mental weakness when it came to my nightmares. Troubled dreams were the direct result of a weakened mind incapable of controlling its own thought processes. I was always punished severely whenever he learned of them. Now that Katsu had arrived, I hoped he wouldn't allow my father to lay a hand on me, but I didn't want to discuss my nightmares with my betrothed unless I absolutely had to.

A tap on the door broke me from my quiet musings, and conversation between Saigo and Kenji stopped.

"Enter," Saigo called out.

One of my guards opened the door.

"Princess, your father has summoned you. He wishes for you to meet him in his receiving room as soon as possible."

I felt a chill sink deep within my bones. I wanted to run to my rooms and hide away for the remainder of the day, but I knew if my father was interrogating someone for information it might be an opportunity to gain some helpful information for Akane, and it was the first time since Katsu's arrival that I had been given such an important opportunity.

"Does Katsu know about this meeting between myself and the emperor?"

He had made it very clear to my father that I would no longer participate in any further interrogations.

"No, Princess."

I nodded. "We need to keep it that way, if you understand my meaning."

His eyes narrowed, and he nodded his understanding.

"Be safe, and don't take any unnecessary risks while you're gathering your information." Saigo gave my hand a squeeze.

Kenji gave me a supportive smile laced with worry but refrained from saying anything. I had always suspected that he somehow knew the extent of my father's maltreatment, and if he did, then I was grateful he refrained from discussing it with my brother.

Feeling strengthened by their concern. I rose from my chair, squared my shoulders, and left the room.

I may have been putting on a brave face, but I was very practiced at that. On the inside my stomach clenched in knots while anxiety, and apprehension threatened to snuff out the breath in my lungs. I had a strong desire to run to Musubi and never return to the palace again.

As I walked with my guards, my wish to get to know them better resurfaced.

"Please, what are your names?" I whispered.

The guard who had summoned me missed a step, most likely surprised at my addressing him.

"I am called Yao, Princess. The man on your left is Chan. We are honored to be of service to you." He kept his voice lowered.

I recognized the danger of conversing with my guards as we traversed the winding hallways through the palace toward my father's receiving room, but I felt a pressing urgency to know these men who risked so much for the rebel cause.

"Will you be waiting for me when I have finished?"

He looked at me sideways from the corner of his eye and nodded.

We finally arrived at the doors of the receiving room. As they opened, I felt Yao give my hand a quick, encouraging squeeze. It was a bold move to make, considering men were not allowed to touch me. Without looking at him, I smiled a half smile to acknowledge his kindness, and then walked with purpose through the heavy ivory doors.

My father already paced the room. A shroud of anxiety mixed with excitement coiled tightly through his person. Whatever he had summoned me for must have been important for his guard to have dropped. Generally, I never had much success in getting a handle on his emotions. Of course, he usually tended to remain angry and hostile, and I never needed to rely on my empathic abilities to sense when he felt like that.

He stopped his pacing and rushed to me, not even giving me a chance to bow to him as protocol dictated. "It took you long enough to arrive," he muttered in a harsh voice. Grabbing my arm, he walked to the right of the room and opened up the door to his study, a room he used to entertain dignitaries and his most trusted officers.

The ivory walls of the room were layered with paintings of ancient warrior kami such as Bishamonton and Hachiman. The frames were painted with real gold leaf, and the furnishings within the room matched the opulence of the framed paintings. Golden silk cushions were placed in a circle in the middle of the floor. Underneath the cushions the area was covered in gold matted flooring. White candles with gold floral patterns were held aloft by thin, tall holders and spaced evenly around the room. Incense burners hung from each corner of the room, letting off a sharp scent of wild cherry blossom.

Japanese characters were inscribed in gold across the ceiling as a means of protection against my father's enemies. I thought it all superstitious nonsense, but if the prophecy was real, and nekomata did in fact exist, then who was I to turn my nose up at the idea of magical properties emanating from Japanese symbols?

Two of my father's higher ups in his army sat on the floor with various injuries needing attending. I recognized one, General Li, a man just as power hungry and cutthroat as my father. I had healed several of his injuries before and disliked the way he looked at me during the process. He was in his fifties, large and muscular from countless years of service in the battlefield.

The other general was a mystery to me. I had not yet met him and was sure I wouldn't like him when I did. He looked quite young to have ascended the ranks in my father's army, and to be the beneficiary of a healing by the emperor's daughter was a high honor indeed, at least, according to my father. The man looked to be in his early thirties.

Akane hadn't yet requested my services for gathering intel, but I recognized the opportunity presented to me and decided now was as good a time as any to see if my idea would work. I needed to be extremely careful, however. My father watched me like a hawk during these healings.

"General Li, you have already met my daughter," my father said. He turned his eyes on the other soldier. "However, you, young Ojin, have not had the opportunity to benefit from The Healer's ministrations. Let us start with you first since your wound is more serious than Li's."

The two men bowed their heads in acknowledgment, and my father released me. I kept my head and eyes lowered as I made my way to the younger man. All the while, I could feel the older general's eyes staring at me. I knelt on one of the gold floor mats in front of the soldier, and without acknowledging him, placed both hands on either side of his head and closed my eyes.

His injury was painful to be sure, but in no way life threatening. Usually the men my father brought here for me to heal were fatally wounded or their injury prevented them from fighting ever again. I couldn't understand why I'd been summoned to heal something as minimal as a cracked rib and a dislocated shoulder. It wouldn't afford me much time to search the man's memories, but I started the process anyway, transferring memories from a few months back until now, absorbing the information and then returning them quickly as I healed the man's injuries. I made certain to draw the healing process out for as long as I possibly could without raising any kind of suspicion from my father.

Not only was it strange to be summoned for a healing of this nature, but as I attended to the soldier's cracked rib, I encountered another curiosity. The man's blood contained foreign entities attempting to bond with the blood cells. They looked harmless, and upon further examination, appeared to have their own healing properties. The entities lit with the touch of my ki and began bonding to the blood cells, strengthening them in a way my ki failed to recognize. I looked at the rest of the entities that had not yet bonded and searched for more answers.

The tiny lights within them circled around my ki and the intelligences attempted to impart the information I was seeking.

"What is taking so long, Daughter?" my father growled.

I startled, sending a pulse of emotion through the man's body and with that emotion the rest of the entities and intelligences bonded to the blood cells, pulsating with life and strengthening the organs.

I pulled away from the man. "I...Father, I sensed some abnormalities within his blood stream. It doesn't appear to be a threat, but I wanted to ascertain what must be done with it."

"Yes, yes," my father replied, flicking his hand in the air as if this were old news to him. "We are experimenting with some new herbs, a tonic to fortify the body. That is all." He paused in his explanation, and I wondered that he had actually condescended to answer my question. Usually he ignored me. "Anything else?" He shifted nervously, allowing his control to come crumbling down around him. His apprehension rushed over me, leaving me to wonder what he was up to. He was obviously lying, but why? I felt wholly confused by this strange turn of events.

"He had a cracked rib and injured shoulder, which I easily

dealt with."

"Very good." He nodded. "Now to the general."

Very good? Had he just paid me a compliment? I felt unbalanced by his unusual behavior.

He impatiently nodded and motioned for me to move to my left. I swallowed as my stomach churned. I did not like touching General Li or his ki. Both felt slimy and corrupt. I reluctantly moved toward him and then closed my eyes to avoid becoming trapped within his dirty glance.

Once again the injuries were slight, almost superficial. A fractured left wrist. The general was right handed. He could have easily fought without the use of his left wrist. His injury would not buy me much time. I rushed to absorb the last few months of his memories and managed to do so even faster than I had with the first man.

Just as I prepared to break the connection, I sensed the same types of abnormalities within his blood. I hoped that maybe the intelligences present would be able to impart whatever information their existence represented, but the minute I moved to touch them and explore the situation further, they lit with a blinding light, coursing throughout his entire body, and then immediately bonded to the blood cells. It was as if my ki triggered some kind of chemical reaction.

I felt uneasy at the thought. I released the general and rose from the floor, moving to my father's side as my mind spun with question after question, not to mention an enormous amount of information. It would take me a moment to form the memories into an appropriate time-line and spot the details, if any, that might be of use to Akane. Fortunately, the amount of memories I absorbed were less than what I was used to. I gave my father a quiet acknowledgment without feeling the usual heaviness of absorbing someone's entire lifespan.

The matter of the foreign entities within the soldiers' blood streams was a mystery I would certainly share with Akane. Though the entities were friendly, almost familiar even, I had a terrible feeling they were meant for some darker purpose. I highly doubted my father was concerned with developing tonics to help strengthen his soldiers. He simply wasn't a thoughtful, caring deity.

No. This was something different.

"That will be all, Daughter. I will escort you out."

I bowed to the men and exited behind my father. He gave me no explanation, and I asked for none. Asking him questions at this point would only raise his ire and suspicion, and the less curiosity I exhibited the less attention I drew to myself.

Yao and Chan were waiting for me outside the double doors. After my father dismissed me, they took me speedily to my room. I beckoned one guard to enter, while the other stayed outside.

"Yao, I need to meet with Akane as soon as possible. I have much to share with her, and feel it important that she receive this information as quickly as possible. Can you get a message to her and let her know it is vital she meet me at the ruins about thirty minutes before my training with Musubi this afternoon?"

"Absolutely, Princess."

I nodded and then bowed at the waist in response to his bow. He turned swiftly and left the room. I heard him murmuring something soft to Chan and then said more loudly, "The Princess wishes to eat in her rooms this afternoon. I shall send for her maid immediately."

I figured that louder part was for the benefit of any spies lurking about, and to explain the guard's absence.

It was still early morning, and my "educational veil training" wasn't scheduled until mid-afternoon. I needed to organize my thoughts and sift through the information I had received. I lay down upon my bed, closed my eyes and reviewed the first man's memories. Most of the information was unimportant, though the maps with markings I viewed might be valuable. I wondered if the markings on the maps indicated where various troops were stationed. If so, I would need to share all of those locations with Akane.

One particular memory held some appeal, however. From the

young commander's point of view, I watched a man with a commanding presence approach him and the group of highly ranked officers. He held a large glass container filled with a dark, red liquid. He looked vaguely familiar, but I couldn't quite place him and decided to worry about it later so I could focus on the memories flashing before me. He poured the contents of the container into several cups at the table and handed one to each of the men in the room.

"To your health, gentlemen. Let us hope this concoction works as well as His Imperial Highness claims it will."

From the commander's point of view I recognized General Li in the room, and four other men of varying stations, each draining their cups and lowering them to the table.

"When will the bonding take place?" Li asked.

"As soon as the king can send for you, though there will need to be some reason for your audience with The Healer. Who wishes to be summoned first?"

I felt the commander's hand rise like it was my own. I saw Li volunteering out of the corner of the commander's eye.

"Excellent," the strange man said.

He moved quickly, faster than the young man's eyes could follow. The commander doubled over in pain as his rib was cracked and his shoulder dislocated.

I pushed myself out of the memory, not interested in feeling the commander's injuries any longer. I knew I would see the same scene played out from the general's point of view if I decided to skim over his memories. I couldn't imagine why the men had injured themselves on purpose to force a healing, but it didn't bode well for the future.

My meeting with Akane couldn't arrive fast enough.

A firm knock at the door startled me from my thoughts.
"You may enter," I distractedly responded. I fully expected one of the guards to peek their head through the door, letting me know my message to Akane had been dispatched. I was a bit startled to see Katsu walk in and shut the door behind him. The silence that followed his entrance felt a trifle awkward. He looked at me as if he wanted something, but his emotions let me know he was uncertain and, more surprisingly, a bit uncomfortable in my presence.

I studied him intently, trying to puzzle through the source of his awkwardness by reading his face, but his handsome features refused to give up their secrets. The firm lines of his jaw and high set of his cheek bones were pleasant to look at. I hadn't developed strong feelings for Katsu, but even *I* could appreciate how handsome he looked.

"Was there something you needed?" I finally posed.

My voice effectively ended the strange staring match we were engaged in. Katsu blinked a few times as if to pull himself together, and then he tentatively approached me.

"I recognize it is quite unusual for me to enter your rooms without a chaperon," he stated.

I quirked an eyebrow, wondering what he would have thought about my unchaperoned trainings with Musubi.

Oh, by the gods, why couldn't I stop thinking about that man?

"Katsu, I'm certain my virtue is safe in your presence, whether we have a chaperon or not."

The light smile that raised the corners of his lips was quite breathtaking. It made me wish that I could give this man a chance. Perhaps I could convince him that our union would be best served here, taking care of the empire and traveling when needed. If Katsu understood how badly the empire had been neglected, and the importance of the rebels' noble cause, he might be persuaded to join us and overthrow my father's reign.

My thoughts returned to Musubi, and my heart sank. Even if I succeeded in convincing Katsu to join our side and followed through with the union, I would always be miserable, wondering what kind of future I might have shared with Musubi if I hadn't already been betrothed to someone else.

"You place an unhealthy amount of faith in my willpower. Why, I could close the distance between us," he took a few steps forward, arriving directly in front of me, "take you in my arms," he stunned me by reaching forward and lightly wrapping an arm around my waist, "and do exactly what I wanted to do when I saved you in the woods almost a month ago."

I might have become nervous and pulled myself away, if I hadn't noticed the mischievous look on his face. I gave him a shy smile as I realized he merely teased. His emotions were completely blocked off, so I only had his countenance to go by.

"You're just being playful," I said, though his arm around my waist felt warm and secure.

His small smile slowly left his face as he placed his other arm around me. "Am I?"

I couldn't tell if he posed the question to me or himself. A sharp sense of longing slipped through the wall he usually held tight. I couldn't tear my eyes from his as I watched his thoughts play across his face. He seemed to be battling some conflicting emotions that centered solely around me.

I didn't know for certain how Katsu truly felt about me. I didn't know if he had resigned himself to his fate and sometimes forced himself to pay more attention to me, as if to give the idea of our union a chance, a strange need to fulfill his duty and play his role to perfection. Or perhaps he actually felt something more than just a sense of duty. Maybe he longed to find a sense of belonging and acceptance much the same way I did despite our union remaining an order and not simply a choice.

He leaned his head forward a little, and I nearly panicked. I had never been kissed before. I had no idea if I wanted to be kissed. My inexperience was something Katsu expected, but I was certain over his lifespan he had been with many women. I couldn't imagine he would have remained alone, waiting for the moment when we could be together. How could I compare to those other women when I was so terribly naïve?

He rested his forehead against mine, giving me a brief respite as I tried to come to terms with our physical contact, his close proximity, and the way my heart raced even though I didn't want to feel anything for him.

He breathed in deeply, and then placed a lingering kiss on my cheek. "You're trembling." His voice sounded gruff. "Do I frighten you, Mikomi?" He pulled back. His eyebrows furrowed with worry.

I looked at the floor. "No, I'm not frightened. I'm simply not used to...to being touched by a man...I mean, I don't know how to react...I..." Why couldn't I form one coherent sentence at the moment? I didn't love him. I knew I didn't, but his presence affected me nonetheless.

He lifted a hand and brushed back strands of hair from the side of my face, tucking them behind my ear. I felt a warm tingle at his touch and used all my will power not to shiver in front of him.

"Mikomi, please look at me."

I did as I was told and raised my eyes to his.

"I know this is all very new to you, but I wonder if you would allow me to—"

There was a knock at the door and the guard said, "Your meal has arrived, Princess."

Whatever Katsu had been about to ask, and whatever courage he seemed to have gathered was interrupted. He pulled away from me and walked to the door. Opening it, he beckoned the servants to set up the food in the center of the room where a table low to the ground stood surrounded by a few red cushions.

I was relieved that our conversation had been cut short. His intensity had been overwhelming.

"May I eat with you, Princess?" Katsu asked. My stomach tightened further, wondering if I would be able to handle more alone time with him, but I nodded my consent. I knew it really hadn't been a question anyway. He had come to my quarters for a reason. It wasn't that I didn't enjoy his company, but I felt hopelessly confused as to how I was supposed to respond to his hot and cold behavior.

I needn't have worried about the intensely charged atmosphere. Once the meal had been set and Katsu and I began eating, it seemed that whatever question he had wished to ask, and whatever moment we had been about to share, would not be brought up again.

The moment was gone.

"I wondered if we might train a little today before your outing with Kenji," he said after serving me some roasted fish. "You've never actually trained with my sword, and it is going to be important for you to become familiar with its energy and how it relates to your own healing powers."

I nodded. "Of course, I am certainly happy to learn more."

"What do you know about the sword thus far?" he asked.

I searched my memory, attempting to dredge up the few lessons Kenji had forced upon me before giving up once he realized that I was steadfastly in denial about my prophesied future.

"The only thing I am positive of is it is used to strengthen weak areas within the veil."

I could tell Katsu was not happy with my ignorance on the matter. "In order to understand how the sword strengthens the veil, you must learn what its powers are." He shifted on his cushion. "The sword is directly connected to the health of the veil. Our First Parents knew the veil would eventually weaken against the never ending onslaught of the demon god, requiring a massive amount of energy to sustain the line between the world of those who have passed on and those who are living."

"How did they find that kind of energy?"

"That question pertains to your healing powers. When you connect to someone's ki you're connecting directly to the life force or essence of that individual. What do you sense during these connections?"

I thought about it for a moment and could come up with only one answer.

"Intelligence."

Katsu smiled and nodded. "Correct. Everything, down to the smallest particles of life have intelligence and can function to create some of the world's most magnificent creatures with the right amount of guidance. Within these intelligences you have unlimited amounts of power and energy, and a person's ki is the purest source of energy available. And where does their ki go when an individual passes on?"

My eyes widened as I realized where this conversation was going. "Their spirits move through the veil to the other side. In other words, on the other side of the veil are millions of spirits, life forces that continue to progress and grow with power due to their increase in intelligence."

Katsu smiled. "Exactly. Their energy is what sustains the strength of the veil, but in order to harness that energy and help pinpoint it to where it is most needed, there has to be a conductor of sorts, something that can penetrate the veil, absorb the energy and channel it into the fabric of the veil, thereby strengthening it."

"So those we have lost to the other side of this veil, they are literally all around us, just participating in a different way and on a different plane than we are." I thought about this new information and felt certain I wasn't going to be happy to receive an answer to the question I posed next. "If this sword is able to channel power to heal the veil, why am I needed?"

"With every new recruit, the demon god receives power from their ki as well, and the balance between a life force that has chosen good over that of one who has chosen evil is quickly tipping. There are no longer merely one or two places that the veil is weakened at any given times. Amatsu plans his attacks all at once in several locations. The sword alerts me to these breaches when it lets off a bright golden glow, and I am led to them through the power of the sword, but I can only fix one weakened area at a time due to the fact that the sword cannot handle more power than it was made to." He reached a hand across the table and softly touched mine. "Your ability to take a person's ki and guide them into healing themselves is exactly the kind of procedure you would use with the veil, but you would be doing it on a much grander scale with thousands of individual ki available for you to guide."

I swallowed hard, unable to imagine having thousands of ki all responding to my every instruction. "How would I accomplish this?"

"First, you must learn to feel the veil around you. Once you are able to do so, you will be able to sense where it is weakening. We hold the sword together, and you use our combined, soul mated ki to channel your power through the sword in order to connect to the spirits on the other side. The sword then becomes an amplifier of your gift, enabling you to communicate and guide thousands of ki, teaching them how to use their energy to repair and strengthen all of the weakened points at the same time instead of having to do so one by one."

"I didn't know our ki would be used together."

Katsu looked down, seemingly uncomfortable. "We haven't talked much about your ascension. On your eighteenth birthday we do what is called a binding ceremony where our souls are bound together forever. Once that is accomplished, you will be ready for your full ascension as a kami, having a ki as powerful as that of any other immortal being."

"If my ki already heals my body, why am I still considered half mortal? What is it that you do that brings me to full immortality?"

"Once we are bonded, I use my ki to heal the half of your ki that is mortal. I won't go into the details of how at the moment since we are still five months from the ceremony, but I can assure you, once you are a full kami you and I will have no problem healing the veil together."

"Forever." I hadn't meant to say it as if it were some kind of prison sentence, but I couldn't consider it anything else. "And what if I fail, Katsu? What if the prophecy is wrong, and I'm simply not powerful enough to heal the veil with you?"

Katsu brushed my hand with his as if to encourage me. "The prophecy is not wrong, Mikomi. I promise you, you will be ready for this when the time comes."

"But what if I'm not? What if I can't?"

"Then the veil will fall, the demon god will win, and this world and all of humanity will be thrown into the hands of a bloodthirsty, power hungry god."

I felt the full weight of my responsibility nearly crush me where I sat, and suddenly such mundane activities as eating food or conversing with Katsu seemed trivial and out of place considering the severity of the consequences that would follow if I didn't fulfill my part in the prophecy.

"Mikomi, you must have more faith in yourself. You won't fail. *We* won't fail."

I looked into Katsu's eyes, felt the truthfulness of his words behind the emotions seeping through that ever present wall of his. His sincerity, his belief in me was humbling, and I felt certain I would never be the kind of person to deserve it. Not when I desperately desired to run away from my responsibilities and into the arms of a man far different from this warrior god seated before me.

"Would you like to hold the sword? Get a feel for it and its energy?"

I nodded.

Katsu stood up and pulled a long straight sword from his saya. The blade, though made of steel, seemed to glow with a vibrant, gold light. The hilt was silver and simple, without ornate carvings or embellishments. It really was the most unassuming weapon, one I never would have considered sufficient for healing the veil if I didn't know better.

"Do you also use this sword in battle?"

"I do. It is one of the few weapons that has the power to fight against the forces of the demon god. Nekomata are easily dealt with."

He motioned for me to stand beside him. I left the table and crossed over to his side.

"Now, take the sword by the hilt, and with the point touching the floor, I want you to close your eyes and connect to it."

I raised my eyebrows. "Connect to it? But it is metal."

Katsu smiled knowingly. "Take the hilt and you will see what I mean."

I did as I was told, bringing the point of the blade to the floor as I marveled at its lightweight feel considering its size. Once I closed my eyes, I attempted to connect with it just as if it were a living, breathing entity.

I felt a slight stirring from the sword and then a strange intelligence brushed my consciousness, latching on to it and allowing me a connection. I might have dropped the blade from the unexpected sensation, but the connection I experienced was overpowering my senses. With it I felt an energy and power buzzing through me. Soon I felt other energies and forces moving toward me at an alarming rate, all hoping to latch on and communicate to me something important, but I couldn't understand their meaning nor their intent, and I wasn't used to so many life forces connecting with me all at once.

I quickly broke from them, and, without meaning to, dropped the sword to the floor. I was breathing heavily and looked at Katsu, wondering if I had done something wrong. He simply gave me a smile and bent down to retrieve the sword. Considering its importance, I wondered if I should have been punished for my careless treatment of it.

"There were several energies responding to you, correct?" he asked as he sheathed the sword.

I nodded, still feeling slightly out of sorts. "How will I ever be able to channel so many ki at one time?"

"Because you will have me. As one who is not full kami, the weight of those intelligences would be too much for your mind to handle, but as a kami bonded to my ki, my energy will be at your disposal to help strengthen your abilities. You will find that this will not be so daunting a task." He gave me a tender, but firm look. "This is why we must practice, Mikomi, and why you must learn to feel the veil around you without the use of the sword, and without assistance of those that are near death themselves." He took my hand in his and rubbed his thumb across the back of it. "We must develop these skills before your ascension."

The need to escape the mounting pressure building within my chest was quickly becoming the only thought I could hold on to with any kind of clarity. If I thought the salvation of the world had been too great of a responsibility it was because I had never experienced the kind of responsibility the veil placed upon me. With so many intelligences clamoring for my guidance and direction, I couldn't begin to understand how I would ever survive the process.

And for eternity?

I'd never considered myself special in any way. My healing power had been a natural extension of me, like an appendage or the permanent color of my eyes. I could use it to help others, and in that I had some measure of control, some source of happiness and fulfillment. I couldn't begin to imagine how I would ever turn from healing people in need to healing a veil for the rest of my existence. I understood my responsibilities. I knew that everything rested solely upon my person, but did it have to? Would I be trading in one prison sentence for another once I married Katsu and left this empire behind me?

I needed to be noble, self-sacrificing, and duty bound, but I felt too small and insignificant, too overwhelmed as I learned more about my future role as The Healer.

"I think perhaps we have done enough for one day. The power you were exposed to can be draining, even for a kami, and you are still half mortal." Katsu studied me intently, looking concerned. "Perhaps it was too much, Mikomi."

I shook my head. "No, it was important for me to know. I needed to know." It wasn't the best in the way of reassurance, but it was all I could say without breaking down and begging Katsu to choose someone else. Someone less selfish and cowardly. I closed my mouth tight and endured my panic and anxiety in silence.

Katsu gave me one last searching look and then nodded, clearly satisfied with my response. "I will leave you to rest then. Until tomorrow?"

"Yes. Of course."

He surprised me by leaning down and placing a gentle kiss upon my forehead, and then he disappeared through the door.

Akane was waiting for me at the ruins as requested. She sent Yao and Chan to one of the abandoned buildings for light refreshment, and as a way to ensure they didn't hear anything that would put them at more risk than they already were.

I agreed wholeheartedly, recognizing their lives were in danger should the emperor ever discover where their loyalties lay, and how they aided my involvement with the rebels.

Akane didn't waste time with pleasantries but delved into the matter at hand.

"Mikomi, I was quite worried about your message. Has your father discovered your involvement with us?" she asked.

"No. Nothing like that. If he had, I most certainly wouldn't be here. Most likely I'd be in a cell somewhere. Something strange happened today."

I explained in detail the healing my father had summoned me to perform and the unusual entities in his officers' different bloodstreams. I also discussed the memories I had absorbed. All the while, dear, supportive Kenji stood by my side, his agitation growing with each word that passed my lips.

Our first order of business was to utilize the map she brought with her so as to notate the areas that had been similarly marked within the soldier's memories. With that accomplished, we moved on to the more distressing part of their memories and the unorthodox meeting with my father and his men.

"In these memories you absorbed, your father's officers were injured on purpose in order to receive an audience with you?" she asked.

"Yes, and I can only assume that whatever substance existing within the drink they imbibed has something to do with why."

"Perhaps it is the drink itself that contained these entities you speak of," Kenji offered. "Though how they would assimilate themselves within the blood is puzzling and a bit unsettling. It almost sounds similar to a process used by the demon god before he was cast out by our First Parents."

I quirked a questioning eyebrow a him. "What process, Kenji?"

My tutor shifted his stance and leaned heavily against his cane. Without thinking I touched his arm, connected with his ki and eased the pain in his joints all within a matter of seconds. He gave me a rueful yet grateful look and then moved on to his explanation.

"After the creation of the world, the kami and all other forms of life, there began to be divisions of power amongst the kami— roles assigned by our First Parents to keep the balance of nature and the world in which nature exists."

I nodded, remembering the lessons he had taught me from a tender, young age.

"At that time, Amatsu-Mikaboshi was one of the noblest of our First Parent's creations. He felt that his role of welcoming souls into the afterlife was something only a minor kami should be in charge of. He mentioned his grievances with our First Parents, but of course they knew which kami were best suited for which tasks. They created them, after all. Dissatisfied with this,

Amatsu began to seek out the powers of creation himself. He wanted to build worlds and have kami of his own to influence and order about."

I listened intently, realizing that this part was all new to me.

"He lacked the knowledge to create kami the way our First Parents had, and so he began experimenting on humans."

"Kenji, I've never heard this part of our history before."

"That, my dear, is because it is not common knowledge. It wasn't anything our First Parents wanted other kami to attempt."

"Then how *did* you come across this information?"

"In your father's library, to be quite honest. There are several tomes there, ancient records of creation and kami history that I've never seen anywhere else. I assume they were placed there long ago by the very first emperor of this land and then forgotten over the ages."

"What were these experiments the demon god performed?" Akane interjected.

"To put it simply, Amatsu wasn't interested in turning mortals into kami through the use of his own ki. He might have lost his own immortality by slowly healing humans. There was no guarantee that the humans would accept the change, and the process would have taken much too long either way. He decided to find out what would happen if he had them drink his blood."

"His blood? I don't understand how that would do anything?"

"Kami blood holds life altering properties. Legends of the fountain of youth can be traced back to the idea that immortality is achieved through a magical elixir gifted from the gods. A kami's blood contains particles of their ki. Intelligent organisms that are capable of changing the chemical properties of one's blood. Once imbibed and bonded to a human, their blood is changed from one of mortal to that of an immortal within seconds."

I began to feel a sinking sensation within my stomach. "What do you mean bonded?"

Kenji rubbed the back of his neck. I sensed he was beginning to link my story and his explanation together and didn't like where our conclusions were taking us.

"Once a kami's blood enters a human's bloodstream it will do very little to benefit the body unless the blood is bonded to the humans' through another kami's instruction, but this can only be done by someone capable of connecting to another's ki and..." Kenji trailed off. The process he explained was disturbingly similar to the healing I had shared. "By the gods, Mikomi, your father is creating his own kami, and using you to bond his blood to theirs."

"Not just his own kami," Akane whispered, "his own *army* of kami. With all of his soldiers benefiting from this elixir we'll be fighting a full militia of kami by the end of the year, and no weapon on this earth will be capable of killing them." She looked to me, eyes wide with terror. "If he succeeds, we'll never accomplish our mission to overthrow the emperor. We'll never survive this war."

"It's far worse than that, I'm afraid." Kenji worried the knob of his cane with both hands. "This battle between you and the emperor is a minor annoyance compared to the battle he is most likely planning once Mikomi ascends as a full kami and marries Katsu."

"What are you saying, Kenji?" I asked.

"With you gone, there will be no reason for the rest of the major kami to allow him to rule this empire. He's going to attempt what Amatsu tried to accomplish in the very beginning."

"What's that, exactly?" Akane asked.

But I had a very good idea. I felt sick inside as his words dredged up pictures of bloody battles and the complete destruction of the empire.

Kenji chewed on his lower lip before reluctantly answering.

"World domination."

There was silence as all three of us tried to digest this new revelation. I sensed hopelessness and fear from Akane, and then a wonderful, resilient sense of determination. Her emotions evolved into that a truly hardened warrior. She stubbornly refused to wallow in her fear for too long. I admired her courage, though I felt it might be wasted on a lost cause.

Kenji's emotions covered a wide spectrum of worry and fear for Saigo and myself. I wasn't surprised that his feelings didn't reek of selfish fear or pity for himself. Kenji was too good to think of himself when those he loved were endangered. The guards hadn't been privy to the details of our conversation, and I was happy they had been spared the worry. They were good men with enough on their plate.

"What do we do?" I finally asked.

"How many men were in the room drinking this concoction? Do you remember?" he asked.

I shook my head. "There were several other men in the room. I can't remember the exact number."

"One thing is certain, child. He will need to call upon your services again in order to bond his blood to these other soldiers. What exactly did you do when the bonding took place?"

I thought back for a moment. "I was trying to understand what exactly the foreign entities were, and when I reached out with my ki to touch them, that's when they bonded."

"Will it be possible for you to heal the emperor's men without having any contact with those foreign elements?" Akane asked.

"I can certainly try. It will be difficult since their blood is saturated with the emperor's, and any healings that take place may need instructions for intelligences within the bloodstream. If I have to heal severe bleeding or internal bleeding, there may be no way of avoiding them."

Kenji nodded. "Do the best you can, child. The emperor is going to use your skills as frequently as he can before the day of your ascension. If you can undermine his plans without him being the wiser, we may be able to avert this eventual disaster."

"This will be a good opportunity to continue searching the minds of his minions. If you find anything of value, please send me a message immediately." Akane placed a hand on my arm. "Make sure you are careful, though. If your father truly plans to rebel against our First Parents like this, then it is clear he will not hesitate to harm you if you get in his way."

"He won't get rid of me. He needs me to heal the veil. If Amatsu is able to free himself and join us in this realm, my father will be facing some rather fierce competition. He needs me alive, and he can't kill me, anyway. My immortality ensures that he can't, but you are right in assuming that he will do much worse if he feels I have fought against him."

"He cannot find out, then."

"No." I grabbed her hand in mine. "He cannot."

We heard a scuffling noise from a building behind us. Akane quickly dropped her hand and pulled her katana from its saya. Musubi appeared from one of the ruins, throwing broken pieces of rock along the ground as he went. He fixed his eyes on Akane's defensive stance, and a wry smile sprang to his lips.

"Expecting trouble, are we?" he said as he approached our gathering.

"Just being hyper vigilant. Something you taught me years ago." Akane sheathed her sword and gave him a long-suffering look. "Though I sometimes wonder if a battle with the emperor's men is preferable to that of dealing with you and your brooding moods."

Musubi wrapped a playful arm around Akane, leaving me feeling slightly jealous. "I never brood, nor do I have moods. Now, what are you doing here, Akane? Planning to watch our training session? Or are you feeling rusty and in need of some review?"

Akane spun under Musubi's arm. "I promised myself I would never suffer another one of your torturous training sessions, Musubi, and I meant it. She's all yours." Akane nodded toward me and then gave me a wink. She sprinted to her horse, leaping upon it quickly and barreling away as if she were afraid he might force her to stay and participate.

"I'll be over here, Mikomi, reading my life away." Kenji patted my arm and turned toward a broken building that looked as if it might offer some considerable shade. He lifted a small satchel from the earth and gingerly moved away.

I had tried to avoid eye contact with Musubi ever since his

approach, knowing full well I would become flustered and crippled by my emotional and physical response to him, but it couldn't be helped as he walked closer and then stood right before me. I met his gaze with trepidation.

He misunderstood the reason for my look when he let out a mischievous chuckle and said, "You are right to fear this session, Mikomi, for I have no intention of going easy on you." His gaze traveled the length of me, and my body shivered in response. "After all," he continued, placing a warm hand at my waist, "Akane *did* say you were all mine."

Now both of his hands were at my waist, pulling me closer as I fought to contain my response to him. He gave me one last lingering look before a naughty glint pierced his eye. Before I knew what was happening, my kimono had been unwrapped, stripped from my person, and thrown to the floor at my feet. My black body suit hugged my curves. I felt heat creep up my neck and blossom along my face.

He surveyed me with immense satisfaction as I sputtered for some kind of reprimand. His emotions, for once, were void of the anger I was so used to. "I tell you, Mikomi, I could live to see a thousand more moons and never *ever* tire of ripping your clothes off." He took in my fierce expression and let out a boisterous laugh.

Little did he know, a part of me would never tire of it either.

12

"**T**oday we are going to take a small break from your *katana* and focus on methods you can use for self-defense if ever you must go hand to hand with your enemy," Musubi said as we stood facing one another. "I hope there will never be a situation in which I am not there to protect you, but if such occasion should arise, you must be prepared not only to be on the offensive but on the defensive as well."

He paused for a moment, and I nodded that I understood. He continued, "Mastering fighting techniques can be a long, grueling process because most people are unable to tune in to their own inner energy or ki."

My ears pricked at this. "What do you mean exactly?"

"Many individuals are unable to recognize that the art of defending oneself is not simply a physical show of prowess, but more importantly a mental one. Your ki, the most powerful part of your true self, rests within your *hara* or center, and your center," he said, coming closer and resting his hand against my lower abdomen, "is just two inches below the navel. This is also your center of gravity."

I swallowed hard as the warmth of his hands seeped through my thin undergarment. He must have felt the heat as well. I felt a sharp emotional shock pulse through him, and then he rapidly pulled his hand away. He seemed to need a moment to recover himself before he could speak, and he avoided making eye contact with me. I was relieved. I was sure if he had wanted to, he would have found my feelings for him written all over my face.

"It is important that we fuse both physical and mental energies together, and bridge that gap between mind and body so that both are working harmoniously with one another. It is a difficult thing for many to do, but it's necessary if you are to master total control." He took two steps back and faced me, finally looking at me, his face an indifferent mask. "To develop the mental skills necessary for controlling your body you must work on a process called centralization. You must focus on the subjective at first. Any troubles you are experiencing or worries and problems you have yet to resolve will be looked at dispassionately, almost as if you are viewing them from behind a screen. They are present but separate. I want you to close your eyes, think of one problem you have yet to resolve, and consider it without allowing it to affect your emotions."

I did as he asked, and the first problem to pop into my mind dealt solely with my father. I wanted his love and acceptance and had never found a way to earn it. The memories brought pain and bitterness to my heart, but I did my best to push those feelings aside and look at my problem subjectively.

From an outsider's point of view, one would look at the situation and recognize that the emperor had never been interested in being a father but in gaining power. I was a pawn. I had already acknowledged this time and time again, but the fact remained it ate at me and my own feelings of self-worth.

However, to look at it dispassionately, I realized that all of those years I spent seeking approval had been wasted on a man who had never sought for my love and approval in the first place, but who relished in the power and control he had over me and everyone else in his life. It made no sense to feel worthless when my father's idea of worth was based upon the amount of power he held within his hands.

I had never been strong enough, capable enough or honorable enough in his eyes, but for all the things I valued and the characteristics I treasured, my own beliefs, actions and character, by definition, made me strong enough, capable enough and more than honorable enough to be The Healer.

I am The Healer, and my father is not.

The moment I accepted my own identity and worth I felt a strange clarity click into place. I opened my eyes and looked at Musubi as he studied me with a commanding intensity. I wasn't sure how he knew that I was ready, but this connection between us might have had something to do with it.

"Very good," he said. "It usually takes students much longer to accomplish that first step. Now, the next type of centralization is objective. You've centered yourself internally, and now you must keep a clear and centered view of what is happening around you. You must be as impartial with circumstances surrounding you as you are with the internal conflict you just dealt with. For example," he held his arms out presenting himself, "what do you see when you look at me?"

I narrowed my eyes, wondering if this was a trick question. I couldn't respond the way I wanted to. It wouldn't have been appropriate to tell Musubi that I saw a handsome warrior, deeply troubled by his past. I couldn't tell him I saw a man I wished to love and take care of, a man whose future could be bright if he allowed me to heal what, within his past, had been broken.

I self-consciously cleared my throat as I realized I had been staring for far too long without giving a response.

"I see a tall, armed man."

Musubi pulled his sword from his saya and crouched forward with the sword held above his head. "And if a man such as I were to come at you with a sword, what would you see?"

I swallowed. "I would see a wicked blade, an intimidating aggressor and a skilled warrior I couldn't possibly overcome."

Musubi dropped his stance and pointed his sword to the ground. "I am merely an object in motion, Mikomi. No matter my size, strength or intimidating presence, an object in motion can always be effectively neutralized so long as you do not allow what you may perceive as threatening to hypnotize your mind and emotions. Without the power of your mind you cannot efficiently direct the power of your body. Your thoughts and perceptions cannot be affected by how I appear. You remain centralized so when an opponent attacks you, you can maintain impartiality, recognizing that your aggressor is simply an object in motion."

"Are you telling me you're not an intimidating figure when brandishing a sword?" I was trying to tease him and lighten the mood. For some reason this session felt more emotionally charged than the others had, though it was less physical in nature. I was uncomfortable with Musubi's direct look constantly piercing my faked indifference toward him. There was a strange tension building between us, and I wanted to scream as loudly as possible in order to break it.

Musubi's lips quirked into a smile. "I will always be an intimidating figure, but it is my job to train you to look past all that."

"And what do you see when you look at me?" I teased again. I bent low into the same position he had and brandished my imaginary sword.

"A beautiful, capable woman." He said it without a pause, and based on his emotional response to hearing his own words, he wasn't very happy with himself. Still, he kept his eyes on mine.

I slowly stood. Bringing my arms to my sides, I tried for another joke. "Well, with that glowing recommendation, I certainly won't be intimidating anyone on the battlefield."

Musubi dropped his sword and approached me. His frustration with himself and his reaction toward me was palpable at this point. He couldn't seem to find his *own* center, and his guard remained lowered, unleashing his intense feelings. It felt as if he closed the distance between us against his will, like some invisible line had connected us both, reeling him forward despite his own internal battle. He placed a hand at my waist, and lifted the other to softly brush a strand of hair from my forehead.

"On the contrary," he said in a hoarse voice, "there is nothing in this world more intimidating than a beautiful, capable woman."

My breathing felt slightly labored as the emotions we were both trying to repress began to intensify. My feet stayed firmly glued to the grassy blanket beneath me, but I wanted to turn and run away before this unbearably charged tension between us overcame my good sense, forcing me to lose all inhibitions and throw myself into his arms.

Musubi's wall had crumbled, and he was like an open book now. He couldn't have thrown up any walls against my empathic abilities even if he had wanted to, and I was grateful—grateful to know that I wasn't the only one who felt this pull, this overwhelming connection we shared. Grateful to know I wasn't the only one affected by our time spent together. It was knowledge I never would have gleaned otherwise, not with Musubi's ability to become cold and indifferent.

He fought it, though. His desire for me became overshadowed by a dark anger that seemed to penetrate whatever light our connection brought to the surface. I knew the exact moment when that anger snapped our connection in half because Musubi was able to take a step back, and my ki cringed at the backlash our severed connection produced.

It felt as if a great knife had hollowed out my insides as Musubi abruptly turned from me and walked back to his sword. He bent forward, picked it up and then kept his back to me while he sheathed it. He continued facing the other way, and I saw the exaggerated rise and fall of his shoulders as he took several deep breaths. Once he turned around to face me, his wall was up and his mask firmly in place.

I had no idea if I would be able to dislodge it again.

"Once you have found your center, you are ready to focus your own inherent energy or ki. Your inner energy is an extension of your will and ability to neutralize an attack. I wish I could tell you that you won't have to injure or possibly kill anyone who may attack you. This is war, and the emperor's men will kill you if given the chance, but it is more important for you to subdue your attacker and evade the ensuing confrontation altogether. The extension of your ki will play a very large part in your ability to do so."

I did my best to focus on what Musubi was saying, but I was

still reeling from everything left unexplored and unsaid between us.

"I want you to stand straight and tall, but relaxed, allowing the weight of your upper body to descend naturally. Focus on that weight being maintained at your core in your lower abdomen, and keep still as you find your center. It matters very little how long it takes for you to achieve this so long as you do."

"How will I know when I have found this balance within myself?" I asked, feeling confused, overwhelmed, and affected by his presence.

"You'll know when you no longer feel the need to ask."

I wasn't happy with his evasive answer, but I closed my eyes and focused on relaxing my upper body, finding my center and focusing on that one spot within me. I considered Musubi's speech of impartiality, a dispassionate look at my own life's crumbling circumstances, and knew at that moment I needed to rein in my emotions where Musubi was concerned or I would never accomplish the task he had just set before me.

I wasn't sure how long I stood, perfectly still, focused on one point within myself where my own ki's energy pooled together, but I soon heard Musubi's voice as if from a great distance giving me more instruction.

"I want you to draw a thin stream of air through your nose, and allow it to fill the whole of you before exhaling out."

I did as I was told, and for several minutes I felt as if I were in my own world where nothing could penetrate my focus and clarity.

I heard Musubi's voice, again from a great distance. "Open your eyes, Mikomi, and tell me what you see."

I opened them slowly and wondered if Musubi had placed a dark cloth over my eyes. It took me a moment to realize the sun had set completely, and we were blanketed in darkness with only the light from the moon giving me any sense of where I stood. I couldn't believe so much time had passed when it felt as if I had only been meditating for mere minutes.

I scanned the darkness, searching for my teacher, and found

him standing next to me.

"How much time has passed?" I asked.

"Four hours, Mikomi." He sounded angry, but I failed to understand why until he spoke again. "Never, in my entire life have I ever had a student find their center and focus their ki as quickly as you have. Your ability is almost inhuman."

My thoughts raced for some kind of logical explanation. "I'm a woman of medicine, Musubi. It is important for me to understand the energies surrounding myself and the person with whom I am treating. This is merely a natural extension of what I already do."

I waited, hoping my explanation might be sufficient. My eyes were nearly blinded as a torch was lit. Musubi stuck it in a hole on one of the broken buildings. He then returned, looking troubled and pensive.

"Are you really going to berate me for exceeding your expectations?" I asked, arching my eyebrow at him.

He looked startled for a moment, and then a slow smile spread across his face. "I suppose I should be used to it by now, little healer."

I gave him an answering smile in return. "Perhaps you do not give your teaching methods enough credit."

He took my hand in his and softly rubbed his thumb against the inside of my wrist. I decided right then and there that finding my center was going to be an invaluable technique whenever I found myself in his presence.

"Or perhaps you're more capable than either of us supposed." The torchlight glinted against the frosty blue of his eyes.

"And this troubles you, Musubi?"

"More than you could possibly know." He lifted my wrist to his lips and softly kissed it before releasing me. "We shall continue our training tomorrow. Goodnight, little healer." He disappeared before I could overcome my shock at the affection he had demonstrated. I stood in the torchlight, unwilling to leave this brave new world I had joined, this part of my life that had become so important to me. I wanted to stay in those ruins with

Musubi for the rest of my life, forget about my heavy burdens and responsibilities as the only individual on this earth capable of foiling the plans of a powerful demon god.

I stared at the flickering flames of the torchlight as it created intricate shadows against the stone wall, and my eyes filled with unshed tears. I didn't allow them to fall, however. Instead, I turned my back on the flames consuming the torch-wood and found Kenji and my guards waiting patiently to accompany me home.

"**Y**our body cannot create new life if your own life is so sorely depleted," I said as I examined my new patient in Daiki's tavern. She was a young girl, fifteen at most, and suffering from what most of my father's subjects suffered, a severe lack of food. Her body could not produce enough nutrients and hormones to continue with her pregnancy. There were many things I could do with my gift, but I couldn't create nutrition out of thin air.

I did my best to strengthen the mother's bodily functions and that of her baby's and then handed her several coins, instructing her to use them to buy what she would need in order to feed herself and her child.

She gave me a grateful hug and left the tavern through the back door. I stared after her and worried about her future and that of her unborn child.

"You cannot save everyone, Mikomi," Daiki said as he sat down next to me.

"Daiki, I'm The Healer. Technically, the only thing I'm supposed to do is save everyone." I rubbed my tired eyes with the back of my hand. I had slept fitfully the night before, even with Aiko's sleeping draught. Visions of Musubi and Katsu at war with one another stayed with me all throughout the night, and my day had not gone much better.

Katsu's sword had notified him of a weakening in the veil far away from our location, and he had departed immediately, leaving a brief note explaining his departure. I couldn't understand why his failure to visit me to bid me farewell should irk me so when I didn't have feelings for him.

My training with Musubi had consisted of more meditation. I think it was his way of preventing us from having further discussions or maintaining eye contact for any length of time. He was determined to keep me at arm's length during our entire session. It left me feeling dissatisfied and irritable.

"Were you able to leave the palace easily?" Daiki asked.

"Yes. With Katsu gone and my father visiting dignitaries in a different part of the province, I have no one who might unexpectedly demand my presence." I turned to study my friend, noting the dark circles under his eyes. "Daiki, you look tired. Is everything well with you and your family?"

"Well enough. I'm merely having trouble sleeping lately. New babies have a sleeping schedule all their own."

I smiled as understanding hit me. "Yes, I can imagine sleep is now considered a fleeting luxury."

We both chuckled at this and then sat in companionable silence for a few moments.

It didn't take too long for my thoughts to travel back to the young lady I had just helped.

"I hope she will be able to continue with her pregnancy. The money I gave her should be sufficient for her needs. I wish I could have done more."

"Hatsumi and I will look out for her. Her husband is with the rebels right now, but I know he checks in on her every now and then."

I shook my head. "These people cannot continue like this. How many more will starve to death, and how many more soldiers will be slaughtered due to my father's tyrannical rule?" I rested my head on the table, feeling dejected. "How do we stop this, Daiki? What is healing the veil going to accomplish if people in my kingdom are dying from things as unnecessary and preventable as starvation?"

Daiki placed a hand on my back and gave it a comforting pat.

"You are needed here, Mikomi. I've told you as much. You could change all of this for these people, and you have access to the information the rebels need to take down your father. I have faith that between you and the rebels, we'll see an end to this insufferable situation."

I nodded but kept my head against the cool wood table. I didn't want to ponder on all the things Akane and Daiki expected me to accomplish. I just wanted to close my eyes and imagine my life as someone else.

"Is there something else troubling you, Mikomi? You seem fatigued, and your ki doesn't usually allow you to feel that for long."

My eyebrows narrowed as I thought about Daiki's observation. "You're right. I'm more tired than usual, but I can't account for it. It feels as if my ki is struggling to replace necessary nutrients within my body, but I'm not certain what I could be lacking. I haven't changed what I consume."

"But you have been more physically active than you're used to. Perhaps you need to replenish your body with a heavier meal."

"That's true. I'm sure things will improve if I eat a little more with each meal."

"You must keep up your strength. Who knows when you'll need it?"

Daiki's words felt like a warning, a dire prediction even. An awful sense of foreboding hit me. My father was due to return tomorrow, but Katsu would be gone another week at least. I felt safer with him in the palace, as I knew it would be easier for my father to summon me without worrying about Katsu's interference. I needed to continue gathering information for the rebels, but I dreaded what I had to go through to get it.

It couldn't be helped. I had to let go of my fear and trepidation where my father was concerned and focus on how advanced his plans for building a kami army were. If at all possible, I needed to heal his men without bonding his blood to them. I had no idea if it was even possible, but trying would be the only way of finding out.

I wanted to get the whole thing over with as quickly as possible. Little did I know, my father's summons would come much faster than I expected.

As I stood within the emperor's meeting room, I felt a kind of subdued anxiousness begin to build within me. There were three men this time, all of them recognizable from the memories I accessed yesterday. My father hadn't wasted any time in arranging another meeting. I had no doubts about the source of his men's injuries. I knew they were purposely inflicted by that man who had brought them my father's blood. The man's familiarity nagged at me. I knew it was important to remember, but I simply couldn't access it due to my unusual feelings of fatigue.

My mental processes had been remarkably slow, though I had changed my diet in the hopes of correcting the problem. Last night, after returning from the village, I ate more than I was used to, and at first it seemed my efforts were working. Then I awakened this morning, feeling slightly off balance again without the energy necessary to correct the problem with my ki.

I tamped down my worry on that subject and turned my attention toward the soldiers and their superficial injuries.

"I need you to heal these men as quick as you can," my father ordered.

He didn't bother explaining why such silly injuries needed healing, and I didn't expect him to. It was understood that any order he gave must be obeyed. I was greatly relieved that Katsu had not yet returned from his travels. Though it sorely tempted me to use him as a shield, I knew the information I gathered for the rebels was monumentally more important than my own fear of my father and his men.

The three soldiers were also commanders of various sections of my father's militia. All men of higher classes, all from wealthy families. I stepped over to the one nearest me, an older man, perhaps in his late fifties, and reached for his oily head. Connecting with him was unpleasant. His ki was dark and slimy. Mentally, my entire being cringed, but I pushed through my initial reaction and assessed his situation.

Just like before, minor injuries. I also noticed those foreign intelligences within his blood and wondered if I could get around them and still pull off a healing. I tried it with his ribs first, but everywhere my ki focused, the entities would bond to the blood. After healing his rib, his left wrist and a bruise upon his kidney, I had inadvertently managed to bond all of the foreign matter to his blood. It was almost impossible not to.

I felt frustrated but tried not to dwell on my failure, taking the opportunity to scan his memories for something useful. I didn't find anything within the last several months that might be helpful. I disconnected and approached the next man, just as old and just as oily. His ki wasn't any better, either.

The same frustrating process ensued with my trying to heal his injuries without bonding his blood to anything foreign and failing miserably. Scanning his memories produced nothing, and I moved on.

This next one was young. He couldn't have been more than twenty-five, astonishing to have flown up the ranks in my father's army at such a young age. He looked upon me with some fascination, and I could read his emotions like an open book. He was clearly excited for this process to take place, and I knew why. Becoming a full kami was nothing to sneeze at. A life of immortality was a gift that few men would be willing to turn down given the opportunity. I worried what these men must have bargained in return.

My father wasn't one to grant favors, and the honor of becoming a full kami, no matter the method, was something no mortal had ever received. I wondered exactly how much blood and how many bondings would need to take place before their bodies were perfected. Once? Twice? I shuddered to think I would be continually called upon to help build an army of formidable immortals for my father. He alone was formidable enough.

I placed my hands on the young man's temples and closed my eyes. His ki was young and vibrant, but tainted. He had committed many despicable acts while climbing the ranks of my father's army. It explained much and fueled my desire to stop these bondings as best I could. Immortality in the hands of these monsters would no doubt lead to an eventual hell on earth that no human would ever wish to suffer through.

His shoulder was badly dislocated, which was easily remedied without my powers. I lifted my hands from his temple briefly and wrenched his shoulder back into place, smiling internally when I heard a loud pop and a stifled groan from my patient.

I would no doubt get an earful from the emperor with that stunt, but it prevented me from having to use my ki and inadvertently bonding the entities within his blood stream. I pondered over what to do about the broken ankle and decided to skip it for a minute and briefly skimmed through his memories, most of which were unpleasant. I hoped to never find myself alone with this young man.

As I reached the end of his memories, I picked up some information that so badly startled me that I nearly broke off my connection and went running out of the room, intent on finding Akane. They had discovered the rebels' main base of operation within an area of the woods that most never ventured into due to how dangerous the deeper parts of the forest were. Perhaps that was why the rebels chose it in the first place.

My father had finally uncovered the camp he'd been looking for.

I was going to have to warn Akane about this impending invasion of their camp as soon as circumstances allowed. First, I would need to fix this awful man's ankle without bonding my father's blood to his. I connected to his ki, deciding that the best way to get around the bonding was to simply break my connection with him the moment I gave his ki instructions.

I would have to be quick about it, but it could work. I inhaled deeply, preparing myself for the possibility of failure and then gave his ki the most basic instructions necessary for sealing the crack in his ankle. I mentally pulled back before his ki could communicate with me as to whether it understood or not.

Keeping my hands on his temples so as not to give anything away to my father, I tentatively reconnected, wanting to catch a quick glimpse of what had occurred, as if I were peeking through a small window into a dwelling that wasn't my own, hoping to avoid detection. The break had healed immediately, and the foreign entities still floated around aimlessly.

They hadn't bonded to the young man's blood cells. I ripped my mind away the minute I knew for certain. My hands lowered to my side, and I kept my focus on the matted floor beneath me, avoiding eye contact with the soldier.

"It is finished?" my father asked. His voice rang out hollow and cold after the dead silence that accompanied my healings.

"Yes." I waited, knowing I wasn't allowed to rise until given permission.

"Then leave us."

I rapidly complied, rising from my knees in one smooth motion, backing toward the door in a low bow and then turning and fairly running through it. I scurried toward my rooms with Yao and Chan shadowing closely behind me. I recognized that running through the halls and corridors of the palace with my guards in tow would look odd to any servants in the vicinity, but my worry overruled my reason.

Akane, Musubi, and all of the rebels were in danger. The attack on their main camp was scheduled for tonight.

I left my guards with strict instructions to guard my door and let no one in or out for the rest of the day. With my father's meeting concluded and Katsu not due back for a few more days, I felt there was little chance of anyone summoning me or demanding proof that I was indeed within the confines of my own rooms.

It was a necessary risk at this point. If for some reason I was discovered missing, I would take my punishment upon my return. I couldn't allow Akane and her men left unaware of the emperor's discovery.

Lives would be lost if I failed.

I slipped out of my window, grateful for the direction it faced and the lack of soldiers within the area. Sneaking out of the window in broad daylight was in no way ideal, but desperate times called for measures unthinkable, and climbing out of my window at this time of day was most definitely that.

Once I alighted on the grassy ground, I waited for any signs or sounds of patrols around the area, but after a few moments of silence I was able to skirt my way around the back toward the gardens. The opening to the forest and then subsequent road ahead resided toward the back of the garden.

The door was never guarded because no one knew about it except me. It was something I had crafted on my own for a truly grave emergency, and today was the first time I felt that such an emergency warranted its use.

Snaking my way along the hedges was easy enough. Hardly anyone ever entered these gardens unless accompanying me. I dodged behind hanging clusters of cherry blossoms and did my best to keep hidden as I finally weaved my way past the large pond, trees, abundant flowers, and statues. Once I reached the area I was looking for, I took a small pin from hair and pricked my finger, producing a few drops of blood.

I rubbed the blood along the large green leaves that covered the entire back wall. The leaves immediately responded to the energy within my blood by pulling in on themselves and separating from the rest of the wall, creating a small opening that I could squeeze through.

Kami blood was a powerful tool I used in communicating with all forms of intelligent life, including all plant life, and even though I was only half kami, my particular blood was recognized by the vegetation within this garden.

Once I passed through, I waited for the hedges and leaves to knit back together before turning my back on the palace and continuing on down the path toward the ruins. My first hope was that someone, either Akane, Musubi or possibly a member of the rebels, was stationed there—someone I might warn immediately.

It took me fifteen minutes on foot to reach the ruins, though I ran as fast as my legs would permit. Doubled over, I fought to catch my breath, all the while listening for any sound of approach from Akane or Musubi.

I breathed in deeply and searched the area, but knew it was useless. My lessons with Musubi weren't scheduled for another two hours, and there was no reason to suspect Akane would be here this time. She didn't always meet me before my lessons.

I stared past the ruins toward the shrine honoring the god of love and marriage, the Shinto temple rising up behind it and the forest eagerly waiting to swallow me within its depths.

There was nothing else to be done. I couldn't wait for Musubi to join me at the ruins. I was going to have to access those memories I'd stolen and navigate my way through the forest toward the insurgents' main base of operations.

And I was going to have to do it by myself.

T he forest of Yanbaru had never before bothered me, but this particular forest was different. The forest of Mimasaka was vast in depth and width, by far the largest part of the kingdom of Kagami, and host to several woodland animals both large and small.

There had also been rumors that unnatural, magical creatures existed within these woods, creatures that didn't take kindly to outside interference or unwanted trespassers.

The rebels had chosen wisely in their desire to remain hidden and undiscovered. Even seasoned soldiers balked at the idea of delving too far past the outer boundaries of the forest.

I didn't fear the legends and stories, but I did fear the large animals that I knew existed within these woods. It wouldn't do to be mistaken for unsuspecting prey. That would cut my noble escapade short. Another problem I faced had to do with the distance I needed to travel. There was simply no way of knowing if I would be able to navigate the forest with time to spare. If I had found a way to steal an imperial horse, this would have made my situation much easier, but I was going to have to travel through the forest on foot with no guarantee that the pathway before me would be clear. There was no guarantee I'd even find a path.

Squaring my shoulders, I headed toward the shrine. A flash of memory hit me, and I thought of the white cherry blossom Musubi had given me the first time I came here. Though I had avoided the area most of my life, my first memories of the shrine were some I would always treasure. I quickly made my way past the Holy Cherry Tree, and sprinted toward the temple, drawing my kimono up around my knees to avoid tripping over the hemline. I rounded the front and headed to the right, rushing into the forest before I had a chance to change my mind. The canopy of trees was like a thick blanket covering the sky, shutting out most of the light, and leaving the leafy forest bed shaded and chilled.

I kept running, determined to move as fast as possible, hoping to rely on my body's ability to heal itself in order to replenish and rejuvenate my cramping muscles as my journey progressed. I continued to use the memories I'd obtained like an internal beacon. Whenever my direction went off the correct path, my mind would send new images to guide me back to where I needed to be.

The terrain was rocky at best and nigh impossible to cover when tree roots and foliage became the only thing covering the forest floor. It was necessary for me to slow my pace and watch my footing to avoid tripping and spraining an ankle. It would have healed to be sure, but every second would make a difference between arriving at the camp in time or arriving amidst a bloody battle.

After tripping over my own clothing for the millionth time, I finally decided I'd had enough and stopped long enough to struggle out of it, throwing it to the forest floor and hurrying forward, clad in nothing but my black, form-fitting undergarments.

It was amazing the difference that made.

Within an hour of traversing the forest with only the young soldier's memories for guidance I came upon a wide, thunderous river. I stopped short as I reached the ledge of the embankment and looked down upon the thrashing rapids twenty feet below.

I felt overwhelmed by this new development. I hadn't realized I would be expected to cross a body of water, but the directions gave every indication that I needed to continue forward rather than skirting around to try and find a narrower place to cross.

I decided to go down river for a few yards first. I had no way of knowing if the waters would grow calmer, but I was hopeful that might be the case. Swimming across the frothy, turbulent current would have been foolish and suicidal, and I had no way of climbing down the embankment unless it eventually leveled out downstream. As I continued along the bank, I spotted what looked to be a rope bridge attached to the round base of a tree on my side of the river, which then crossed over, connecting to another tree on the other side.

Upon closer inspection, I noted the rope itself looked fairly reliable, but the wooden planks weaved into the flooring of the bridge were warped and cracked. If this was a bridge used for traveling, it had certainly seen better days. I hesitated for a moment, fearing the consequences if the wood proved to be as unreliable as it looked, but in the end I knew I had to cross. Lives depended upon my arrival, and I couldn't remain on this side of the river, trapped by fear and uncertainty.

A decision had to be made.

I firmly grabbed both sides of the rope bridge and tentatively stepped onto the wooden planks. The bridge bobbed and dipped slightly as it compensated for my additional weight, but after a moment it straightened out and held firm with only a slight groan. I let out the breath I hadn't realized I'd been holding and slid my right foot forward. After a moment I shifted my weight forward upon it and lifted my left foot in the air, freezing as the bridge slightly swayed. The groaning noise came again, but I had to admit the bridge was quite sturdy despite its shabby appearance.

I began stepping forward with a bit more confidence, gradually increasing my speed with each board that supported my weight. Before long, I had traveled more than halfway across the bridge and felt certain I would reach my destination in time. I'd managed a few more confident steps when I heard a strange snapping sound to my right. I looked to one of the ropes attached to the plank of wood I was standing upon and noticed that several threads appeared to have unraveled.

Before my brain could latch on to the precariousness of my situation, the supporting rope snapped and the plank beneath me gave way. I felt myself abruptly drop through the bridge's underbelly, and only managed to prevent myself from catapulting into the tumultuous river below by grasping the wooden boards in front of me. With the lower half of my body dangling off the bridge and my arms gripping the small crevices between the planks, I wasn't sure how I would manage to pull myself up.

I took two deep, steadying breaths and then used what little upper body strength I possessed to pull myself further up and forward, but the minute I strained forward I heard another loud crack and then a snap. I looked to my right and saw that the board I clung to was beginning to fold under my weight. Freezing in place, I waited to see if it would hold and then tried to reach my left arm forward to grab the next plank ahead. The minute I shifted my weight I heard another sickening crack and felt the plank I was clinging to drop an inch or so as the supporting rope snapped almost completely in half.

This could not be happening! How was I to rescue an army full of rebels if I couldn't even manage to save myself from this rickety bridge?

Amidst the roaring of the water and my own heartbeat pounding within my skull, I thought I heard someone calling my name. I squinted my eyes and looked to my left, across to the other side. There, standing on the riverbank, looking just as handsome and wonderful as ever stood Musubi with an awful, panicked expression on his face.

I didn't know how he had found me or what had brought him to this particular place, but I wasn't about to waste time asking. I saw him cup his hands around his mouth and then his strong, comforting voice floated over to me.

"Mikomi, do not attempt to move again. You will only make your situation worse. I will come to you."

I might have acknowledged his words with a nod of my head, but even that movement could have sent me toppling the rest of the way down. I didn't fear the river, I was an excellent swimmer, but I did fear drowning. It had happened more than once when I was younger, and though my ki quickly and efficiently expelled any water that my lungs inhaled, the process was painfully frightening. My father had used it against me several times as a child.

I felt the bridge sway a little as Musubi placed his feet on either side of the ropes, avoiding the planks altogether and walking along the cords weaved through the sides. That course of action would have been a wiser method for me to have employed, but how was I to know the boards would be so treacherous? My mission to save an army wasn't exactly foolproof.

My anxiety and fear lessened as Musubi closed the distance between us. Once he was towering above me, he bent his head forward and reached for me.

"Give me your hand, and I will pull you to safety. Just try not to jerk as you do so." I slowly raised my hand and felt his warmth surround me as he pulled me up through the broken planks and into his arms.

I wrapped my arms around his neck as he pulled me closer to him. His breath warmed the side of my face as I felt him place a small kiss there. The contact was surprising, but I was too relieved to be in his arms, and more than grateful for the excuse to remain so close to him.

"Thank the gods. I must have aged a thousand years when I spotted you on this damnable contraption. And then to watch you fall before I could get to you and warn you."

His arms held me tighter as I felt him shudder. I buried my face in his chest, reveling in his closeness. Honestly, I would have fallen through a thousand bridges to procure this kind of response from him.

"Yes, if I had plummeted to my death you would have been made a widower without ever having truly been married."

Musubi barked a short laugh, one filled with relief. He placed a light kiss on the tip of my nose and then rested his forehead against mine. "I'm just glad I reached you in time. If I hadn't come when I did…"

He broke off and looked at me as if he'd had some kind of epiphany. The stormy blue of his eyes became filled with such a strong look of yearning, I felt myself leaning forward, completely ensnared by the power of his desire. His heated gaze held mine for what seemed like an eternity, and then a loud snap quickly brought us back to the present.

Musubi blinked twice and then seemed to get his bearings. "I may have rescued you from your fall, but we must still travel across the rest of this bridge. Wrap your legs around my waist, and I will take you back in the direction you came from."

I nodded and did what I was told. Squeezing my eyes shut, I took comfort in the warmth and strength of his body as he carefully negotiated his way across the other half of the bridge.

"Going for a stroll, were we?"

"Not exactly." I lowered my feet to the grassy bank, lifted my head, and pulled back a little in order to see his face. His eyes were bright with amusement, and the corners of his mouth turned up, ready to deliver a smile I was sure I would never recover from. "How on earth did you find me?"

"I was on my way to meet you for our training session. Was this some desperate attempt to get out of it?" He gave me a smirk. "Nearly getting yourself killed hardly seems reasonable when all you really had to do was let me know you were ready to quit."

My eyes narrowed. "Of course I wasn't going to quit. Stop looking so hopeful."

He laughed as his smoldering eyes continued their hypnotic hold on me, pulling us closer until I was sure he was finally going to kiss me. I could sense him struggling with his emotions, wanting to hold me, to touch me, but fighting some inner turmoil that had no name, no face, and no way for me to push against it.

His eyes hardened, and his emotions were suddenly blocked

from me as he released me, stepping back and crossing his arms over his chest almost as if he were using them as a shield to lock his heart and feelings in place. His face stiffened for a moment, and then he looked angry. I felt wholly confused by the change in him.

"Would you mind telling me why you are out here, traipsing about by yourself in such a dangerous part of the forest?"

"*This* is the most dangerous part of the forest?"

"If you're in it, then yes! You can't possibly think that any part of this forest is safe for a young, unaccompanied woman. Why on earth are you this far in to begin with?"

And just like that my purpose, my entire rescue mission, came crashing down around me. I'd been so caught up with Musubi and the fact that my near death had dislodged that hardened wall about his heart that I had completely forgotten my reason for being out here in the first place.

"I came to warn you and Akane. The emperor knows the location of your main camp. His troops are planning an attack this evening."

Musubi's eyes widened, and he shook his head. "Impossible! None of our people would ever share such information. How in the world could the emperor have found out our location, and how would you have gleaned this knowledge?" He eyed me suspiciously.

I realized I hadn't thought this whole scenario through. It would look terribly suspicious for a woman, even a wealthy one, to know the emperor's military secrets. I scrambled fast for something plausible to tell him.

"I...I...am sometimes summoned to the palace to treat his servants and wounded soldiers. It is another reason why Akane wished for my help. She was aware that I would have access to this type of information."

With every word I spoke, Musubi's face grew darker and his body more rigid. "Unbelievable. I cannot fathom how you or Akane could be so stupid as to put yourself in such a dangerous and precarious situation."

"I can take care of myself," I stated stiffly.

"You can barely cross a rope bridge without falling to your death," he shouted. "How do you expect me to believe that you are capable of retrieving highly classified information from the most powerful kami in this empire without being caught, tortured, and killed?"

"I'm here, aren't I?" I shouted back. I advanced toward him, refusing to allow him to put more distance between us. "I'm standing right here, with information that will save hundreds if not thousands of men. Do not, for one second, label me as incapable just because I was unaware that a perfectly sound looking bridge had faulty flooring."

"You are too involved," he shot back. "It is bad enough that you heal men considered seditious traitors to the empire, but you're learning to fight as if you think you will ever see battle, and you're actually spending time with the emperor and his soldiers. You are at the heart of this conflict." He grabbed me by the shoulders and shook me hard. "Can't you see there is a chance you won't survive it?"

The tormented look in his eyes made me feel as if he was already emotionally preparing himself to lose me. Which was ridiculous. He didn't even consider me his.

Did he?

I raised my hand and let my fingers softly trace the slight curve of his cheekbone. He drew in a sharp breath, but he didn't pull away, and he didn't let me go.

"I know this is dangerous," I said. "I know there is a chance I could be caught, I could be tortured, or I could be killed." Musubi shook his head at that, readying himself to say something, but I placed a finger to his lips and held it there. "I know a number of things could go wrong, and the outcome could be fatal, but Musubi, a number of things have already gone right, and many people have already been saved." I could feel my voice rise with the power and intensity of my own words. "The emperor is corrupt, drunk with his own power and greed. He cares nothing for his people, for this empire or even for his own family, and though this may be a losing battle, one that has no hope of ever ending in our favor, it is a battle I am willing to fight. So long as I have two hands for healing, two feet for moving and this heart continually beating, I will not stop fighting until Emperor Fukurokuju is no longer capable of hurting anyone ever again."

I hadn't realized my finger was still resting lightly against his lips until I felt them, warm and gentle, as he kissed my finger and then the inside of my wrist. He guided my hand, palm open against his cheek and covered it with his own.

His eyes seemed to devour me with their intensity, and I felt heat suffuse my entire body.

"I can see there's no talking you out of this, so I will continue to train you, and I will continue to protect you. But I warn you, Mikomi, the minute I become aware that your life may be in danger, I will take you away from here and never allow you to return."

"Ridiculous! You would have to remain with me always in order to make good on that particular threat."

His eyes narrowed, but his lips held a hint of a smile. "I can't think of any better way to pass the time than in your company, Mikomi, especially if it means forever." He kissed the inside of my wrist again, and then turned around and headed for the bridge.

My heart soared at his words, but I had to remind myself that he was most likely teasing me again.

"Where are you going?"

He turned back. "I'm assuming you would like for me to go warn everyone at the camp before they're all slaughtered? Otherwise, you're traveling into the woods and nearly falling through a dilapidated rope bridge to your death will be all for naught, and quite anticlimactic, I might add."

I placed my hands on my hips and narrowed my eyes at him. "You had better not take all the credit for this rescue, Musubi. When it comes to glory, men can be quite stingy."

He chuckled softly. "I trust you will make it home without

incident?"

"I think I can manage." By the gods, it wasn't as if I was completely helpless. I tried to keep the indignation from my voice but knew I had failed when his laughter carried across the distance between us. I couldn't help but feel fortified by it.

"Then I will see you tomorrow, little healer, and don't think for one second I'll be going easy on you. I don't care how adorable you look with a fake sword in your hand."

I crossed my arms and glared at him, feigning displeasure, when really his delightful teasing warmed me to my very soul. He laughed one more time, gave me a wink and then nimbly crossed the rope bridge within seconds, disappearing around a bend in the river. I felt cold and empty once he was gone.

15

I t had only taken a few hours to return to the palace, and by that time night had fallen. Sneaking into my room proved to be a much easier task. I had just climbed through the window when I heard a loud commotion at the door.

"The princess wishes to be left alone for the remainder of the evening," I heard Yao declare.

"I don't care what the princess wishes," Aiko fairly yelled. "You'll allow me in there this minute before her father comes to summon her himself."

Oh, no! What could my father want at such a late hour? Shouldn't he be sitting in his rooms, waiting for word about the attack on the rebels' camp? I grabbed a thin robe from my closet and wrapped it around my quaking form, and then ran to my door, opening it before Aiko could cause a scene.

The minute I did so, both Yao and Chan gave me glances filled with relief. I nodded to them, hoping my look would convey the success of my mission. I then turned my attention to my maid.

"Aiko, what is going on?"

"Your father's guards found me on my way to your rooms and informed me that the emperor needs to see you immediately. It seemed serious, and I don't want you to suffer another..." she broke off, clearing her throat and then glared at Yao and Chan. "I would not wish your father to become displeased with you."

"All right. Allow me to get dressed, and I will be there as quickly as I can." I was loath to perform another healing for any of his men, and wasn't sure I would have enough energy to avoid bonding any more kami blood due to my own physical exhaustion. I didn't want to consider the possibility that I might be summoned for another interrogation, but with Katsu gone, my father was free to do as he pleased again without any interference.

I only hoped once I arrived at his study, I would be able to do whatever needed doing as quickly as possible.

∞∞∞∞

I bowed from the waist the moment my father entered the room.

"We've no time for that, Daughter. I have an urgent matter that must be attended to immediately."

My heart sank so low I thought it might never rise again. I followed my father out of the room, but instead of heading to the lower level of the palace where his interrogations usually took place, he led me up to a higher level and, to my surprise, straight to my mother's quarters. I followed him through her guarded doors and stopped just inside. I had rarely been allowed to visit my mother's rooms, and I felt extremely uncomfortable. My father walked over to the bed where my mother lay and knelt down next to her.

"I told you this cannot be allowed to happen," my mother said, speaking to my father. She then began to cough roughly and covered her mouth with a white cloth. Her breathing sounded wet, heavy, and labored. I knew she had been suffering with a cough several weeks ago, but this was much more serious. Her condition had gone unchecked.

My father had never been a very attentive husband, so his concern in this matter was most peculiar.

"And I told you that this empire cannot function without the symbol of an empress here at my side. We are already experiencing too much trouble with the rebels. If anything untoward should happen to you, I will have a full revolution on my hands. You know the people love you and hate me."

"Who do you think is to blame for that?" my mother hissed and then coughed into her cloth again. When she pulled it back, blood was soaking through the cloth. Now I felt concern.

"You will allow our daughter to heal you. I will broach no argument on the subject."

"She is not supposed to use her powers to heal anyone but herself. Don't think I am not aware of your abuse where her gift is concerned. You use her to carry out your dirty work while I have done nothing but sacrifice to make certain she fulfills her destiny. I will not allow her to waste her talent on me, simply because my healing will benefit your position as emperor."

Her coughing began again and became so severe I was sure her lungs would expire. I wanted to help her. Of course I did, she was my mother, but I had no wish to sit next to her and feel her hateful eyes upon me, knowing that every moment I healed her was a moment she would spend despising me with all her heart.

"You will allow this, Chinatsu. I command it. She is in no danger of losing her ability to fulfill her destiny."

I remained where I was as I listened to my parents argue back and forth. The only thing interrupting them was my mother's terrible coughing fits. They were people I had spent my life obeying without question. To have them contradicting one another's orders left me feeling torn and somewhat indecisive, but in the end I would do exactly as my father requested, for I knew what the consequences would be if I didn't.

"This is ridiculous. We are wasting time." My father beckoned me forward. "Mikomi, you will heal your mother, and you will disregard any comments she might make to the contrary," he bellowed.

My mother glared at him. I had to admire her bravery. I was so frightened of him when his anger reached this level, but she sat there sick and weak, fighting him with what little energy she had left.

"Perhaps once I have healed her, you might consider allowing her ascension to take place in order to avoid any more of these illnesses?" My suggestion was soft and tentative, but one hopeful look from my mother made me realize how long she had been waiting for such an event to take place.

I was suddenly enraged that my father had never made good on his promise. This whole situation never would have occurred in the first place if he had been willing to help her ascend as a full kami immediately after giving birth to me, instead of using that promise as leverage to keep her in line.

"Fine," he said in a gruff voice.

My eyebrows rose at that, surprised that he wouldn't even argue the point or berate me for speaking without permission. The severity of my mother's condition must have escalated to a dangerous level indeed.

"Mother, if you would permit," I said, tentatively reaching out toward her head. She slapped my hands away.

"Don't you dare touch me," she hissed.

"You will allow this, Chinatsu, or so help me I will beat you unconscious with my bare hands," he threatened.

The anger my mother felt was beginning to overwhelm me. I needed some distance from her to avoid absorbing any more of her emotions, but I didn't dare move from my spot, knowing full well my father's anger would be waiting for me.

When she stayed silent, I raised my hands again and placed them on either side of her head. I couldn't connect to her at first. She desperately fought me, despite my father's threats—threats I knew he would make good on. I continued to push through whatever block she had placed in front of me, and eventually I connected with her ki, but by the time I did so, I was fairly worn out. I had never endured such a difficult connection with anyone else. Moving aside my mother's icy will was as insurmountable as moving a boulder with my mind.

There was something about my connection with her that felt wrong. I realized I'd only managed to penetrate part of her ki; her own mind had closed up completely. I let it go for now but knew once I ascertained what was happening within her body, I would need to push through whatever mental walls she had put up against me.

I could feel most of her pain, but her anger was terribly distracting. I knew how little she cared for me, but I didn't want to feel it, not like this. Not ever. Forcing myself to focus, I searched for the source of her illness. Her lungs were filled with some kind of infection, but I had never healed anyone with an infection like this and couldn't identify it. All I really knew was the pain I felt in her chest, and her temperature was dangerously high. The infection was the cause and needed to be dealt with, but without full access to her ki, her indomitable spirit wouldn't allow it.

I suddenly heard a loud hacking sound and realized my mother was having another coughing fit, forcing her to let down her guard. I seized my moment and connected to her fully. I wasn't prepared for the next wall I encountered once I started giving instructions. My mind beat soundly against a door of impenetrable, cold glass.

The veil! I found myself struggling against the veil. I was so shocked by this that I lost my connection and opened my eyes.

"Well? How soon can we expect a full recovery?" my father asked.

I stared at my mother. Her eyes were shooting daggers at me, and I could only stare. She was going to die. My mother couldn't recover from this.

"Mikomi, you will answer me or—"

"She won't recover," I said softly.

"What was that?"

"I can't heal her. The veil won't permit it. She's meant to die."

The silence that came after felt heavy, dark, and threatening. I'd never witnessed my mother show any fear, and even now, this news did nothing to change her demeanor or her attitude toward me, but I could sense real fear emanating from my father. Without my mother to keep his subjects at bay, there was nothing to prevent them from joining the rebels.

"I gave you an order, child, and you *will* obey me."

"I wish I could, but I can't. The veil is present when I connect with her ki. She is not meant to survive this disease."

I felt a kind of numbness engulf me as I said it. I loved my mother, or at least the idea of her. She'd given birth to me, but that was all I could give her credit for. In the end, we were perfect strangers, and I think I hated her for that. I didn't want her to die, but even if I could have saved her, she would have resented me for it.

My father didn't hesitate to handle the situation the way he handled everything else. I felt his hand clamp down upon the back of my neck while his fingers dug into my skin. My back and neck stiffened automatically, but I knew better than to try and fight him off.

"The veil is not my problem, it is yours, and if you don't find a way to get around it, I will have your tutor, Kenji, executed right before your eyes."

He shoved my head forward and stepped back. My father always followed through with his threats. If I didn't find a way to save my mother, then Kenji would be dead within minutes.

I quickly grabbed my mother's head despite her weak protests and forced a connection. My panic must have been all consuming because my mother's resistance was batted away within seconds. I hit the veil again and mentally searched for a way around it. I could find no weaknesses, no holes or thin spots that might break under the mental tension I threw at it. My efforts became less controlled and more frantic when I thought about what the result would be if I failed.

I shoved my mother's ki to the foreground and communicated with the veil directly. My father got whatever he wanted through brute force and intimidation. I didn't like his methods, but I was willing to give anything a try. Instead of finding a way around the veil, I was going to have to push through it. I started by pressing my mind against the glass wall, and then I continued to add more pressure. I wasn't going to stop pushing or shoving until I broke through, no matter the outcome.

I wasn't sure how long I was at it before I felt a small give in the glass wall, but I took advantage, even though sweat trickled down my face and my body shook uncontrollably. The wall became more pliable as if it were melting under the force of my determination. I gave one more desperate push and exploded through. I felt my body jolt at the pressure being released, but I didn't have time to analyze it. Instead, I immediately began instructing the tiny intelligences that made up her lungs to fight the infection and eliminate it completely.

I watched as the infection in her lungs began to die off and disappear, slowly at first and then more rapidly as more of the intelligences within her lungs responded to my instructions. The scarring on her lungs began to heal, and any residual blood was absorbed and restored to its rightful place within the body.

My mother's body temperature dropped to its normal level, and her chest pain vanished. I wanted to disconnect and pull away from her, but I no longer had control over my own body due to how badly it was shaking.

I thought I heard yelling and a loud scream, but anything happening outside was muffled and too distant for me to follow. Suddenly, my connection with my mother was severed, and someone roughly jerked me backward.

I opened my eyes and saw Katsu's stormy face staring back at me. I wondered why he had returned when he wasn't due back for a few more days.

"You cannot stop this, Katsu. I forbid it," my father yelled.

Katsu stood to his full height, towering over my father in the process.

"You have to be the most ignorant kami our First Parents ever created. Have you learned nothing about the veil and the consequences for breaching it? Do you truly value power over your own daughter's life? Do you have any idea what you could have done?" Katsu was yelling. I had never before seen him so angry. "You cannot ask this of Mikomi. If someone is meant to die then that is final. Forcing a healing like that is dangerous and could have caused serious damage. Her body was already rejecting the process when I arrived."

I felt something wet dripping on my hand. I glanced down. Red drops of blood smacked my skin and spread on contact. I lifted a hand to my nose and felt warm liquid dripping down my fingers. Then the warm liquid began to drip from my eyes and my world turned red. I could hardly find my voice to bring it to the attention of those present, but I didn't feel the need to panic either.

"Katsu," I whispered, but he didn't hear me.

"If she had managed to break through the veil, if she had even managed to get close to weakening it, the damage to her brain would have been immeasurable."

Interesting. Maybe that was why droplets of blood from my nose and eyes had turned into a slow, steady stream.

"Fortunately for all of us, it is virtually impossible to break through the veil."

I had to laugh at that, although I wasn't sure why I found it so funny.

"I'm afraid that's not entirely true," I stated in a loud voice. "Not only was I able to break through the veil, but mother's illness has healed completely."

I heard Katsu gasp and my mother scream.

Chaos ensued, with my father barking orders about finding a physician. I thought that amusing since the only competent physician in the palace was me. My mother's screams were frantic, begging for my father to heal me, something I found to be equally humorous. I couldn't think of a being less qualified to mend or heal anyone.

It was impossible to see what was happening due to the blood seeping out of my eyes, but my hearing wasn't affected at all, which made all of the yelling and screaming amplify the pounding pain within my skull.

I felt feminine arms wrap around me, and my mother whispered something unintelligible as she rocked me in her arms. All this time I wanted her to show me some kind of affection, and it took my imminent death to achieve that kind of milestone.

"Quiet," Katsu roared.

I felt him place hands on either side of my head and then sensed his presence within my mind, but the pain didn't allow me to focus for much longer, and a strange, insistent blackness began pulling me away from him.

I fought it at first. The darkness scared me, and I wanted to take advantage of the nurturing contact I was receiving from my mother. I wasn't able to put up much of a fight, and once the darkness touched me, I felt peaceful and weightless. The pain existed, but felt deadened somehow, and I found myself wanting to accept the darkness.

Eventually, I gave in and let go, sleeping under a curtain of endless night.

"When will she wake up?" I heard Saigo ask.

"I'm really not sure," Katsu responded in frustration. "The damage she sustained when she broke through the veil was extensive. I can't believe she managed to accomplish something so mentally demanding without dying immediately afterward. Even now, I'm not sure that I healed all of the damage her mind sustained."

If he was trying to comfort my brother, he was making a huge mess of things.

"I tried reasoning with the emperor, Katsu. I even tried to prevent her from connecting with me, but he threatened Kenji's life, knowing her attachment to him to be a weakness for her. Foolish girl."

I wanted to return to my own personal oblivion after hearing my mother's criticism. I'd saved her life, but she didn't care. I realized nothing I did, short of becoming The Healer, would ever be enough for her.

"It isn't your fault, Highness. It isn't Mikomi's fault, either.

She had no idea what the repercussions would be if she actually succeeded. She only knew what they would be if she failed, and as I understand it, Kenji is considered a valued member of the family."

"That he is," Saigo said. "If I had been in her position, I would have behaved in the exact same way, foolish or not."

I knew I could always count on my brother to defend me.

"Where is the emperor now?" my mother asked.

"I believe he is in a meeting with some of his generals. He actually had the nerve to demand that Mikomi be brought to his quarters once she had awakened. If he thinks I'll allow him near my betrothed again, he's insane."

A soft giggle escaped my mouth as I managed to open my eyes a crack. "Don't let my father hear you accusing him of insanity. He'll throw you into the nearest dungeon." My giggling returned, and I found that I couldn't stop. It must have been contagious because Saigo joined in and attacked me on the bed where I lay immobile.

"I knew you would be all right, sister. You have too much spunk to let little things like fatal injuries prevent you from bouncing back." He kissed the top of my forehead, and I smiled. I could only make out his outline. Everything else was a bit fuzzy.

"Thank the gods." I heard Katsu say under his breath. I heard him slide whatever he was sitting on closer to the side of my bed. He gripped one of my hands in his. "I don't know what I would have done if the damage to your mind had been irreversible."

I managed to turn my head in his direction and forced my eyes open a little wider, but everything still remained fuzzy.

"Is my mother well?" I asked.

"Of course I am, you silly girl." I sensed her approach my bed, but she stopped just before she reached it. I released Katsu's hand and lifted it toward her. I guessed I was hoping that somehow her feelings toward me had changed. She hesitated for a second, then patted my shoulder stiffly and turned away.

"She'll make a full recovery, and that's all that matters," she flung over her shoulder as she left my room.

Not many things were capable of crushing me so completely, but at that moment, as my mother walked away from me, I felt a piece of my heart shrivel and break.

"Yes, I suppose The Healer is all that matters," I mumbled.

"Don't let it hurt you, Mikomi," Saigo said, attempting to console me. "You know Mother has never been one to show affection."

I stayed mute, deciding now was neither the time nor the place to share with him our mother's previous remarks about her feelings toward me. I certainly wasn't going to discuss it in front of Katsu.

"How do you feel?" the warrior god asked. He reached for the hand my mother had refused and tightly grasped it. I squeezed his hand and felt grateful that he was at least showing some concern, even if it was only meant for The Healer.

"I'm feeling much better, thank you." I turned my head to try and look at him and managed to pry open my eyes a little more. His face was coming into focus, but the edges were deformed and fuzzy. I heard his sharp intake of breath as he looked at me.

"Mikomi, the whites of your eyes are completely red. Do you feel any pain?" He was trying to remain calm, but I could tell he was worried.

"Her eyes are red?" Saigo turned my face to look at me and grimaced. "Does it hurt?"

"Not really." I wondered why everything else within me had healed. "I'm having trouble seeing as sharply as I once did, but I'm sure my body will correct itself, now that I am feeling better."

"Yes, let's hope that is true."

"How long have I been unconscious?"

"Three days," Katsu said.

I went from a prone position to sitting straight up. "Three days? I have never been sick that long. Why would my body have taken so much time to heal?"

Katsu placed his hands on my shoulders and guided me back down. "I am happy to answer your questions, but I want you resting while I do so. You had a very close call, and I'm not entirely certain that you are completely recovered, especially with how your eyes look. There seems to be some residual damage."

"What happened to me exactly?"

"You injured yourself by attacking the veil. There are laws in death just as there are in life, and when the natural order of the Universe is tampered with, fatal consequences are usually the result. If I hadn't come when I did…if I hadn't been able to stop the bleeding within your brain…" Katsu took a deep, calming breath and grasped my hand again, bringing it to his lips and placing a soft kiss there. "I'm just not sure what I would have done."

I was astounded. I knew it was possible for kami to use a small amount of power to heal someone, but I had never thought that Katsu would do something like that for me.

"You healed me? You sacrificed some of your power for me?"

"Of course I did, Mikomi. You're The Healer. Did you really think I would just stand back and watch you die?"

At first I had been overwhelmed with emotion to think that Katsu would risk his immortality to heal me. That he might care that much for me, but my heart sank at his explanation. Of course, he would do everything he could to save The Healer. It was his duty and his destiny to share a life with me, whether he wanted to or not, and Katsu, above all else, was a kami sworn to fulfill his destiny. I had to wonder if my title as The Healer made it impossible for anyone to really love me.

I knew my brother loved me and Kenji loved me, but that was familial affection, not the kind of love between couples that, if strong enough, could join them in a way no other love was capable of. Would I ever experience that for myself, or would a union with Katsu always be about duty, honor and fulfilling one's destiny?

I wanted to cry, but I didn't want to do it in front of my betrothed. I didn't want him to think me ungrateful regardless of his motives for saving me.

"Perhaps, I could be left alone to rest. I think if I sleep just a little more, I will recover completely."

Katsu and Saigo agreed it was a good idea. The warrior god left my room first, giving the back of my hand a light kiss before leaving. He no doubt felt it his duty to show some signs of affection. I didn't even know how to interpret his behavior toward me. I never had.

Once Katsu left the room, Saigo turned to me.

"I realize that you are tired from your ordeal, but you must be informed. One of the guards had a message for you from Akane, and when he discovered that you were ill, he gave the message to Kenji. I have it here."

I couldn't imagine all the things I had missed if I had truly been unconscious for the last three days. That meant I'd missed three trainings with Musubi, three chances to see him and be near him. Now I really wanted to cry.

"I'm surprised Akane has not received any knowledge of my condition. She usually knows the goings on within the palace better than anyone."

"Your condition has been kept very quiet. Katsu worried that people within the empire would panic if the severity of your injuries were known."

Yes, Katsu seemed to have a handle on everything, although I couldn't fault him for his cold, hard logic. "Would you read the message to me, Saigo? My eyes are still having problems focusing."

He nodded and pulled out a small piece of parchment paper, reading it aloud. "Meeting tomorrow evening. Same place as always. Burn immediately."

"When was the message delivered?"

"This morning. It will be dusk within the hour."

"Saigo, I have to find a way to get to that meeting, but I doubt very highly that Kenji will be able to impress upon Katsu the importance of my educational outings considering I almost died."

"Yes, I doubt Kenji would even consider it himself. He's been very worried about you."

My heart warmed at that, but the problem still remained. If Akane needed me, then there was no help for it. I would do all that I could to make it to that meeting. A small grin spread across my face as an idea took root.

"Saigo, how do you feel about pretending to be me tomorrow evening?"

My brother grinned widely.

"I honestly can't think of anything more exciting than dressing up in one of your kimonos and hair wigs."

I slapped his arm as he moved into a feminine stance.

"Honestly, you think I'd allow you to actually walk around impersonating me? I'm supposed to be in bed. I want you to be my body. Just lie in this bed with one of my hair wigs covering your head and keep your back turned to the door."

"Sounds easy enough. What happens if your maid, Aiko, comes in?"

I pondered that for a moment.

"I will instruct the guards to allow no one in my rooms for the rest of the evening."

"That could work, but it also means you will have to go to your meeting unaccompanied. Are you sure you will manage?"

I nodded. "Granted, I'm no samurai expert, but I've learned some very valuable exercises that will help me defend myself. I should be just fine, Saigo."

He looked worried, but I could tell the idea of helping me sneak out was an exciting one.

"How will you leave the palace?"

"The same way Akane did the first night we met her. Out my window."

"You'll be able to descend from the roof without any problems?"

"I've managed it before."

"Just make sure you are back before the following morning, sister. I'm not certain how Katsu will react if he finds you gone and me snoozing in your bed, but I would rather not find out."

"Agreed. We shall both be careful." I leaned back against my pillows, feeling exhaustion descend. "I've slept for three days straight, and yet I feel as if I could sleep even longer still."

"Then you most likely should. You may not be used to the same kind of fatigue we mere mortals suffer from, but I have found it is always wise to listen to one's body."

I gave Saigo a rueful smile. "You're only half mortal."

"And still it does me little good." He gave me a rueful smile in return. "It is late afternoon and will be dark within a few hours. Get some rest, sweet sister, and we will plot and plan your rendezvous with Akane later."

I watched as Saigo exited my rooms, and then let out a heavy sigh. I couldn't afford to allow my breaching of the veil or its awful consequences to affect my health for long. I was still a spy for the rebels, and learning to protect and defend myself was important. I shifted in my bed, and a sharp stabbing pain shot through my arm.

I withdrew it from underneath my silken bed sheet and stared in shock at the small cut within the crook of my arm. It looked as if it had scabbed over at one point, but my movements had ripped the cut open and blood dribbled slowly down my arm.

I couldn't quite grasp what was happening. Never in my life had I ever had such a minuscule cut remain on my person. Incisions like these healed within seconds, but it was clear my ki had struggled to heal something as simple as this.

More disturbing was wondering how on earth I had received such a cut. Had it occurred when I was delivered to my room? I grabbed a small cloth from my nightstand and placed it within the crook of my arm, staunching the small amount of blood flow and applying pressure. The movements had taken their toll and weakened me, another worrisome development. Since when did simple, everyday movements make me feel as if I'd just sprinted for several miles? I ignored the stinging pain in my arm and closed my eyes, allowing blessed oblivion to claim me for just a little while longer.

16

I could feel the sunlight, warm and inviting, seeping through the cracks between the shutters of my window as I slowly began to awaken from a fitful night's sleep. I didn't want consciousness to take me, considering the wonderful dream I'd had involving Musubi.

I could have lain in bed with my eyes closed for hours thinking about the way it felt when he touched me. I could have slept and wondered at the sadness he held trapped within his heart, a sadness that needed my help for release, but I soon became aware of another presence in my bedroom.

I opened my eyes and turned my head to the right, surprised to see Katsu sitting on the floor next to my bed, anxiously looking at me.

He reached for my hand when our eyes connected and let out a shaky breath. I sensed his emotional turmoil, but he reined it in quickly before I had time to fully understand the source.

I sat up, fearful that something terrible had happened. "Katsu, what is troubling you? Are you well?"

He pulled my hand to his cheek and placed it there for a moment. "I am well, Princess. I have been worried about you ever since you sustained the injury to your brain. I gave up the fight to sleep and came in here to sit by you and make certain you were well."

"You've been here long then?"

"No, just a few hours. I just...I needed to reassure myself that you were still breathing."

He let go of my hand, but I kept it against his cheek, running my thumb along his brow and cheekbone, touched that he would have been concerned enough about my well-being to sit beside me and watch over me.

I marveled at this caring compassionate side coming through. He was abrupt and indifferent with me in public, but in private he tended to disarm me with his behavior. He let out a soft gasp as I ran my fingers through his jet-black hair, and I nearly pulled my hand away, wondering if perhaps I had been too forward. His emotions stayed locked away, not allowing me to know exactly what he was feeling.

"As you can see, I am still breathing, and everything about me is functioning properly." I held my hands out to either side to emphasize my point. Katsu rose to his knees, bringing himself eye level with me.

"Everything is not okay, Mikomi. Your eyes are still red. Your body should have corrected this by now. I am worried that not only was there damage to your mind, but to your ki as well."

I considered his idea and thought it probable. If my eyes were still suffering from breaching the veil, then there was something very wrong indeed, and there was also that mysterious cut to consider.

"Is there anything that can be done to discover the extent of the damage? Any way to repair it?"

Katsu inched his face closer to mine. "There is, but it will involve crossing certain personal boundaries. It might make you feel..." he searched for the right word, "...uncomfortable. Do you mind if I connect to your ki?"

I couldn't understand why Katsu would feel this to be a shocking personal boundary to cross. "Katsu, you connected to my ki a few days ago to save my life. Why would this make me feel uncomfortable?"

He lowered his eyes, looking a bit uncomfortable himself. Then he raised them and gave me a look longingly desperate. I thought I saw fear and uncertainty cross his features, but then he grew determined, as if he had just made an important decision. "You might feel uneasy with the way I have to connect with your ki."

Now I was curious, but I also felt a bit impatient, trying to draw Katsu out and discover his thoughts and feelings depleted what little energy I still possessed.

"You are an honorable kami, and I trust that you will handle my ki with as much care as you took in saving my life. Please do what you think is best and connect with me anyway you must."

The corner of his mouth turned up into a grateful half smile. "As you wish, Princess." He placed both his hands on either side of my face, an action I already anticipated. I didn't anticipate what happened next.

Instead of closing his eyes to concentrate, he leaned forward and tenderly kissed my lips. I didn't have time to react before I felt his consciousness enter my own, searching for my ki and embracing it with his.

It was different than any connection I had ever made with the people I healed. They were never as aware of their ki as kami were, and no one's ki had ever reached out to hold mine the way Katsu's did. Once he found it, I felt him deepen the kiss and by doing so deepen the connection. A slow warmth spread from my spine to the tips of my toes as he continued searching for the damage.

I could tell the moment he found it because his ki spread out and covered the area, completely encompassing it in white, healing light. For some reason I wasn't responding to Katsu's instructions and suddenly the bright light seemed to backfire, sending shock waves that blew our ki apart and ripped through our bodies.

My vision blurred as I opened my eyes and found myself displaced from my bed and cradled in Katsu's arms. He was leaning his forehead against mine, taking in heavy gulps of air.

"I don't understand this. I can't understand what happened. I found the damage, and I could have fixed it, but there is a blockage of some kind."

I reached up and placed a hand on his cheek, attempting to comfort him. "Is it a blockage of the mind? Did I put it there, or did I shut you out unintentionally?"

He shook his head, worry lines creasing his face. "No. This is completely different. It's as if I have no access to your soul. Damaging someone's ki is difficult to accomplish. It only happened as a direct consequence of your breaching the veil, but soul mates are able to balance each other's ki. We have access to one another's souls and can heal the damage sustained on any level so long as we are connected with one another. Your ki didn't respond to mine. It was as if your soul didn't recognize me."

I stared at him wide-eyed. "What does that mean?"

"I don't know, but we must uncover the cause of this barrier, or you will never be whole again, and without the full strength of your ki, you'll never become a full kami." He lifted me effortlessly back on my bed, and it was then that I realized I wore only my undergarments. Katsu didn't seem to sense my embarrassment. He was too distracted by his failed attempt at healing me.

He stood up and strode toward the door.

"Where are you going?"

He turned to look at me. "I must speak with Kenji and see if there is anything recorded on this matter. We must find out how I can breach this barrier. If you feel up to it, I would like to continue our practice sessions after breakfast."

Without so much as a farewell, he exited, leaving me to wonder if he had even thought twice about the kiss we had shared or if it had affected him in any way. It saddened me to think that my first kiss had been given for the purpose of healing me instead of loving me.

I arrived in the gardens with my guards early. If there was a chance Daiki had left a note for me, I needed to be there to retrieve it without Katsu's watchful eye hovering over me. I didn't need to worry about what the guards did or didn't see since they were loyal to Akane.

I walked straight for the fist-sized rock snuggled next to one of the trees. Lifting it up I stuck my finger inside the small compartment chiseled into the center. I smiled when I felt a small piece of parchment tickle the tip of my index finger. I gripped the end of it and slid it out, swiftly stuffing it within a pocket sewn inside my kimono. I then replaced the rock.

Footsteps approached, and I startled to see both Katsu and Kenji directly behind me.

"Kenji, are you here to watch me practice?" I gave him a weary smile he didn't seem capable of returning. Worry lines creased his forehead.

"Katsu shared with me the extent of damage your ki has sustained and his inability to heal it. I am quite baffled by this, Mikomi, but I am even more concerned with your well-being."

"I'm sure there has to be an explanation for the blockage Katsu encountered," I said. I was putting on a brave face, but inwardly I was concerned. If my ki no longer functioned at full power, what kind of consequences would that hold for the future?

I wasn't concerned about never becoming a full kami. My father may have unintentionally given me an out in all of this. I couldn't fulfill the prophecy if I didn't become immortal. On the other hand, I wondered what would happen if I were injured slightly or even seriously. If my ki couldn't heal the whites of my eyes, what hope did I have that it might heal other injuries of a more serious nature? And what of the rebellion? How would I ever heal Akane's men?

"Come here, child, and let us experiment for a moment." Kenji reached his hands out and grabbed both of mine. "My hip is feeling poorly. I think it best if we see what your ki can do with physical pain."

I looked at Katsu, waiting for permission to proceed and hating myself for doing so. He folded his arms over his chest and nodded, barely making eye contact with me before focusing on

Kenji. I didn't know what to make of his standoffish behavior but thought it best to simply comply with Kenji's request, rather than analyze Katsu's ever changing moods.

I let go of Kenji's hands and placed them on the graying hairline of his temples. Closing my eyes, I connected to him, but the connection felt fuzzy, as if my mental sight had been impaired in some way. I continued forward despite the disheartening handicap and located the inflammation in the joints of Kenji's hips. I instructed his ki to minimize the inflammation and block the pain and discomfort he felt.

He took several seconds to respond, and when he finally did, the healing progressed at a sluggish rate, as if it were unclear as to the specifics of my instructions. I found that I had to use much more energy to accomplish something as simple as relieving joint pain. By the time Kenji's ki had completed the task, I could feel droplets of sweat parading down my hairline. I opened my eyes and shakily released my hold on my tutor.

Unfortunately, holding onto him was the only thing that had been keeping me upright. The moment I let go, I felt my legs buckle and would have collapsed backward into the shallow pond if Katsu's reflexes had not been so quick.

I leaned against him, breathing heavily.

"Why, was that so difficult?"

Kenji studied me for a moment. The tension in his face and body made me nervous. "Katsu, connect to her now and see what happens when your ki touches hers."

He was already holding me, so turning his head and pressing a gentle kiss to my lips happened before I was ready for the intimate contact. Entering my mind and connecting with my ki occurred within seconds. He moved to a specific point, in a place where my brain had been injured and folded his spirit over mine in an attempt to surround the fractured area. The minute he touched it, my ki writhed in agony and fairly flung his spiritual force to the background, severing the connection immediately. He didn't even get a chance to produce that warm healing light I had felt before.

When I opened my eyes, I realized we were both sitting on the ground with him cradling me in his arms once again.

"Katsu, what happened?" Kenji asked, kneeling down next to us.

"I couldn't even make contact with her. The minute my ki touched hers it instantly repelled me. I can heal her physically, but I can't heal her spirit, and as her soul mate, this is something I should have access to."

"I think I may have an idea of what is blocking your connection, though I can't be sure until we give this situation some time, but I think the more she heals the less capable her ki is of receiving light or help. Her energy is used to doing this on its own, but it takes a certain level of energy for spiritual connections between soul mates to take place. The answer, hopefully, is that she must stop healing long enough for her ki to retain the strength necessary to accept you."

"You think it is as simple as that?" Katsu asked.

"I certainly hope so. Only time will tell at this point, but might I suggest that you suspend her veil training for a week or two? I can continue with her educational outings in the meantime."

"Yes, Kenji. I think it a very good idea." Katsu sounded a bit relieved, even felt it. I sensed that before he threw the walls back in front of his emotions. Kenji's were just as disturbing. He acted as if he had just solved all of our problems, but his emotions bounced from worry to fear to outright panic. I needed to talk with him but didn't know how to end this session with Katsu. Fortunately, he did it for me.

"I must take care of some business matters with your father, Mikomi." He easily stood, taking me with him and gently setting me on my feet. "In the meantime, I want you to rest for the next week or so, and we'll try again."

I nodded, and hoped for both our sakes that Kenji's prediction became a reality. Katsu lifted his hand and tenderly brushed his fingers against my cheek. I shivered slightly at the contact and gave him a smile I didn't feel. Then he dropped his hand to his side and walked swiftly down the path and around the bend.

"We have a serious problem here, Mikomi," Kenji said the minute Katsu was out of earshot.

"You don't think I will have recovered enough to accept his healing?"

"Worse. Everything I told him just now was a complete and total lie."

My mouth flew open in surprise. "What do you mean you lied? Is there no way for Katsu to heal me?"

"Absolutely none, I'm afraid. Your ki is damaged, and you tire more easily. If Katsu had waited to have you practice on me later this evening, you most likely wouldn't have struggled as much as you did just now, but when he told me what happened when he tried to heal your spirit, I knew I needed to come up with a plausible scenario fast."

"Kenji, I still don't understand. Why would you lie to him? What is it you're not telling me?"

Kenji worried his cane in both hands before answering. "Katsu's inability to heal you has nothing whatsoever to do with your ki needing rest in order to accept him. Your ki will never be able to accept a healing from his."

"Why on earth not?"

Kenji swallowed hard. "He isn't your soul mate. The prophecy is flawed. "

I stared at him in stunned silence, having no idea how I might respond to such an unbelievable declaration. I might have rejoiced at the thought that I would no longer be forced into a marriage with Katsu if what Kenji said was indeed correct, but the look on my old tutor's face gave me pause.

"How do you know this?"

"Your ki would never have rejected a healing from your true soul mate. It shunned Katsu because it doesn't recognize him. Your spirits do not belong to one another, and as a result, he can never hope to heal you."

"What does that mean for the future, Kenji, for the healing of the veil?"

Kenji shook his head, his eyes wide with worry. "We've missed something in the prophecy. If you and the warrior god are not soul mates, then you can never become a full kami. Your soul mate is the only one who can help you complete the full transformation."

My thoughts swam with questions. "If Katsu is not my match, then who is?"

"A very good question, but there is another I must pose that is far more troubling. How will you and Katsu heal the veil if you can never be united?"

Epilogue:

Tie Hart

T he heart monitor attached to Hope Fairmont beeped slow and steady. Her breathing remained regular, and her MRI had come back normal. Any impartial onlooker would have assumed she was sleeping, but Tie knew better.

All of the monitoring was unnecessary, yet Tie had agreed with James Fairmont, Hope's father, that it was better to allow their group to believe her unconscious state was due entirely to breaching the veil, though this was far from the truth.

He leaned forward in his chair and rested his elbows against Hope's hospital bed. He tenderly took her hand in his own and brought it to his lips. She stirred ever so slightly but showed no other signs of awakening. Soon she would remember everything, and that knowledge filled him with equal parts of excitement and dread.

He had waited a millennium for this!

She would know him as he was a thousand years ago, but would she wish to be near him once she remembered everything that had transpired? He didn't think so, and that thought, more than anything, terrified him.

He thought of a simpler time, a time when he stood in a clearing surrounded by cherry trees and taught a mysterious, beautiful woman the art of the samurai. He would've given anything to have those moments back.

He closed his eyes and let out a tired sigh. "Angie, you should go home and try to get some sleep."

"Like hell!"

Tie opened his eyes, surprised at the look of indignant outrage on Angie's face. She sat in the chair opposite him on the other side of Hope's bed, clinging tightly to her hand.

"Angie—"

"Save it, Cupid." Angie pointed a finger at him in warning.

Her emerald eyes gleamed a bright green as she glared at him with a ferocious intensity. With her flaming red hair tousled about her head, back-lit by the setting sun coming through the windows, she was an intimidating figure to behold; a beautiful, fiery goddess in her own right.

He tried to keep the corners of his mouth from curling up in amusement and thought it best not to correct the "Cupid" remark she'd just thrown at him.

She poked her finger in his direction again. "If you get to stay, then so do I."

Tie shook his head. "I'm her soul mate."

"I'm her *best friend*."

"I think soul mates trump best friends."

"In what realm of *ridiculous* would that ever be possible?" Her nostrils flared in anger.

Tie wondered if he should continue pushing her buttons. It was better than sitting here, thinking about the unknown future they were headed toward. He decided to try reasoning with her instead.

"I just think it would be best—"

"Stop talking! Unless you can sit here and tell me what it was like all those years after Hope's mother died. Unless you can talk to me about her hopes and dreams, her favorite color, her favorite movie, whether she likes pepperonis or Canadian bacon on her pizza, every performance she ever gave at Expresso, every tear she ever cried and every horrible outfit she ever had to be talked out of, you do *not* get to sit there and tell me what you think is best in regards to *my* best friend."

Tie studied Angie intently, acquiring a new respect for the girl. She reminded him of a sweet, stubborn, courageous friend he'd once had a very long time ago.

"Fine, but please remember that what you've heard discussed between James and myself cannot be shared with Victor or Chinatsu."

Angie's shoulders visibly relaxed. "Like I could ever be that stupid." Her eyes narrowed. "How do you think Victor will take it?"

Tie quirked an eyebrow at her. "Why? You worried about his feelings? Are you starting to like him?"

"Just because I admire the way his rear fits into his blue jeans doesn't mean I like *him* personally."

Tie had to chuckle at that, though he noticed some tension around Angie's mouth.

"We just have to keep this quiet. I'm fairly certain that Hope and I aren't legitimate soul mates."

Angie gave him a shrewd look. "Legitimate? What the hell is *that* supposed to mean?"

He pulled his hand from Hope's as he heard the door to her room open, but relaxed a little when he saw James step in.

"Is it your turn to guard her, then?" James asked.

Tie studied Hope's father, noticing the dark circles under his eyes and the worry lines surrounding his mouth.

"Yeah. This is *my* shift." Tie gave Angie a meaningful look, but she leveled him with a challenging glare. "I told Victor I would take over for the rest of the evening since he has more veil strengthening to do somewhere in England. To be honest, I don't see any nekomata returning for a while now. Not with Victor traveling as often as he can to strengthen the various weaknesses in the veil."

James nodded but kept his eyes on Hope. "Do you know how much longer this is going to take?"

"I know she has a lot to remember, and she has to do it gradually. The shock of her first life colliding with her present will take some getting used to. I continually check her progress, and her life force always lets me know how her vitals are, far better than the technology you have around here." Tie nodded to the heart monitor and IVs attached to Hope's body.

James gave him a rueful smile. "Habit, I suppose. I just want to know she's okay, and it makes it look as if she's really in a coma. I'm assuming you still want Chinatsu and Victor to believe that." He walked around the bed and sat down in a chair next to Angie.

"I do."

Tie studied him carefully, worried James might fall over from the exhaustion plainly etched upon his features. He knew Hope's father had slept very little since the latest nekomata attack at the football field.

"Where's Kirby?" Angie asked.

"He's staying with Ms. Mori right now, refusing to go back to his own mother, although I'm sure we'll have a fight on our hands when his mother realizes he no longer has leukemia."

"That mother of his best not mess with me. I will go postal on her worthless a—"

"Angie, have you had anything to eat yet?" James asked.

Tie stifled a chuckle. Angie, whether at her best or worst, was always entertaining.

She gave him a sour look. "I see both of you are trying to get rid of me."

James patted her shoulder. "Hope would never forgive me if I allowed you to miss a meal."

Angie rolled her eyes and stood. "As if the doughnuts in the food dispenser could ever be considered *real* food. Any takers?"

"I would rather have something from the cafeteria," Tie said, knowing it would take her much longer to get there. He needed some time alone with James.

"Oh, would you now? Why don't I just dash down to the local *Olive Garden* and pick you up some Chicken Fettuccini Alfredo while I'm at it?"

"If you don't think it would be too much trouble." Tie gave her an innocent smile.

"Unbelievable," Angie grumbled. "Who knew kami could be so high maintenance." She stalked out of the room, leaving

James and Tie to their conversation.

"I need you to explain to me again what you did to Hope and how this process works." James looked at his daughter, and Tie thought he saw a small tick jolt at the base of the man's jaw. He was not handling this well.

"When Hope healed Kirby, she damaged her brain just as she did the first time she healed him. It's lucky I got to her first. I was able to heal her easily enough, but she was beginning to slip away mentally. Her life force was trying to travel to the other side of the veil. When my life force connected with hers it created an anchor for her, a trail for her to follow back."

"Then why hasn't she done that yet?"

"It's not that simple, James. You have no idea what Hope is up against once we go back to Kagami. She has to remember her previous life. She has to remember how she felt, what she experienced, the customs, the culture, the people, the…relationships." Tie swallowed a tight knot forming in his throat. He took a moment to compose himself and continued. "There are many things she will not be able to fight against if she doesn't have the necessary knowledge backing her choices and decisions. I guided her back from the veil, but I instructed her ki to open that other part of her mind that stores memories, even memories of past lives."

"Why didn't you let Victor or Ms. Mori do this once you brought her back? We could have verified that she was fine."

"She is fine." Tie insisted. "I promise you, her mind is completely healed, but to answer your questions, I don't trust Chinatsu. She's only interested in forcing Hope to heal the veil. Victor…well, let's just say neither he nor I are anxious for Hope to remember her past or the circumstances surrounding her death. I knew he wouldn't help her to remember, but I also knew he was incapable of doing so."

James' eyes narrowed. "Why? Why can't he do what you have done? Why can't he open her mind as you have?"

Tie let out a heavy breath and looked at Hope, the one person in the world who truly loved him, the one person in the world who had managed to save him from his own self-destruction.

He reached for her hand again and held it up, palm and fingers flat against his. A bright, iridescent glow spread out from their contact, and a black cherry blossom slowly sprouted and unfurled from the tips of their fingers. He heard James gasp in surprise, and Tie turned his head to look at him.

"The prophecy has decreed that Victor and Hope must marry, but he can never heal her completely, never hope to help her ascend to a full kami, never join with her to heal the veil and never..." he choked back a tired sob threatening to escape, "...never restore to her the very memories that encompass the beauty, strength, and humility of who Hope truly is." He watched as the black vine from the cherry blossom circled its way around both their wrists, binding them together as it had over and over every day since she had been admitted to the hospital.

"Why?" James asked, clearly desperate for more answers. "Why has everything changed?"

Tie watched as the black blossom continued to tighten the binding between Hope and himself before answering.

"Because a thousand years ago, I committed the worst kind of betrayal and forced upon Hope something she never would have chosen for herself." He pulled his hand from the woman he loved and watched as the black blossom disappeared, leaving dark wisps of magic in its wake. "I forced her to sever her tie with Victor and bound her soul to me. She's mine now, forever, and even if I wanted to, I could never let her go."

Deep silence permeated the small space between Tie and James, interrupted only by the steady beeping of Hope's unnecessary heart monitor.

Thank you for reading *The Black Blossom*. I hope you enjoyed it. Here is a Sneak Peek of *The Grass Cutter Sword,* Book 3 in *The Healer Series*.

PROLOGUE

Edana, 700 A.D.

The day Edana died was much like any other, and yet her heart was filled with love, hope and happiness, cherishing the moments spent with an individual who had promised her an eternity of happily ever afters. With Katsu by her side she would never be subjected to death, illness or even injury. His gift of immortality granted her the opportunity to continue what she felt was her divine duty: to warn others of their own unnecessary deaths, receiving visions of how best to help them so that they too might live their own versions of a happily ever after. More importantly, however, she would finally have what she had yearned for most of her life: unconditional love from a man who valued her, not because of her own supernatural gifts, but because she was simply Edana, and he was simply Katsu.

Before sneaking out of her small, thatch-roofed hut to join Katsu forever, she stole a kiss from her sleeping mother. The contact gave her another reassuring vision of how her mother's life would end; in her sleep ten years from now, her spirit leaving her body as naturally as it had first arrived. There existed no better way to slowly slip through the veil than by natural causes.

Edana felt relieved to never experience the crushing burden of warning her mother of some unfortunate accident or possible harm done to her by another. The best deaths were the ones fated to all of mankind, and she need never interfere with those.

She stole away into the darkness of pre-dawn to meet with Katsu at the appointed place and time; a small bluff overlooking a beautiful chasm of rocky green foliage and a tiny, rippling stream of sparkling azure. She wrapped her woolen shawl closer about her person, though she hardly felt the cold of the morning due to the warmth spreading from the love within her heart.

She was first to arrive at the bluffs and had a moment to breathe in the cool, crisp morning air, pondering on the circumstances that had brought her to this point. Only a few months had passed since she first met a wandering merchant by the name of Musubi, but the months blurred into a cacophony of emotional discoveries and eventually hope. He had wandered into her village with obvious purpose in his air and speech. Though his accent was strange and his appearance even more so, she had felt compelled to help him locate a young woman by the name of Thesbis. He left the nature of his business a secret, but she didn't worry about his motives for his eyes were kind and his manner sincere.

When she accidentally bumped into him without receiving a vision of his death, she had been overcome with shock and then an unrelenting curiosity. Contact with another human being always resulted in a vision of demise, whether natural, accidental or sinister in nature, but no visions manifested themselves in the presence of this intriguing man.

In the weeks that followed, he sought her out more frequently, and she was only too happy to oblige, enjoying the presence of a man who allowed her to feel normal and accepted for once in her life. Though she exercised caution when initiating contact with him, every time he touched her she was blessedly free of any and all visions dealing with the manner of his death. She soon began to wonder if Death feared taking him.

The day his friend Katsu came for a visit would mark the beginning of the end for her, though she hardly knew it at the time. The announcement that she and Musubi planned to marry was just as much of a surprise to her as it was to Katsu, and an unwelcome one by the look on his face. Though she ruefully realized she had never discouraged Musubi's interest in her, her heart ached at the idea of marrying a man who had become a dear friend to her and nothing more. To marry him solely because he gave her a blessed reprieve from her visions would only end in her unhappiness and his. It wasn't enough to build a marriage on, and yet what other options did she have as the village witch and outcast?

Katsu remained in the village while Musubi left to make preparations for their wedding, promising to return within a few weeks to fetch her. During that time it seemed to Edana that Katsu felt it his duty to look after her on behalf of his friend.

At first, he merely observed her as she worked in her garden, offering to lend a helping hand in cultivating the few vegetables she and her mother enjoyed. His regular visits gave them both the opportunity to broach different topics of conversation, some of a more serious nature, while others filled with the most wonderful sense of levity and true fulfillment. Though she had grown to know and care for Musubi, her heart longed for Katsu's conversations and his opinions on any and every topic available. In short, she simply longed for him.

A day before Musubi's return, Katsu made his usual visit to her home with some surprising information to share.

Musubi and Katsu were gods, chosen to perform specific tasks in this world, never to have soul mates of their own. He warned her of the endless life Musubi intended to impose upon her, and the possibility that she might not survive her own ascension as a kami. Even now, she remembered their conversation in vivid detail.

"Why are you warning me of Musubi's deception?" she asked. "He is your friend, is he not? How can you slander his name if you are as close as you say?"

"I merely wish to warn you, Edana. What you will be forced to give up and the risks involved are things that you must be aware of. It is only fair that I impress upon you the gravity of this decision so you may ask yourself if immortality is what you really want."

He moved closer and took a piece of her red hair in his hand, wrapping it around his finger and then gently giving it a small tug. The gesture brought with it emotions she had never once experienced with Musubi.

"Please do not misunderstand me. Musubi is one of my oldest friends, and I greatly love and respect him, but he has spent all of his existence helping humans find their soul mates, the one person on this Earth who can make them completely whole. He cannot help but long for that himself, and I cannot blame him for taking the one thing he has never been allowed to have."

"And what one thing is that?"

Katsu's eyes held Edana's as he quietly stated, "Love."

She swallowed hard, feeling a rush of heat spread across her cheeks. She took a step back, waiting for the rapid beating of her heart to subside and then drew in a steadying breath.

"What if I wish to take those risks and give Musubi what he's always wanted?"

Katsu closed the distance between them again. "If that is your desire, then I will not stand in your way. You needed to be apprised of all of the facts. I couldn't remain silent, even if Musubi is my best friend. It seems wrong somehow, just as it is wrong to keep hidden my own feelings concerning you."

Her mouth went dry at what she thought he insinuated. "I don't understand your meaning."

He gave her a calculating smile. "If you want to risk your own mortality, shouldn't you be risking it with the right person?"

"And Musubi isn't right for me?"

"He is blinded by his feelings for you, but I believe he knows that you two are not meant for one another."

"Then who am I meant for?"

Katsu looked genuinely puzzled for the first time. "According to Musubi, you are an enigma. He has received no clear reading on you and assumes he can take you for himself. If that is true, however, and the fates have chosen no one for you to love in this life, why not join a kami for all eternity...so long as he is the right kami for you."

"You believe that kami to be someone other than Musubi?"

He smiled wide and placed his hands at her hips, drawing her closer to his person. "The right kami will ensure your immortality. Aligning yourself with one whom you hold no true love for will end in certain death. I believe the only kami you are meant to love is me. With our union, there will be no risks to your survival."

Katsu's words should have alerted her to the truth right then and there, for he had never come right out and divulged the true nature of his feelings. He never once expressed his love for her, but merely hinted at it. Yet she was too carried away in her own feelings for Katsu to consider he might have ulterior motives.

No. He had laid his trap perfectly, and Edana willingly fell into it. For the first time in her life she experienced that wonderful, terrible, earth-shattering level of love that blinds the sight, deafens all reason, and strips the heart bare for all the world to see.

Standing on the bluffs overlooking the wide chasm and trickling stream beneath, Edana still awaited a happily ever after that would never come.

"Edana." Katsu's gruff voice took her by surprise, and she turned around with a radiant smile upon her face, one that slowly slipped away once she beheld his furious countenance.

She rushed to him. "What is it? What has happened?"

"You did it, did you not? You informed Musubi that you held no love for him, that you would never marry him."

She looked at him in confusion. "I wasn't quite as heartless as that, but yes, I told him exactly what we discussed earlier. While I love him as a dear friend, I must be true to my heart and follow it wherever it may lead, and it leads to you, Katsu." She placed a gentle, loving hand on his cheek, but he abruptly pulled back, steeling his eyes and glaring at her instead.

The disturbing change in him baffled her beyond anything she could comprehend. Where had the man she cared for disappear to?

He stood before her with an indifferent, almost triumphant expression upon his face. "I knew you never loved him. Just like any woman, you are quick to switch your loyalties to whatever circumstance betters your situation."

The hurtful accusations speared the very center of her heart and crushed her spirit. "I cared for him," she cried, "and I will always consider him a dear friend, but I feel nothing more than sisterly affection for him. I didn't refuse him without good cause."

"You did exactly what I stated you would do, exactly what I warned him you were capable of. He needed to understand what he risked his immortality for. What kind of friend would I be if I didn't expose you for the unfaithful, loveless woman that you truly are?"

Edana's heart broke with each vicious word Katsu uttered. They inflicted the highest amount of pain. He wielded them as a weapon, like tiny shards of glass capable of penetrating her most tender and vulnerable places. She cried heavy tears as she slumped to the earth. "I love you, Katsu. Whether you believe it to be true or not, I love you more than I thought it possible to love anyone or anything."

"You love what I offered you. You love the thought of achieving an immortal state risk free. You love yourself more than the idea of being true to my friend." Katsu's anger on behalf of Musubi blazed across his features. "He shied away from telling you the truth until you had no choice in the matter, but I knew that to be a mistake. Your eye could be turned just as easily as the next woman's. It is not his destiny to be saddled with such a woman as you. Nor is it mine."

Edana fell to her knees and lifted her hands in supplication. "Please, Katsu. You know this isn't true. You know I had no intention of following through with a marriage to Musubi. Even if you hadn't come along."

"I know no such thing. All I see is a faithless woman who will never have the chance to hurt my friend again. Goodbye, Edana."

∞∞∞

Katsu 700 A.D.

An enormous amount of regret engulfed Katsu as he threw such hateful words at Edana and began to walk away. He convinced himself of her guilt. She deserved to be abandoned for so cruelly abusing the affections Musubi offered her. She deserved her own heartbreak for throwing aside Musubi's love just as easily as she would Katsu's if a better offer ever came along. He knew how these human women operated, and he had set out to protect his friend no matter the cost or the collateral damage. He was determined to save his friend from the kind of heartbreak he had witnessed a thousand other mortals experience in his expansive lifetime. He would save Musubi from his own fruitless desires, from the possibility of losing his own immortality.

To save his best friend's life.

And he had!

He damn well had!

Why, then, did a massive hole rip within his chest as he continued to create more distance between Edana and himself?

He pondered the idea of returning to her side, apologizing for the subterfuge, and at the very least helping the young girl to understand why a union between the two of them verged on the other side of impossible.

He steeled his resolve further, recognizing his own weakness where a pretty face was concerned. There were plenty of other women to revel in before the day was through, but Edana he would cast off forever.

In the end, did it matter who he spent his time with? Eventually, he would be saddled with his own fate; tied to The Healer and trapped in an arranged, loveless marriage for the rest of eternity. Why not live life to its fullest now?

A terrified scream knifed through his musings, causing an unfamiliar sense of fear to course through him.

Edana!

He raced back the way he had come, reaching the bluffs with lightning speed, but unable to spot Edana anywhere. Turning in circles and surveying the land spread out before him, he came to an unacceptable conclusion, one which filled him with stone cold dread. He inched himself closer to the cliff's edge, hoping against hope that his fears might not be realized. At the bottom of the rocky chasm he saw Edana, broken, bleeding, and barely alive.

He dove to her side, hardly paying any attention to how he arrived or the temporary damage his fall inflicted upon his own body. He focused solely on Edana, wishing only to arrive at her side and save her before her heart drummed its last beat.

When he reached her, her eyes took on a glint of recognition for just one precious moment, a moment that filled him with hope, relief and...love! He batted away the emotions, knowing he couldn't afford to be distracted, and placed his hands on either side of her head. Just as he connected to her sweet spirit, she slipped away from him, away from his touch, away from his desperate grasp, and away from the surprising feelings her absence in his life evoked. Her bright spirit slid from this life to the next, through the veil and on to the other side where he would never be capable of retrieving her.

"Edana," he cried, shaking her though he knew it was pointless. "Edana...please, I..." Katsu wrapped his arms around her broken body and pulled her to his chest, not even attempting to muffle his sobs. The pain of her loss attacked the entirety of his ki, a terrible ripping sensation that shattered his senses and hollowed him from the inside out.

She killed herself. Threw herself over the cliff's edge because of him, because of his refusal to love and accept her. He hadn't truly believed her professions of love, not until that very moment. The realization made him shake harder as he rocked back and forth with her in his arms.

He failed to notice the soft glow of his sword each time it accidentally made contact with Edana's skin.

Someone shouted from the distance, and then Edana was wrenched from his arms.

"What did you do?" Musubi yelled. He held her close to his chest and placed a hand to her head. Katsu ached for his friend as he watched his eyes roam over Edana's form, frantically searching for a flicker of life, a spark of light within her.

He knew what Musubi encountered when he attempted to connect to Edana.

Nothing.

Absolutely nothing.

When Musubi opened his eyes, Katsu, the great warrior kami, felt his heart break further. Not only had he lost a woman he hadn't been aware he loved, but through his misguided desire to save his best friend he had just managed to lose him as well. He hadn't a clue as to how to make amends for his enormous mistake, and no viable resource for bringing Edana back to life.

Musubi's voice shook. "Katsu, what did you do?"

He knew he must own up to his part in all of this. He had to admit that Edana's death was his fault, and he willingly did so, feeling the ache of that one truth.

"I told her I never truly loved her. I was testing her to see if she loved you and intended to remain faithful to you. I..." He took a deep breath as Musubi pulled Edana closer, wiping away the blood from the side of her face as if that might somehow bring her back to them. "I was trying to protect you, Musubi. If you had lost your immortality to a woman as fickle as the ones I've encountered I would have lost you forever."

Musubi's anger hung heavy between them. "So you concocted this little plan of yours to save me from myself? After all of these years, I finally found someone who wasn't fated for any other person, someone whose soul belonged to no one else. Untethered." He whispered that last word to himself. "And I actually cared for her. I..." Musubi's voice caught on a sob and his shoulders shook.

Katsu swallowed the guilt and grief his actions had caused, attempting to hold back his own devastation at the loss of Edana. This wasn't about him or the realization of what he'd lost. This was about what Musubi had longed for since the beginning of his creation. A soul mate, someone to love, someone who could love him in return, and his friend now believed that love to be lost forever. It wasn't something Musubi would soon recover from.

Neither of them would.

"I didn't know she intended to take her own life when I told her the truth. Musubi, please, I didn't realize she had actually—"

"What? Fallen in love with you? Why not, when so many have before? When so many other human women have watched you walk away from them with their hearts broken and their own worst fears suddenly realized. To ruin countless women who will never be accepted by another man or even open to accepting one themselves." Musubi broke a fist through a massive rock beside him, his anger a foreign emotion Katsu had never before witnessed. "What made you think Edana would be any less devastated by your deceit? These women have never been fickle of heart, Katsu. That role has always been played by you."

Katsu shut his eyes as the truth of Musubi's words began to sink in and take root within his conscience. He was right, of course. His behavior with human women had been less than stellar, rebelling against the idea of being shackled to The Healer for the rest of his existence. He had taken his love life in his own hands and made of it what he would for as long as the fates might permit.

He had the sure knowledge that for better or worse he would

never be alone once he united himself with The Healer. The gift of a soul mate had not been something he fully appreciated until seated there, watching Musubi rock Edana back and forth in his arms, knowing that the god of love and marriage would have given up far more than his own immortality to experience, for even a brief moment, that overwhelming feeling of love.

To love and be loved in return. It was all Musubi had ever wanted.

And Katsu had stolen it from him. At least, he thought he had. But Musubi had never come right out and said that he loved the girl. Not even when Katsu had attempted to dissuade him from his foolhardy plans.

"I didn't know...I...I simply didn't believe her when she professed her love for me."

The words did little to comfort his old friend as he held Edana and glared daggers of hatred at Katsu. He felt a sudden jealousy take hold as he watched the woman he loved being held in the arms of another. He knew it was foolish to react that way, recognizing he was nowhere near worthy to claim her as his own. He still couldn't fully comprehend the level of attachment he held for a woman who was now dead because of his duplicitous behavior, yet he wanted to prove a point in order to make his original intentions justifiable in some way.

"Did you really love her, Musubi, or was she simply a woman without a soul mate?"

Musubi's eyes darkened. "How could you possibly suggest such a thing?" he spat out. "I never before dreamed I could care for a person the way I did for Edana. I loved her, Katsu."

As did I.

The thought surprised Katsu due to its strength and intensity. As he sorrowfully watched his best friend cradle Edana's limp form, all of his good intentions shriveled and died. Nothing could ever justify his actions, and no amount of excruciating regret would ever bring her back.

∞∞∞

Amatsu Mikaboshi - The Day of The Healer's Birth

Amatsu paced back and forth amongst his several followers, seeking a way to punish one or possibly all of them for the now obvious mistake he had made three centuries ago. That the fault lay solely in his corner did little to dissuade him from abusing whomever he might choose.

"Tell me again," he said, his voice deceptively pleasant and calm. "Tell me exactly what transpired the moment The Healer was born."

Quaking on bended knee, the nekomata kept his head down and gazed upon the blackness of the stone floor.

"The moment Empress Chinatsu delivered The Healer into the world of the living, pressure built within the room housing The Black Blossom. It compressed the air and space within the chamber, and then it exploded outward, shaking the entire room and knocking me to the floor. When I collected myself and checked for damages, I noticed its petals had whitened along the edges."

"And everything you have done to blacken it has failed?"

The nekomata hesitated before answering. Admitting any type of failure invited repercussions of the worst kind.

"The blossom refuses to welcome the darkness it lost. Even now, the white tips of the petals are gaining ground." Amatsu stared at the top of his minion's head, fuming at the only possible conclusion this new development signified.

"The prophecy is flawed." He let out a rueful chuckle, mentally berating himself for never once considering that the translated prophecy might hold grievous errors, the kind of errors capable of negating thousands of years worth of planning. But shouldn't he have foreseen such a possibility? Wasn't it just like his Parents to have allowed the prophecy to be flawed in the first place? What better way to thwart the thwarter than dangle a distraction, a red herring, and watch him hang himself with it?

He didn't consciously remember taking hold of his minion's head or realize the pain his hands inflicted until the nekomata's shrill cries finally penetrated his embittered musings. It hardly encouraged him to let go of the vile creature. It wasn't as if the nekomata could be killed with his bare hands, but the pain he inflicted certainly allowed him to channel the fury coiled within.

Eventually, he let go, surveying the slumped nekomata in disgust and then promptly forgetting him. The blossom he stored within his keep stood as sentry, a type of barometer attached to Musubi's heart and ki. Since his ability to keep tabs on the god of love and marriage remained virtually impossible, he had created his own fail-safe to ensure the darkness within Musubi's heart remained intact. He'd doubted the necessity of it, fully believing that nothing short of Musubi's soul mate might be capable of saving him once the darkness became firmly rooted within his ki. After all, only one kami in the history of creation had been allotted a soul mate, and anyone who understood the prophecy believed that kami to be Katsu.

As had he.

If the princess happened upon Musubi before her marriage to Katsu, the inevitability of their union was certain. Amatsu had no idea what a union with The Healer and the god of love and marriage might do for the veil, but he determined one thing: the princess and Musubi could never come to know one another.

His anger spiked anew at this disturbing development. He had counted on Musubi's part in all of this. Severing The Healer from her soul mate had been vital, the only thing capable of making the prophecy null and void. Afterward, the only other weapon he possessed, and a highly effective one at that, was time. Time used to sufficiently erode and weaken the veil's impermeable wall, and with The Healer his prisoner, and Musubi on the path to becoming a nekomata, he could begin his grand reentry into the world of the living with his arsenal fully loaded.

Only one course of action made sense at this point, now that his meticulous planning had failed. He spoke to all of the nekomata assembled.

"We must capture The Healer before her eighteenth birthday." Eager eyes followed him as he moved across the floor. "My power to send any of you through the veil is extremely limited, and the longest you may remain in the world of the living in your current form is one year, possibly two, before you must return to the underworld or risk disintegrating within the world of the living. You all understand the risks involved? There is no guarantee I will have the power to bring you back."

In truth, Amatsu held no concern for their plight and loathed the idea of wasting an ounce of power returning them to the underworld before the laws that governed life and death eventually righted the wrongs of their presence in the land of the living. If they disintegrated within a year or two it mattered very little in the grand scheme of things.

"She must be captured and brought back here where she will never be capable of joining with her true soul mate."

"Forgive me, sire, but why not kill her when the opportunity presents itself?" The nekomata groveling at his masters feet hunched his shoulders.

Amatsu studied his grotesque follower with disdain. He longed for the moment when he might finally surround himself with beauty instead of death and the constant reminder of his own failures.

"The Healer can be killed with our weapons, it is true, but I have recently made a few startling discoveries concerning the properties held within The Healer's blood and the role The Grass Cutter Sword plays in all of this. If we kill her, the powers of The Grass Cutter Sword will ensure her eventual return. She will be reborn anywhere at any given time. No, it is better to keep her alive, for we know where she is, but more importantly, we know who she is. At this point she is more useful to me alive.

We require an army of kami for the war we plan against Heaven and Earth, but we need a way for all of you to return to the land of the living with your original forms intact."

Without Musubi's dark heart and connections, another kami's participation was necessary to carry out this new twist to his plan. His thoughts immediately turned to that arrogant upstart, Fukurokuju.

The kami had always thirsted for power and position, willingly aiding him in Heaven when war broke out and then changing sides last minute, abandoning Amatsu to this hellish existence. Amatsu intended to make him pay for that stinging betrayal by helping him build up an army. Fukurokuju would realize only too late that the kami army he built belonged to his former ally. Amatsu rubbed his smooth palms together in anticipation of the look on that simpering kami's face when he finally discovered the deceit. It would take great planning and several nekomata to pull something like this off. The veil's walls needed to weaken considerably in order for them to get through, but he had plans for that as well.

After all, if The Healer had the power to strengthen the veil, she must also possess the power to weaken it, cripple it even. He could use that to his advantage when the time came.

"What about the dissenters?" the nekomata before him asked. "What if some of them cross over when we do and kill The Healer before we can capture her?"

Amatsu nearly cursed at this, but held his anger in check. Several nekomata wanted The Healer to die as soon as possible. They believed it would somehow end their own miserable existence. A group of misguided zealots hiding within the ranks of his loyal subjects.

"If they are located, kill them immediately. Your survival depends upon The Healer's blood and her inability to form a union with her soul mate, and if her soul mate truly is Musubi, then we have more than just one kami to deal with."

He bade them all leave for now. Multiple variables needed to be thought through. Details that couldn't be left out and possible contingencies to his planning that couldn't be overlooked were at the forefront of his mind. He had eighteen years to get it right. He felt confident The Healer and a full kami army would be available to him long before the end of those eighteen years arrived.

The Healer Series

The Healer: Book 1
The Black Blossom: Book 2
The Grass Cutter Sword: Book 3
The Prophecy: Book 4

***

Supernatural Treasure Hunters Series

Double Booked

***

The Paranormal Misfits Series

My Fair Assassin: Book 1
My Fair Traitor: Book 2
My Fair Impostor: Book 3
My Fair Invader: Book 4
Book 5 Coming July 2019

Other Books By C. J. Anaya
Written Under The Pen Name Cynthia Savage

Billionaire's Reluctant Wife Series

Marry Your Billionaire: Book 1
Cynthia Savage

Crushing On The Billionaire: Book 2
Jennifer Griffith

Trusting The Billionaire: Book 3
Cynthia Savage

About the Author

C.J. Anaya is a USA Today bestselling and multi-award winning author. She also enjoys assisting authors in writing, publishing, and marketing their books with her helpful non-fiction guides on Amazon and her Youtube channel Author Journey.

She's a huge fan of The Mindy Project, Hugh Jackman, and binge eating any and all things chocolate. Who isn't, right?

As a mother of four awesome children, C.J. is usually helping out with homework, going to gymnastics, or delivering her kids to their karate classes so they can learn discipline, respect, and "...kick some serious butt, mom." She loves writing entertaining reads for everyone to enjoy and dabbles in singing and songwriting for kicks and giggles.

Follow her on Bookbub: https://www.bookbub.com/authors/c-j-anaya

Stop by and say hello at http://authorcjanaya.com

Facebook:https://www.facebook.com/cjanayaauthor

Twitter: CJAnaya21

Made in the USA
Monee, IL
03 September 2023

42078645R00176